MY ANGEL

BEWITCHED AND BEWILDERED

ALANEA ALDER

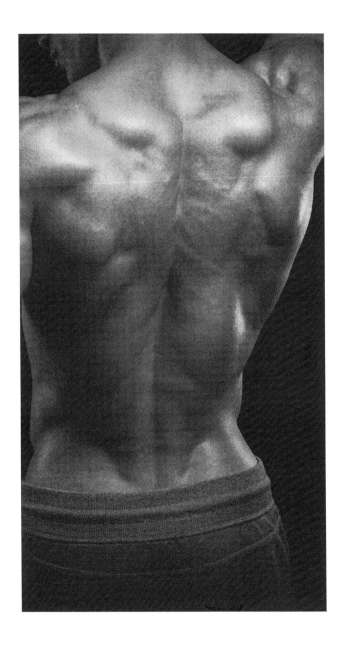

MY ANGEL
Copyright © 2019 Alanea Alder

PUBLISHER'S NOTE
This is a work of fiction. Any names, characters, places and incidents are the product of the author's imagination or are used fictitiously, and any resemblance to actual persons, living or dead, business establishments, events or locales is entirely coincidental.

www.sacredforestpublishing.com
P.O.Box 280
Moyock, NC, 27958
Digital ISBN- 978-1-941315-20-0
Print ISBN- 978-1-941315-21-7
Sacred Forest Publishing

Cover Design and Interior Format

Dedication

~Omnia Vincit Amor~ Love Conquers All~

Remember the best way to conquer
the darkness is to turn on the light.

PROLOGUE

ETAIN STARED INTO THE GOLDEN flames that flickered in the wall-sized fireplace. The warm light usually calmed his soul, but he found that he couldn't close his eyes without seeing the tormented tears of his mate.

Sighing, he sat back in the worn, brown leather recliner and swirled the rare amber liquid in his goblet. Fae wine outside of Éire Danu was hard to come by, but lucky for him he was favored by their queen.

He took a sip and breathed through the warmth expanding from the wine as it traveled to his stomach. Usually, it only took half a glass to chase away the worries of the day. He was on his second bottle, with little effect.

For the dozenth time, he raised his cell phone and stared. He had never once asked for help in all the long, lonely centuries he had been in Noctem Falls. It made him feel like he was failing to call now.

He shook his head. This was his future mate. His pride be damned. She deserved every protective measure he could call to their side. With his thumb, he pushed the number two. After several rings, a soft voice answered.

"Hello?" his baby sister sounded half awake.

"Hello, Allia."

He heard her gasp. "Etain! Are you well?" she paused. "Do you know what time it is?" she demanded, sounding more like her usual spitfire self.

"I may need some help baby sister," he admitted.

"Who do I have to kill?"

He pulled the phone away and stared at it checking the number. Frowning he put it back up to his ear. "No one." He scowled. "Who is letting you fight?" His second call would be to her twin and his other younger sibling Ailain.

She humphed. "My only big brother in the entire universe is calling me at two o'clock in the morning for the first time in years. Years Etain!" her voice rose an octave and he winced. "Of course someone needs a beat down and if you're even thinking of bypassing me and calling Ailain I will come there myself to kick you."

Etain's mouth twitched. "By the gods, I have missed you."

She sniffed. "I miss you too. When are you coming home for good? Surely your duty to the queen has been fulfilled by now."

He chuckled. "It was fulfilled a long time ago little one. I stayed because I saw hope where once there was nothing but fear and I wanted to ensure that hope had a chance to bloom."

"Then why call? What is going on?"

"I believe my mate in on her way to me and

could be in danger. Many things are happening right now in the city."

"Your mate? Oh Etain! That's wonderful news. What do you need from us? Should we come help?" she volunteered.

"No!" he barked. Images of his two precious siblings getting hurt or sick flooded his mind.

"You don't have to take my head off. I was offering assistance you know."

"It's not safe for the two of you to come here."

"But it's safe enough for you to be there?"

"I am a warrior. Besides I do have other fae here who can help. Belenos, Eoson, Vindonnus, Daire and Sulis also serve as unit warriors."

"Which Sulis?"

"Sulis Vi'Erlondon, Sulis Ri'Orthames is assigned to the Zeta Unit in Lycaonia."

"I always get those two confused. How did that happen? It's not common practice to name children after anyone, we're too long lived for it."

Etain chuckled. "The younger Sulis was named after his *athair*. Our Sulis walked around with his chest puffed out for months." He shook his head at the memory.

"Ailain and I have been training. We could help as much as the other warriors," she offered.

"Don't make me call father."

She snorted. "Go ahead. I bet it would be faster to come here explain everything, visit with mother and return, than to get him off the phone." She was quiet, then continued in a softer tone. "They miss you every day."

Etain swallowed hard. In truth, he missed them as well. Leaving the shining city of the fae had been hard, leaving his family painful, but leaving them both had been torturous.

"Can you ask the queen if she has anyone who can come visit for a few weeks, until things calm down?"

She sighed. "Of course I can. That's why you called me isn't it, instead of father? Because I'm her personal attendant."

"That and you're right, if I called father at two o'clock in the morning, I would only be able to hang up the phone with him after he traveled through a portal and stood knocking on the other side of my door."

She giggled. "True. I will pass along your request first thing in the morning. Is that crazy little human well? I know the queen will ask about her."

"She is fine. It amazes me that Meryn has captured the interest of our queen."

"I'm not amazed, do you follow her on Facebook? She is an absolute nut! We all love reading her posts here at court."

Etain shook his head. He wondered if Meryn knew exactly how popular she was, but then again, knowing her, she probably wouldn't care.

"She's even crazier in person."

"Bring her to visit along with your mate. You're long overdue to return anyway."

It was on the tip of his tongue to promise, but he hesitated. If his gut feeling was right his mate would be arriving to help with the children's sickness. If that was the case, she'd be needed here to help treat the children.

"I will bring them as soon as I am able," he promised.

"Etain, brother, everything is all right isn't it?" she asked, sounding younger.

He forced himself to smile and lighten his voice. "Of course darling. If things were truly dire I would be calling the queen herself would I not?"

"No you wouldn't. Don't try to blow smoke up my bottom, I know you. You don't like asking for help, that's why I'm worried, because out of all of us, I know you feel I am the easiest to talk to. That's why I believe things are dire, you'd never ask for assistance otherwise."

He sighed. "When did you grow up?"

"While your huge ass was walking around that dark, horrible city," she retorted.

"I do not have a huge ass," he protested. He smiled when he heard her giggle.

"You know what I mean. I'm pretty tall but sparring with guards always makes me feel tiny."

Etain frowned. "Who have you been sparring with? Does the queen know?"

"Who do you think suggested the lessons?"

Etain rubbed between his brows. "Be careful." He knew he would be calling Ari Lionhart later to threaten his ability to reproduce if anything happened to his baby sister.

"Always."

"Goodnight darling."

"Goodnight brother, may the gods bless your dreams." She blew him a kiss and hung up.

He set his phone down and brought the goblet to his lips.

If only the gods could bless his mate instead, maybe, then his nightmares would end.

CHAPTER ONE

"I AM STARTING A RELIGION."
Etain looked across the breakfast table and stared at the small human. He and Micah were invited by the prince himself to take their meals on Level One going forward. It was easier to get everyone's briefings done while eating, than to have multiple meetings throughout the day.

Aiden's head snapped down to look at his mate. "No."

"My furries need guidance. And, I'm bored." She looked over to Gavriel. "You've been around a while. How do religions start?"

Aiden's expression became more panicked as he realized that his mate was serious. "Meryn, you cannot start a religion. It just isn't done."

She looked up at her mate. "Why not?"

"Because!" Aiden sputtered.

"I think I would be a great religion." She turned to Magnus. "Right?"

Magnus' lips twitched. "There are worse examples of both religions and religious leaders out there. I do believe you could do better than they."

Aiden shot the prince a dirty look before focusing his attention on his tiny mate. "You don't even update your Facebook regularly, how could you run a religion. What are you basing it on?" The Unit Commander sounded absolutely flustered.

Meryn tapped her chin. "Good point. Other regions have martyrs and shit and I don't feel like dying. They're also usually really smelly, and my stomach is finally settling down. I don't need to make myself sick with my own body odor."

Aiden relaxed a fraction. "See, there you go."

Gavriel chuckled. "These things usually evolve over time Meryn. I do not believe you can just announce it on social media."

"But I've worked out my first commandment already," she said brightening.

Eva's eyes were dancing as she leaned forward. "Do tell."

Aiden growled. "Don't encourage her."

The air around Meryn shimmered, and suddenly she was dressed in a black monk style robe and cowl. "Thou shalt not be a douchebag," she intoned in low monotone syllables.

Across from each other, Colton and Declan folded their hands in front of their chests. "Amen," they said in unison.

Adriel frowned at the grinning duo. "These two should stay in different cities. I fear for Noctem Falls."

"Oh Holy One, your latte is ready," Ryuu said placing a tall cup in front of Meryn.

The hood was thrown back before the clothing shimmered to the sweats and tee shirt she had been wearing. "Yes!" She picked up the cup and inhaled reverently.

Kendrick smiled indulgently at Meryn amused by her wackiness. He then turned to Aiden. "She will need another guard. I am commandeering Law and the twins to work in the lab with me."

Meryn frowned. "My acolytes? Why?"

"Because they are twins and can run power between them, amplifying it like a battery. They will be needed," Kendrick informed her.

Etain cleared his throat. "I can watch over her."

Aiden look at him relieved. "Are you sure?"

He nodded. "Of course. My queen holds her in high regard. It would be an honor to guard her."

"Perfect," Law said. "Kendrick told me that we would be delving into old magic. I don't know if I will ever have another opportunity to see it done."

"Does anyone have anything else to go over?" Kari asked looking up from her clipboard.

Meryn raised her hand and waved it. Kari smiled at her. "Go ahead Meryn."

"Y'all's iPads arrived yesterday with the shit ton of supplies that Marjoram strong armed that hospital into donating." She laughed. "I was there when she called, the directors were tripping over each other seeing who could be the most ingratiating because of that asshole who tried to kill Ellie. I could almost hear them genuflecting over the phone." She looked at Ellie. "Your gram is a serious badass."

Ellie grinned wickedly. "I know."

Meryn turned back to Kari. "I already set up the iPads and linked them to our network. They are ready to go." She looked behind her. "Ryuu?"

"I have them here *denka*." Ryuu lifted a small

stack of silver tablets. He handed one to each person at the table. Etain frowned down at his. "What does this do?" he asked.

Meryn shrugged. "What doesn't it do? It can do lists, email, texts, FaceTime, video and audio recording, movies, music, books, internet browsing, lists, database records and more."

Adriel held his in his hands as if it were made of expensive, delicate crystal. "You said that it could also be used with a pen." He pulled out a ballpoint and went to write on the tablet.

"Stop!" Meryn screeched.

Adriel froze. "What?"

Ryuu handed him a thin white object. "I believe you are to use this."

Adriel frowned. "Where is the ink or lead?"

Kari shook her head. "I can show him Meryn. I use a tablet at work."

Meryn sat back. "Neanderthals I swear." She looked at her mate. "I added everyone to the same running contact list including email addresses."

Colton held up his tablet. "Meryn what is the app with the 'V' on it?"

"That's the Vanguard app I launched last year. I had Radek distribute it among his squad first. They forwarded it to every Vanguard they knew of with instructions to do the same. To register they have to meet up with another Vanguard squad for verification then both squads can proceed. Their personal information is then added to my database and I'm able to track them using a built in GPS feature on the app." She became thoughtful. "There aren't many of them."

Rheia smiled. "Of course there are. Radek said

that there were multiple squads per state. Even if there was only one squad per state, that's at least two-hundred and fifty men."

"Well, only eighty-five have registered," she said flatly.

The men around the table became quiet. Colton opened the app. "Why don't we have to register?"

"Because I know you're not feral. That was the whole point of the verification process." Her explanation did nothing to alleviate the mounting tension in the room.

Etain looked to Micah, Grant and Declan. They had many close friends among the Vanguard.

"I'm sure they're just off the grid," Colton said.

"Meryn why didn't you tell me about this?" Aiden asked scowling.

She rolled her eyes. "Tell you what exactly? That your friends didn't want to sign up for my app?"

"Baby, based on what Darren Williams was able to tell you about the current list of Vanguard members, how many are missing?" Aiden asked.

Meryn fidgeted. "About one hundred. According to his latest list, there are thirty-seven Vanguard squads, which equals one-hundred and eighty five members."

Aiden paled. "That can't be right."

Rheia set her fork down. "Does my brother know?"

Meryn nodded. "He said he would work on contacting anyone who is listed as 'unregistered'."

"Unregistered?" Declan asked.

She turned to him. "Those who have been invited to join but haven't followed up."

"Add that to our growing list of concerns," Magnus said, pointing to Kari's new iPad.

"What list?" Rex asked.

Magnus turned to Meryn. "What did you call it again?"

"The SGW list. 'Shit. Gone. Wonky'," she explained. "I moved a copy of that list to the iPads. It syncs among our group. So if someone adds something or solves a problem it updates for everyone."

Magnus nodded. "Yes, yes. Very apt name. Which reminds me," He turned to Kendrick. "Since the twins are reporting to you for the duration, can you have them check the city's refuse tubes? We have had multiple reports of slow or backed up drains. As you know, those two are some of the best earth witches we have."

Kendrick nodded. "I'll get them on it today."

Etain noticed that the prince looked more tired than normal. He had dark circles under his bloodshot eyes. "Sire, mayhap you could rest after breakfast?" he suggested.

Magnus shook his head. "Too much is being added to that damn list for me to rest."

"Don't make me call my grandmother down here," Ellie threatened.

Magnus smiled. "Her company would be welcome compared to what I have planned for my morning." He sat back. "I have meetings with the heads of the Founding Families today regarding the children. Speaking of which, were you able to call your friend?"

Ellie nodded. "Vivi? Yes, I called her this morning actually while feeding Benji. She said that she had to tie up a few loose ends, but she'd get here as soon as she could. Knowing her, that means this evening at the latest. I had barely gotten the words 'Shifter Virus' out when she started asking about the nearest portal."

Magnus' eyes softened at the mention of Grant's new son. "How is our little gentleman?"

Ellie beamed. "He's teething, which means tons of drool and growling. Grant thinks it's adorable," she said teasing her mate.

Grant shrugged. "He is very fierce."

"Where is my godson?" Adriel asked.

"My gram took over watching him during the day. The antivirals that Rheia and Anne brought have bought us some time. Adora along with her mate and son help us monitor the children during the day and we've been rotating unit warriors to stay with them at night." Ellie looked at Grant, who kissed her temple. "We don't want Benji at the hospital anymore," she admitted softly.

"Well duh, that's where the sick kids are," Meryn said breaking the awkward silence Ellie's confession created.

Ellie looked up surprised. "You don't think I'm being a hypocrite?"

Meryn just stared at her. "How? If you were working at a normal hospital, treating an outbreak among kids, no one would consider you a hypocrite for leaving your child at home. It's not your fault everything is cramped in this city. I swear you can't turn around here without stepping on someone's nuts."

Eva chuckled. "Especially when you're aiming for em."

Meryn shrugged. "He had it coming." She

looked at Ellie. "If anyone has something smartass to say about Benji send em my way. I'm your bitch remember?"

Ellie broke out into a huge smile. "How could I forget?"

Aiden groaned. "You don't need to be offering to fight." He looked at Ellie. "Send them my way instead."

Ellie blushed. "Thank you, Commander."

He waved a hand at her. "Trust me, it would be a pleasure to educate some of these pompous windbags."

"Did that mouthy little troglodyte ever challenge you?" Kendrick asked.

Aiden grinned. "Not yet, maybe he's still clucking like a chicken."

Meryn looked between the two men. "So it's okay for you two to cast spells and beat up on people but when I do it, I'm being 'difficult'." She held up her fingers to form air quotes.

Etain sipped his coffee. She had a point. If you took her actions and attributed them to warriors, it wouldn't seem as scandalous. "She has you there Commander," Etain mused out loud.

"My pregnant mate does not need to keep getting into fisticuffs with impudent tunnel escorts and exposed to spell making components," Aiden refuted.

Meryn stared. "Did you just seriously use the word fisticuffs?"

Aiden ignored her. "She should be concentrating on eating healthier and getting more rest, for our child's sake."

"Meryn two-point-oh happens to like pudding

and coffee thank you very much." Meryn sat back crossing her arms.

"I noticed you ate a normal breakfast this morning," Rheia pointed out.

Meryn blinked and looked down at her empty plate. "It tasted good today."

"It's because I doused everything in cinnamon," Ryuu said stepping forward to take her plate. "Marjoram's suggestion seems to be working, though, we may need to stock up on more cinnamon."

Meryn stuck her tongue out at her mate. "Ha! There! I am eating better."

Aiden smiled and pulled her onto his lap. "I'm very proud of you baby."

Bethy turned to Ryuu. "I don't think that will be a problem. The vendors on Level Six adore her. With all the rumors running rampant about our pregnancies, they will be tripping over themselves to donate."

Aiden looked at her. "What rumors?"

Bethy looked at him surprised. "You mean you haven't heard?" Her eyes glanced around the table. Etain shook his head when she looked at him. "None of the warriors have heard anything."

Kari sipped her coffee. "I have heard some things, but I bet you have heard more. The people here trust you more than anyone," she informed Bethy.

Bethy blinked. "Oh. Well, as most of you know a pregnancy is a sign that a couple or in our cases, our House has been blessed by the gods. Despite there being a sickness here in the city, most still view Uncle in a positive light. On this level and within our circle of friends, there are four pregnancies, plus little Benji. Most of the city believe that Uncle is favored above all others by the gods, especially with my pregnancy being out of season. It has helped more than you know to keep political rumblings to a minimum."

Eva snorted. "If you call that mob that marched on our bar-b-que minimal rumblings, I'd be afraid to see what could happen."

Bethy turned to her friend. "That was just a portion of the Noble and Founding Families. Remember, they represent a small percentage of the city. The average citizen outnumbers them sixty-to-one."

"Holy shit!" Eva exclaimed. "That's close to twenty thousand people based on the little I know about the Noble and Founding Family numbers, where are all these citizens hiding?"

Bethy looked confused. "They aren't hiding. They are on their levels of course."

"There's no way twenty thousand people go to Level Six and I missed it," Meryn argued. "I have cameras now."

Bethy exchanged looks with Magnus who shrugged. She turned back to Meryn. "Why do you think they all go to Level Six?"

Meryn held up her hand and began counting off on her fingers. "Food. Shopping. Food. Entertainment and food."

Bethy laughed. "Meryn, each level is self-sufficient and trade directly among themselves for foods and goods. Going to Level Six everyday would be like going out to eat every night."

"And?" Meryn asked as if unsure of her point.

Bethy sighed. "Meryn, normally people don't eat out every night."

Meryn looked around the table guiltily. "Oh. Well, I didn't either before I met Aiden," she said quickly. "I cooked a ton of Hot Pockets for myself."

"Don't remind me," Ryuu murmured.

Etain relaxed back in his chair. "I'm glad to hear that the people still support our prince. It will make patrols go much smoother."

"Agreed." Adriel added.

"So like twenty thousand people huh?" Meryn hedged.

Bethy nodded. "Yes, Meryn."

"So, like these peeps are kinda like homebodies and don't get out much huh?"

Bethy shrugged. "I suppose."

"So, how do we know they aren't sick?" Meryn asked.

Etain felt his heart begin to race. He looked around the table to see varying degrees of horror on the faces of his closest friends.

Ellie, Rheia, Anne and Adriel stood quickly.

"Stop!" Kari shouted holding up her hand.

They turned to her, eyes wide.

"Running out of here with your hair on fire will not solve anything. Obviously if they are ill, they are not reporting it. If you all storm out of here panicked, we will have nothing but chaos on our hands."

Slowly, the four sat back down still looking a bit wild eyed.

Kari stood. "Let us instead have the normal level patrols done by the warriors go door to door for the next few days. We have not done a sweep in a while looking for our errant feral Augustus Pettier, let us use that as our explanation to speak with everyone."

Kendrick rubbed his chin as he stared at Meryn. "How is it that you somehow manage to see things we don't?"

Meryn shrugged and stared down into her latte. "My grandmother used to say that my defective brain focused on the wrong things."

Etain clenched his fists. More than once he had heard comments about Meryn's grandmother, and none of them were good. Having gotten to know Meryn well over the past couple weeks he could only imagine how precocious she was as a child. She would have been a delight to know. It angered him that her upbringing was anything but a happy one. Hearing the gasps around the table at her quiet comment he knew the others felt the same.

"You are not defective Meryn. You are extremely special and should be treasured as the rare mind you are. If I hear of anyone saying otherwise, they will have to face me," Magnus said his eyes darkening to a deep burgundy.

Meryn smiled shyly at his pronouncement while Aiden continued to rub his cheek against the top of her head. "So if I need a favor?" she started, a calculating look on her face.

Magnus smiled, his eyes returning to their normal color. "You have only to ask."

"Will you take me down to the vaults today? I'm kinda tired, so I was thinking we should just take it easy and have some fun," she suggested.

Beside Magnus, Bethy stilled as did Adriel. Etain knew the two of them along with Sebastian were pushing Magnus to rest more. The prince was pale and looked exhausted. A day with Meryn might be just the thing to help him recoup.

Magnus became thoughtful. "I do not know Meryn, so much is happening. I have the meet-ings with the Founding Family members this morning." He strummed his fingers on the table. "I could have Sebastian escort you down so you could pick out your rewards."

Meryn hopped down off her mate's lap and trudged over to Magnus. She leaned over to rest her head on his shoulder. "Please," she asked simply.

"I could very easily go to those Founding Family meetings in your stead Uncle," Bethy offered.

Magnus' eyes went wide as he stared down at her spiky brown hair. His mouth opened and closed several times before he smiled gently. His arm came around so he could pat her on the head. "Of course dear, I will go with you."

Meryn's popped up, and she grinned at him. "Good because I don't know what you consider an heirloom. Plus half of it is probably stuff we don't use anymore. I don't want to pick out a golden bowl only to discover people used to shit in it or something."

Magnus stared, then burst into laughter. Wiping his eyes, he pulled her head down and kissed her forehead. "I will keep you from making such mis-takes." Meryn blushed furiously.

Bethy met Meryn's eyes and mouthed, 'thank you!'.

Sebastian stepped up behind Meryn and ruffled her hair. "I will pack a huge lunch and soft duvets. You can make a day of it, the whole day in fact."

Magnus shook his head. "Surely not the whole day."

Sebastian pointed to Meryn. "You would not want to disappoint the little one would you?"

"Of course not."

Sebastian crossed his arms over his chest. "Then you both are to spend the entire day in the vault, relaxing and resting."

Magnus looked at his niece. "Thank you for taking over the meetings for me darling. Remember if they get too rambunctious to call me immediately."

Bethy looked over at Kari grinning. "I think we can handle it Uncle." Kari nodded.

Etain hid a smile. It was clear who was really in charge on Level One.

Meryn rubbed her hands together as she walked to Aiden and climbed back into his lap. "Time to swim in the gold coins like in *Duck Tales.*"

Etain smirked at Law who was scowling. "Too bad I'm her guard now. I bet you would have loved to see what our prince has in his vault."

"Shut up," Law groused.

"I'm not upset you're jealous," Kendrick said to Law. "Even I wouldn't mind seeing what the prince of the vampires has deemed precious enough to store in the family vault."

Meryn looked at the witches smugly. "I get to go. I even get pudding," she gloated.

Kendrick winked at her. "That's because you're so special."

Micah cleared his throat. "Adriel, with four new adult cases showing up at the hospital yesterday, would you like me to change out the rotations so that the shifters are doing patrols away from sickness? The witches, fae and vampire warriors can help on Level six," he suggested.

Adriel exchanged glances with Rheia and Ellie. They both nodded before Ellie spoke. "That might not be a bad idea. As Meryn pointed out just because we haven't seen any vampires coming forward as sick doesn't mean there aren't any. But we do know for a fact that shifters are susceptible. The last thing we need is for our warriors to get ill."

Grant turned to his mate. "I've been around the kids since day one and haven't gotten sick, in fact, none of the shifter warriors have."

"Let us not tempt Fate," Adriel said.

Grant scowled at his unit leader. "I'm staying with my mate."

"Of course you are," Adriel sighed. "Just be careful."

Grant rolled his eyes. "At this point, I've been covered in just about every type of bodily fluid a kid can produce, if I was gonna get sick I would have by now," he said jokingly.

Ellie turned to her mate slowly her eyes wide. "You're right. You've been exposed to everything from vomit to blood. Why aren't you sick?"

Grant looked surprised at her expression. "Because I eat my veggies?"

Declan laughed. "No you don't, you're a meat and potatoes kinda guy. Sometimes minus the potatoes."

Ellie frowned. "Why aren't you sick?" she demanded again.

Grant looked around to the others. "Do I apologize for this?"

"No, but this does make for an interesting morning in the lab," Kendrick mused.

"Grant as you have just admitted, you have

already been exposed. You stay with Ellie and continue to help on Level Six. The other shifter warriors should be moved to patrols in the city. I do not want to take any chances with their health," Magnus ordered. He turned to Ellie. "When did you say your friend was arriving?"

Ellie smiled. "I bet you she is packing as we speak."

CHAPTER TWO

VIVIAN MERCY STARED DOWN AT her cell phone and chewed on her lower lip. Eleanor Kimball had to be one of the best pediatricians in the world, so there was no doubt in her mind that when the doctor used the term 'Shifter Virus', that's what it was. The only problem was, they didn't exist.

Her seminar about updated lab procedures at the Center for Disease Control had just wrapped up, so she was between projects. There was a fae portal located outside of Atlanta, so she could head to Noctem Falls from there. She just had to convince her squire to tag along.

Why did it have to be Noctem Falls? Why in the hell was Ellie there? Why couldn't it have been Lycaonia?

"Motherfucker," she muttered.

"Vivian, language." A low voice rumbled.

Vivi smiled. If she had a dollar for every time her squire admonished her for cussing she could afford to send him on the vacation he obviously needed.

"You'll be cussing too when you hear what's

going on."Vivi stood and walked out of her office, down the hallway to the small family room where her extremely large squire sat folding her underwear.

Not for the first time in her life she was struck by the contradiction that was her squire. For as long as she could remember Halbjorn Bergson had been at her side. As a child, she always assumed they were related because they both had red hair, everyone in the human world assumed they were father and daughter. It never even dawned on her how unlikely that was since he was a shifter and she a vampire. Growing up she never questioned why a bear shifter squire was raising a vampire child, but once she was old enough to venture out into other paranormal communities, she began to notice exactly how different they were from others, and realized that their small family was an oddity.

For one, not everyone had a squire, and if they did they usually chose one of their own race. Secondly, most children had at least one parent. She had neither, just Hal. He was everything to her. Mother, father, brother, best friend, but most importantly squire. He took care of her and made sure her world kept spinning. She would have been lost without him.

He was also huge, like blot out the sun huge. But that never scared her, if anything he always made her feel safe, after all who would tangle with a six foot eight, barrel chested bear shifter descended from Vikings?

"That was Ellie," she began.

"Oh?" he commented without looking up.

"She discovered a shifter virus."

This had him looking up. He smiled. "Sounds right up your alley, when do we leave?"

She grimaced. "She's in Noctem Falls."

"No," he said immediately.

"But Hal..."

"No. I won't have you waltzing back into the lion's den. I told you a long time ago, we could go anywhere on this earth but Noctem Falls, and I meant it." He put the clothes in the basket and turned to face her. "Anywhere but there."

She sat next to him and wrapped both arms around one of his. "They've already lost a child Hal. She was only five years old."

He inhaled quickly. Her shaggy squire was a push over for children. She continued. "It hit the children first, over a dozen are sick now. You know I can't say no."

He rested his head on top of hers. "I didn't realize Noctem Falls started to have children again."

She smiled. "They haven't. Prince Magnus took in a local wolf pack to protect them from the unexplained murders going on around the country. It's their children who are ill."

She felt it when his breath caught. "Wolves are at Noctem Falls? Are you sure?"

She nodded against his arm. "From Wolftown," she answered quietly.

Cursing he stood and began to pace in front of their coffee table. Being so tall it was a short walk back and forth. "What is Fate up to now?" he grumbled.

"You know I'd rather stay here with you, but I can't turn my back knowing my refusal could result in more children dying."

He stopped and turned to her a sour look on his face. "You already said yes haven't you?"

She nodded. "I wouldn't be the girl you raised had I said no."

"Low blow Vivi," he rumbled.

"Will you come with me?" she asked.

His brows snapped together as he frowned. "Of course I'm coming with you! Let you head off to that city of death alone? Ha! I'd like to see you walk out of here without me girly. You're not too old for me to put you over my knee," he threatened.

She rolled her eyes. He had never raised a hand to her. She doubted he would start now. "If we pack right away we could get there by this evening."

Hal stopped his pacing. "You get the suitcases down from the attic, you know I don't fit through that tiny hatch they built. I'll start organizing your clothes. It's a good thing I just did the wash." He bent down easily lifting the clothes laden basket with one hand.

"Yes, Hal," she said smiling.

"In and out. A quick visit. Do not talk to anyone. The sooner we get back home the better. I don't trust that prince, or the vampires, or anyone in that city," he rambled.

"Yes, Hal," she agreed.

He wagged a thick finger at her. "I mean it missy. No talking to anyone."

She fought against the urge to roll her eyes again. "Just the medical team and those organizing treatment efforts, that of course may include the prince, that's unavoidable."

"Fine, just stand behind me when we talk to them," he answered.

Somehow she didn't think it would work like that, but she wasn't about to argue with him. "Be right back with those suitcases."

"Don't forget to pack your toothbrush," he yelled from the kitchen.

"I know!" she shouted back. She stomped down the hall towards the attic hatch. Smiling she pulled the rope and unfolded the stairs. She would always be six years old to her squire, and she wouldn't have it any other way.

"Hello my name is Sulis Vi'Erlondon. I will be your escort to Noctem Falls." The tall blond warrior gave them a half bow and stepped to one side to clear the way for the portal.

"My name is Dr. Vivian Mercy, and this is my squire, Halbjorn Bergson," Vivi said introducing them.

"Ellie is looking forward to your arrival. She and the other doctors have been working around the clock to figure this thing out."

"Ellie huh? Not Dr. Kimball?" she asked.

Sulis smiled. "Grant only makes Doc call her Dr. Kimball. The rest of us call her Ellie. She insisted."

"Who is Doc?" Hal asked.

"Dr. Nathaniel St. John, our resident physician. Evidently, Grant believed he was flirting when introducing himself, so he isn't allowed to call her

Ellie."

"Ellie is mated?" Vivi asked incredulously. They had spoken to each other that very morning and she hadn't mentioned anything about having a mate.

Sulis nodded. "They met each other right after she arrived. It seems like the warriors are finding their mates all over the place, don't be surprised if you end up with one of my brothers," he winked at her.

At her side, Hal growled. "She won't be getting mated to anyone," he admonished.

Sulis cleared his throat and fought a smile. "Of course."

Vivi regarded him. "You say your brothers, but don't include yourself."

"As much as I would love to have a stunning woman like you as my mate, your aura doesn't shine for me."

"Aura?"

"That's how the fae can sense their mates."

"Vivian perhaps we should head to the city? The sooner we get there, the sooner we can return," Hal reminded her.

Sulis shook his head ruefully. "My apologies for the delay, please step through the portal, I will follow and close it behind us."

Vivi slung her backpack over one shoulder and allowed Hal to walk through first. Seconds later, she stepped through and was immediately overwhelmed by the sun and heat. Hal was at her side in a moment. "Bear with it for a bit longer, the city isn't far."

"Is she well?" Sulis asked as he closed the portal.

Hal scowled at the fae. "She is sensitive to the sun, even if it is setting."

Vivi always hated all the special provisions she had to make in life due to her body's reaction to the sun. Luckily, she could work whatever hours she wished in her own lab.

"Then by all means let us not waste a moment more. Follow me." He took them to the edge of the cliff and held out a hand to her. She shook her head and jerked her thumb to her squire. "If you could help him, I can make it down on my own."

Sulis offered a forearm to Hal, who looked as if he would rather be doing anything other than being escorted by the fae. They floated down to a small ledge. Sulis was about to step forward when the archway began to glow, and the large door swung open by itself.

Sulis' mouth dropped. "It isn't supposed to do that."

"Oh well, I'm heading in." Vivi couldn't wait to get out of the heat. Once inside she was able to relax. The cool air of the stone city washed over her. "Much better." She smiled up at her squire. He only grunted as a response.

"Dr. Mercy, I was told to bring you directly to Level One..." Sulis began.

Hal stepped between them. "And why is that? She is here to help Dr. Kimball not placate the prince."

Sulis shook his head. "The prince is in his family's vault at the moment. He let Drs. Kimball and Albright take over the meeting rooms on Level One for as long as they need."

Vivi tried to peek around her squire. "He did?

Why is he in his vault?"

Sulis grinned openly. "He promised the Unit Commander's mate a reward for all she did in modernizing the city. They have been down there all afternoon. They should be returning to his quarters soon though. Last I heard she picked out a few things. She has him completely wrapped around her finger."

Hal sucked air through his teeth. "Like that is it?"

Sulis straightened, and his face turned frosty. "I would appreciate it if you kept your disparaging remarks about my Unit Commander's mate to yourself. She would never, ever betray the McKenzie, nor would the prince participate in such a disgraceful act."

Vivi stepped past Hal. "He meant no disrespect, but that's usually how it's meant in the human world, unless you are talking about a child."

Sulis inclined his head. "Meryn isn't a child, but, well you have to meet her to understand. There isn't much any warrior wouldn't do to keep her safe."

"I look forward to meeting her. Please show us the way," she smiled at him apologizing again with her eyes.

His icy demeanor thawed a bit. "Of course. If you would follow me." He walked them over to a large hole in the floor.

She blinked. "The transport tunnel."

Sulis nodded. "Heard of it have you? It's very handy if you can fly, very inconvenient if you can't." He extended his forearm again for Hal.

When they arrived on the lower level, she instinctively turned right.

"Dr. Mercy, this way," Sulis called out pointing to the left.

She shook her head. "Sorry." She followed him to a door and waited while he knocked. Moments later, a polished, handsome man opened the door and smiled at them. "Just in time for dinner."

"I'll take my leave here. Good luck," Sulis said, then waved goodbye.

"Please come in, everyone has been expecting you. My name is Sebastian Hearthstone. I am the squire for House Rioux." He opened the door wide for them to enter.

"Come in said the spider to the fly," Hal whispered.

She elbowed him in the stomach and was satisfied at his surprised grunt. She winked at Sebastian, who winked back.

"Don't mind him, his blood sugar is low. My name is Dr. Vivian Mercy, and this is my squire Halbjorn Bergson."

"It is a pleasure to meet you both. Both Ellie and our Broderick have had nothing but wonderful things to say about you. I will show you to the dining room. Prince Magnus and Meryn returned only minutes before you arrived. If you hand me your bags, I will take them to our guest quarters," Sebastian held out his arms.

"We're staying here? On Level One?" Hal asked incredulously.

Sebastian looked at them confusion on his face. "Of course. The lab is on this level, it will make it that much easier for updates, meetings, and meals."

"I'll take our bags if you show the way," Hal offered.

Sebastian inclined his head. "As you wish."

Sebastian walked them down a long hallway off from the main room. "These quarters have recently been expanded thanks to two of our local witches. I think the two-bedroom suite will be perfect for you. They included a kitchenette and a small family room. It is quite cozy." He stopped and opened the door. "Here we are."

Hal stepped in first and looked around. "Nice." Without saying anything else he took her backpack along with the suitcases and went in to put them away in their rooms.

"A man of few words?" Sebastian asked.

"Not when you get to know him," she answered.

When Hal returned Sebastian escorted them back toward the main room. When he opened a large set of doors, Vivi fought the urge to turn around and run. Over twenty people sat at a huge banquet style table. Everyone stopped their conversations and turned to them.

"Vivi!" a voice called out before she was nearly plowed over by her friend.

"Hey EllieBean, I heard you got mated. Forget to go over that little detail?" She crossed her arms and gave her friend the stink eye.

Ellie blushed. "I wanted to wait until you were here." She turned and rushed back to the table to scoop up a small toddler out of a dark-haired man's arms. "This is Benji, my son."

Vivi felt her mouth drop. "Son!"

Ellie thrust the child in her arms. "Grant and I were able to adopt him. Isn't he perfect!" she gushed.

Vivi stared down into two unblinking brown

eyes. She felt a piece of her heart melt away. "Well aren't you the cutest little spawn."

Ellie smacked her arm. "Don't call him spawn."

"She's right Vivi. This little guy is too cute to be called spawn," her squire chastised her.

"Hal!" Ellie hugged the large squire who in turn leaned down and kissed her forehead. A low ominous growl echoed throughout the room. Hal's head came up, and he scanned the table. "Your mate I take it?"

Ellie beamed up at him. "Isn't he wonderful?"

"If he's that protective of you, then absolutely." Hal stared at the man who was glaring at him. "Well pup, stand up and let me see you."

The man stood and stalked over to them. He pushed Ellie behind him and snarled up at Hal. "I am not a pup."

Hal guffawed. "You are, but that's okay. A few more centuries and you'll be able to pull off that little growl."

Vivi wanted to sink through the floor when her squire reached out and patted the agitated wolf shifter on the head.

The growling immediately stopped. "Did you just pet me?" The man asked in a low voice.

Ellie jumped between them. "Vivi, Hal, this is my mate Grant Douglas. Darling, this is my other best friend Vivian Mercy and her squire Halbjorn Bergson." Ellie gently took her son and passed him to his father. Grant visibly relaxed and stepped back cuddling the boy. Hal beamed at him. "You have the makings of a great father. Good for you."

Grant still glared at them but there seemed to be less venom in his eyes. "Thank you," he mumbled.

Ellie pulled her forward. "Let me introduce you."

They sat down and by the time introductions were done Vivi's head was swimming. "Is that everyone?" she asked sarcastically as they took their seats.

Ellie shook her head. "Actually no. Adriel and Micah are wrapping up check-ins with the warriors who had patrols today. They should be here any moment."

"Etain may be late too. He had to swing by the hospital to grab some bandages," Meryn volunteered.

Ellie swung around to face the small human. "Why on earth did he need bandages?"

Meryn spun the butter knife on her plate. "He may or may not have been the victim of my horrible throwing skills."

Ellie's eyes widened. "Good gods, what did you hit him with?"

Meryn's face lit up. "A shit pot! I actually found one. I'm glad I talked Magnus into going with me. I meant to toss it to Magnus, but it kinda drilled Etain in the head. On a positive note, I did find some cool stuff for my rewards."

Declan lost his composure. "Our golden boy was brained by our wacky human with a chamber pot," he held his sides as he laughed.

"It was a sight to see," Prince Magnus added chuckling.

Vivi studied the man she heard so much about. He was nothing like she expected. Hal raised her on stories about the foreboding prince and how he killed to take over the city. The man before her exuded warmth and kindness. She looked over at

Hal to find that her squire seemed just as confused as she felt.

"Sorry we are late everyone, but the meetings with the patrol leaders took longer than antici-pated."

Vivi turned to see an elegant warrior walk in who looked a lot like Gavriel. Behind him a shorter but no less handsome man walked in grinning. "Evi-dently, today's visit by the warriors constituted the only company some of the citizens has received in months." He laughed. "They were hard-pressed to get away."

"At least they didn't nearly get brained to death by a poorly aimed chamber pot," the golden giant teased as he closed the door behind them.

"Vivi, this is Adriel Aristaios, Noctem Falls' Unit Leader, Micah Sageson, the Eta Unit's witch and Etain Vi'Aerlin, Eta's fae warrior," Ellie said intro-ducing the trio.

"I said I was sorry, like at least twice," Meryn protested.

Etain smiled at her. "I know. I am only joking."

As they walked by Vivi was overwhelmed by the most amazing smell. Honey. No. Honey*suckle* and cinnamon. Vanilla and musk. Gods what was that amazing aroma? She stood.

"Vivi?" She heard Hal ask. She ignored him and followed the smell until she was standing next to where the ethereal looking golden warrior sat.

He frowned up at her. "Yes?" His eyes widened as he stared at her chest.

Using her vampiric strength, she used one hand to push him away from the table before straddling his legs.

"Vivi!" Hal called. "What have you done to her?" he roared.

Behind her, she heard chairs falling as men scrambled past her to restrain her squire. She ignored them and concentrated on the man in front of her. "Gods you smell delicious."

"I can see your light," Etain said choking on the words.

She leaned forward and sniffed the bandage on his head. "Honeysuckle," she whispered.

"Vivi!"

She shook her head to clear it of the pleasures promised by the blood pumping through her mate's veins and turned. "Hal!" The woolen bubble that the scent of his blood created popped, and reality came crashing in on her. She hopped off the blond warrior and raced over to where Adriel and Aiden had her squire pinned to the table.

"Let him up, I'm here now," she ordered.

Aiden looked at her dubiously. "Are you sure? He's a strong sonofabitch."

"Yes, I'm sure. Let him go please."

The men let her squire up, and he immediately swept her behind him and backed them against a wall growling the entire time. "He bewitched her. What did you do to her?" he demanded of Etain.

Vivi pushed against her squire's back. "I've met my mate Hal."

He froze, and the growling stopped. He half turned to stare down at her. "What? Are you sure?"

"Yes Hal, she has met her mate, so would you kindly move out of the way?" a polite but dangerous voice asked.

When Hal turned and straightened he was looking eye to eye with the blond warrior. Vivi took a moment to admire her mate's tall, strong body.

"We'll see about this supposed mating," Hal said moving slightly to one side.

"This is like a made for TV movie," Meryn said watching everything with wide eyes.

Etain gently pulled Vivi forward and into his arms. All at once, she was surrounded by his scent again, and she almost moaned out loud. She rested her head against his chest. "It's true Hal. He's mine."

"May I be the first to congratulate you on your mating?" The prince said standing. "Though this may not be the best of times, finding your mate is always a cause for celebration." He turned to Sebastian. "Mayhap some wine will help to relax everyone?"

Sebastian nodded. "Just the thing. Ryuu?" The other squire nodded and followed Sebastian out of the room.

"Halbjorn, will you not sit down with us and get to know your charge's mate better?" the prince asked.

Hal gave a sharp nod. Etain turned with her and led her back to the table. He pulled out a chair for her. When she sat down, he gently pushed her chair in before sitting down himself. Hal took the seat on her other side.

A long silence filled the room.

"Well this is awkward." Meryn announced. Beth just shook her head at the blunt announcement. "What?" Meryn demanded.

"Doesn't announcing something is awkward just make it more awkward?" Ellie asked.

Meryn shrugged. "Probably." She turned to Vivi.

"So why is your squire so 'grrr' about you finding a mate?"

Vivi smiled. Meryn couldn't have phrased the question better. "Because he is my only family. He raised me from the time I was a baby, so the responsibility he feels as my squire is compounded by the fatherly affection he has for me as my parent."

Meryn nodded. "I bet Marius is like that."

Vivi looked at the human. "Not Ryuu?"

Meryn grinned wickedly. "There would be no 'grrr' he'd just kill peeps."

"That is a frighteningly accurate assessment *denka*." Ryuu said, stepping through the doorway from the kitchen. He balanced a full tray of wine glasses effortlessly.

Sebastian followed behind them. Where Ryuu offered white, Sebastian offered red. Once everyone who chose to indulge sipped on their wine the tension in the room did noticeably dissipate.

Vivi frowned when Sebastian handed a small bottle to Hal. "What's that?"

Sebastian grinned. "A gift from Prince Magnus and his brother Caspian. Our Bethy has recently mated, and we understand the turbulent feelings it brings. What you are holding is a sample of aged vampire whiskey, Forbidden Fruit. That bottle, in particular was made from apples harvested right here on Level One, in the Royal Gardens."

Hal regarded the bottle with interest. "Well now." He uncorked it and drank straight from the bottle. His face brightened. "Well now, indeed." He nodded at the prince at the end of the table. "You have my thanks."

While Vivi was relieved that her squire was no

longer in any danger of being executed in the prince's dining room, the overwhelming urge to roll around on top of her mate, preferably naked was threatening her sanity.

She nearly jumped out of her skin when she felt a warm hand settle on the back of her neck. She turned to find her mate smiling down at her. His arm rested on the back of her chair, and his long fingers massaged her neck gently.

"Better?" he asked softly.

She nodded. "Thank you."

"Your comfort and well-being will always be my utmost concern. I will spend the rest of our days tending to your every need," he promised.

"Oh my," she whispered.

"I love the way the fae talk," Meryn said eyeing Aiden's wine glass.

"Though our words may seem grandiose, that does not make them any less sincere," Etain explained.

"I just like it." Meryn stared up at her mate. He sighed and pushed his glass over to her. "Not too much." She picked up the glass and took a sip. "I think I like the white better, the one from the other night that Ellie had."

"That was an import from a vampire clan in Germany," Sebastian explained. "I will write down the vineyard for you."

Meryn handed Aiden back his glass. "As much as I love my little parasite, I wish I could try all the wine Magnus has to offer. I mean, how many people get to experience the depth of the prince's wine cellar?"

Aiden raised an eyebrow at his mate. "Please

don't call our child a parasite."

"A parasite is an organism that lives in other organisms and benefits from the nutrients of it's host. A baby is just a parasite," Meryn explained.

Aiden frowned. "That's not right."

Rheia chuckled. "Technically, she is correct, though it sounds terrible to say it like that."

As Ryuu and Sebastian began serving the dinner's first course Vivi cleared her throat. "Could someone get me up to speed so I can get started in the lab before laying claim to my mate?"

CHAPTER THREE

VIVI GLANCED UP TO SEE if she embarrassed her mate. He winked at her and calmly continued to sip his wine while drawing figure eights on the back of her neck. Did he have any idea the effect he was having on her? She looked back over to him and saw a self-satisfied smile. Yup, he did.

As they ate their dinner Ellie went over the timeline she established from the moment she was called, with Rheia adding bits and pieces from her perspective after her arrival a few days ago.

"So you're saying you didn't see evidence of a possible virus at all until Clara's passing?" Vivi asked.

Ellie nodded solemnly. "Her heart defect is the only reason we were able to see anything at all."

"Shifters do heal quickly," Vivi swiped through the notes on the iPad that the squire Ryuu handed her. In it, were observances from nearly everyone involved. "Whoever put the notes in a group share was a genius."

Meryn nodded. "I know."

"Maybe when you grow up you can go into computer work," Vivi said without looking up. She knew full well that the little imp was an adult, but her smirk was practically begging for teasing. Vivi had to fight a smile when she heard an indignant gasp.

"I am grown up!" Meryn insisted.

Vivi just smiled at her and ignored her protest. She turned to Ellie. "I know you must've had a long day," she glanced over at her mate and sighed. "And the gods themselves know how much I'd like to retire with my mate, but I really would like to get to the lab tonight."

Ellie chuckled. "We'll make it quick."

"I won't," Vivi murmured.

Across the table, Declan laughed. "I can't wait to see her ruffle Etain's feathers. He's always so calm and proper."

The brunette at his side smacked his arm. "Leave them be Declan."

Declan nuzzled his mate. "But Kari, I am happy for my brother. I have to torture him to show him I care."

Kari shook her head and sent her a sympathetic look. "The boys think they are clever sometimes. It comes and goes."

"Ahh. Good to know," Vivi said playing along.

Declan frowned. "I am always clever."

Kari patted him on the arm. "Yes, dear."

Vivi turned to Hal. "Are you okay settling in here?"

"That depends. You are coming back here tonight aren't you?" her squire asked raising an eyebrow.

Behind her Etain leaned in closer. "We'll both be sleeping here tonight. I believe that it is imperative for Vivian stay on this level to work in the lab and I, as her mate, of course will be with her." Hal glared at her mate.

"Don't worry Etain, the twins soundproofed the new guest quarters so you can get your freaky deak on without worrying that the red giant will kill you in your sleep," Meryn announced grinning.

Vivi looked over and met Meryn's eyes. The little midget had gotten her back for the 'being grown' comment. Meryn stuck out her tongue.

Hal heaved a great sigh. "I suppose he can stay with us."

Vivi felt a moment of unease. Her squire sounded like he was saying goodbye. When he looked at her his eyebrows shot up. "What's the matter my little love?"

"I've dated before now, why would meeting my mate be any different?"

Hal waved his hand about. "They were, how would you describe them? Temporary? An amusement?"

"A fuckboy?" Meryn volunteered.

Hal nodded. "I like that term." He looked back at her. "I knew they would come, then go. No pun intended." She gave him a flat look, and he continued. "Etain will stay. You won't need me anymore."

Vivi felt her mouth drop open as her eyes immediately filled with tears. Without thought to decorum, she launched herself at the man who raised her and wrapped her arms around his neck. "I will always need you!" She buried her face against his chest. She looked up as tears trailed down her cheeks. "Am I not your little girl anymore?"

Hal settled her on his lap as he had done a million times before in the past. To him, it didn't matter if she was five or seven-hundred and five. "You will always be my little girl, no matter what. However, you have a mate to tend to you now."

Vivi looked over her shoulder at her mate who watched them patiently. There was no censure or anger in his gaze, only acceptance. She begged him with her eyes. "He's my only family. He is both mother and father to me. I can't lose him."

Etain moved over into her chair and rubbed her back. "Who said anything about him leaving? He is also your squire is he not? I don't know about you, but I'm not the best when it comes to being domestic. I pay a nice motherly citizen from Level Five to clean my home once a week and to do my laundry. I either eat with the men on the Unit Level or grab something from Level Six. If anything, Hal is needed now more than ever." He paused before his face lit up with a huge smile. "Especially if we have children right away as seems to be the pattern lately."

Vivi held her breath as Hal's muscles tensed under her hands. She looked up at her squire, and he stared down at her mirroring the shock she felt. Suddenly, he was grinning from ear to ear. "A baby?" Gently he passed her over to her mate. He was still smiling like an idiot when he poured himself a half glass of the whiskey that the prince gifted him. He raised the glass to the ceiling. "May the gods be willing." He shot back the liquid and laughed.

Vivi looked up at her mate with a sour expression. "You seduced my squire."

Etain shrugged a smile tugging at the corners of his mouth. "It seems that he and I agree on something."

She sniffled suddenly feeling embarrassed. When she looked around the table all she found were varying degrees of affection and understanding.

"Sorry about that display," she said ducking her face against Etain's chest.

"Nothing to be sorry for at all my dear. Your world just changed significantly. If we can help in any small way, it would be a privilege. There is nothing as sacred as the bond between a girl and her loved ones," the prince said smiling at his niece with nothing but affection shining from his eyes. He nodded at Hal. "And nothing more anticipated than a grandchild or grandniece."

Beth smiled. "It could be a grandnephew."

Prince Magnus shook his head. "I do believe your child will be the most perfect little girl, just as you were."

Beth blushed. "Oh, Unky."

Sebastian set a huge slice of cake in front of Hal. "When the time comes, I can show you all the places I ordered from for our Bethy. The things they have for babies now! I could spend all day looking at things online." He sighed happily before leaning down. "Personally, I like the baby duck theme."

Hal chuckled. "I need to order some fabrics right away to get started on baby clothes."

Across the table, Meryn began to choke on her pudding. Immediately Aiden and Ryuu were at her side gently pounding on her back. Looking up she stared at the huge squire. "You make baby clothes?"

Hal nodded and jerked his head toward Vivi. "Granted not for a long time now, but yes, I do sew."

Meryn's eyes were wide. "I know she said squire, but I was thinking more like bodyguard."

Hal rubbed a hand over his bushy, red beard. "I do that too."

Meryn's face contorted. "So you're like a Viking Martha Stewart?"

"Meryn!" Aiden exclaimed.

Hal burst out laughing. "That sums it up nicely. But Meryn, most squires cook, clean, sew and act as a bodyguard. Does yours do any differently?"

"No, but he doesn't look like he eats trucks either," Meryn answered.

"Not in this form at least," Ryuu murmured under his breath as he set a fresh bowl of pudding before his charge.

Vivi relaxed against her mate as her squire laughed uproariously. She could tell he was taken with the tiny, blunt human. She was glad to see the doubt and fear were gone from his eyes, replaced with love and hope. With a few simple sentences, her mate helped her only family smile again.

"Thank you," she whispered into his ear. His arms tightened around her. "There is nothing I would not do for you," He kissed her temple and held her close.

"Vivi, whenever you're ready, we can head to the lab. I'm anxious to see what you make of the magic." Ellie said smiling.

"Magic?" Vivi frowned.

Ellie grimaced. "Using the process of elimination we ruled out a bacterial infection leaving us with a virus as the culprit. That was pretty standard. But what makes this whole thing even trickier is that there is magic *in* the virus. The only reason we could see the virus at all, even using Clara's blood, was due to the sparkling light the particles of whatever spell was used were emitting. I may have missed it altogether otherwise."

"Now's good. Though, I don't have much experience with magic." Vivi stood and cracked her back. If there was magic in the virus she needed to get started right away.

Around the table, Ellie, Rheia and Kendrick also stood. Kendrick kissed his mate before walking over to the door and opening it for them. "That is where I come in. After you ladies."

Vivi looked down at her mate and blushed. "I guess I will see you later?"

He nodded. "I will be in your quarters getting to know your father figure better. He is family now."

"I'll bring the whiskey," Hal offered gruffly.

Vivi looked between the two men of her life. "Have fun." She walked around the table to join Kendrick by the door.

Rheia kissed Colton before snagging a couple of cookies while Ellie kissed both her mate and son. "Don't wait up for me. I'll be along as soon as we're done."

Grant nuzzled the side of Ellie's neck. "Call me when you're ready to come home. I'll come down to meet you."

Ellie kissed him. "I'm sure Emeric can escort me. It is kinda his job."

Grant grumbled under his breath. "Fine, but if anything happens, I won't be happy."

Vivi looked between the two. "What could possibly happen?"

Ellie blushed. "So telling you about the virus was part one of my story." She looped her arms with Vivi's. "As we walk to the lab I'll tell you part two."

"Walk slow so I can eat my cookies," Rheia said. Ellie nodded.

When they reached a long hallway Ellie smiled up at her. "So there may have been a few murders and attempted murders I forgot to mention."

Vivi stopped in the middle of the hall. "What?"

Etain waited until Hal had another drink before telling him about the recent murders and the current security concerns.

The large man stood and began to pace from one side of the room to the other before turning to look at him. "You mean to tell me there's a feral on the loose that can mask its scent due to a necklace made from the souls of poor murdered unborn babes, and both Kari and Ellie were almost killed?"

Etain grimaced and nodded. "In addition to that, we believe the virus was engineered adding a new level of sophistication to the ferals arsenal."

Hal reached for the bottle and poured himself another drink. "I knew we shouldn't have come here. This city has always been nothing but a cesspool of corruption and death." He took another drink. "No wonder the prince looks haggard. The city is about to implode." He looked at Etain. "Where are the Elders?"

Etain stared into his own glass. "They had just

moved back to the city when things started to get bad. Prince Magnus practically had to order them back to the City Estate to keep them safe. Declan still hasn't convinced his brother to leave as of yet. I personally doubt he will, as Kari is with child. She carries the next generation of the Lionhart line. Rex would sooner chop off his legs than leave her here."

"Why not evacuate the women?" Hal suggested.

Etain raised a brow. "Have you met them?"

Hal chuckled. "Stubborn, intelligent, strong and feisty. Just like my Vivi."

Etain smiled. "She is amazing. You did a wonderful job raising her."

Hal puffed out his chest proudly. "She is pretty wonderful isn't she?"

Etain set his glass down. "So, do you feel like telling me how a bear shifting squire ended up with a baby girl vampire?"

The scruffy squire eased into one of the recliners. "She'll tell you when she's ready. It's her story and hers alone."

"I'm her mate," Etain pointed out.

"Exactly. And when she's ready to talk about it, she'll let you know. You'll not get a word from me." Hal shook his head.

"Can you at least tell me that nothing from her past can hurt her? That there is nothing I need to prepare for?"

Hal turned his attention to his glass. "Like I said, it's her story to tell."

Etain collapsed back in his chair. "Marvelous, just what we need. More complications."

Hal shrugged. "Life is full of em." He turned to

him a sly grin on his face. "You know, she started her fertile cycle last week."

Etain inhaled just as he was taking another sip and ended up choking on the whiskey. He set the glass down quickly and pounded on his chest. When he looked up Hal was grinning broadly at him. "So, a girl or a boy? Personally, I'd like one of each to keep me busy. It's been too long since Vivi was a baby, and I miss taking care of a little one."

With a shaking hand Etain downed his drink and reached for more causing Hal to laugh. As his glass was refilled his mind wandered to that childbirth video their commander showed them. He had been joking when he suggested a child, now that it seemed to be an actual possibility, he was scared out of his mind.

Hal clinked their glasses together. "It's the will of the gods."

Etain nodded. "I'll drink to that."

"So why does a scientist have a squire?" Kendrick inquired, raising an eyebrow.

Vivi shrugged. "They're useful. I may have starved otherwise." She looked down to read over the lab notes Ellie handed her. She turned to her friend. "Ellie, could I see the samples?" she asked, ignoring Kendrick's pointed gaze.

Ellie indicated to the counter where Rheia was finishing up the microscope set up. "She's just about done."

Vivi walked over to the long counter. Rheia moved to one side, and she stepped in front of the microscope. Vivi looked down and frowned. Using the dials she moved it left and right before adjusting the magnification. She looked up. "Are you sure this slide contained a sample?"

Ellie walked over. "Of course I'm sure! I labeled them myself." Vivi stepped aside as Ellie stood in front of the microscope and looked through the eyepiece doing exactly what Vivi had just done. She moved the slide about for a minute before turning to Kendrick, a panicked look on her face. "It's gone!"

Swearing in different languages Kendrick stalked over and took Ellie's place at the microscope. He peered through the eyepiece before straightening. Frowning fiercely he looked at them. "The magic is gone as well."

He pulled the slide from the metal clasps. Under his breath he recited a spell making the slide glow for a moment. With his eyebrows knit together he looked at them. "The slide hasn't been tampered with. There's no evidence it was wiped clean or sanitized."

"Some viruses cannot live outside the human body for long. They need the environment the body provides," Vivi suggested.

Kendrick shook his head. "If that were the case the organic part of the virus may die but some trace of magic should be left no matter how minute." He pulled his walkie talkie from his belt. "Frick, Frack, I need you down in the lab."

A few moments passed before a voice answered. "Be right down, just have to save our game."

Kendrick sighed. "Just hurry." He re-clipped the walkie-talkie to his belt. "Gods they make me feel old."

"You adore them and don't try to tell me any different," Rheia said teasingly.

Kendrick shrugged. "They look too much like Keelan for me not to adore them." He chuckled. "And I've been watching over them since they were children. They were so damn adorable at times I couldn't tell them no, when I should have."

"Like when?" Vivi asked curiously.

"Like when I was working on dangerous spells, I almost blew them up a time or two. It's why they remember me bellowing at them a lot. I was scared to death that I would accidentally break them down to a molecular level."

A few minutes later two, tall red-headed men practically fell through the door. Breathing heavily they immediately went to Kendrick. "What's up?" one asked.

Kendrick pointed to her. "This is Dr. Vivian Mercy, she came to Noctem Falls with her squire Halbjorn Bergson to help Ellie with the sickness. Vivian, these two rapscallions are Nigel and Neil Morninglory, technically they are unit warriors, but they need a bit of polishing." They grinned at her looking very young indeed. She waved, and they waved back. Kendrick cleared his throat. "She discovered that the virus is no longer visible, so I'd like for the two of you to amp up your magic as much as you can and pass it through me like last time," he paused. "I see no trace magic either."

The boys' eyes widened and without being asked twice lay one hand each on Kendrick's arms as he stood in front of the microscope.

Kendrick frowned at their hesitation. "Well?"

The one introduced as Neil gulped. "All of our power? Are you sure?"

Kendrick chuckled. "Yes, I'm sure. I can handle whatever you two can produce."

Nigel's eyes lit up. "Wicked!" He turned to his brother. "We never get to play with all of our magic," he said excitedly. Neil nodded then the two of them closed their eyes. Moments later, Kendrick exhaled slowly through his nose as both of his arms began to glow an emerald-green color. He cracked his neck and leaned over to look through the eyepiece. Cursing he stepped back and the boys moved their hands. He turned to them. "There isn't the slightest trace of magic now." He rubbed his arms where the boys ran their magic through him. Scowling he looked from one twin to the other. "I'm adding more lessons to your daily schedule." He let his hands drop. "Where have you two been hiding that much power?"

Nigel and Neil grinned at him before Neil answered. "You taught us."

Kendrick's mouth dropped. "I most certainly did not."

Nigel nodded. "Yes you did. Remember in Storm Keep we were asking you how to pass the warrior test like the others, so we didn't score too high so they would keep us? We started doing it then."

Kendrick's eyes bulged. "You were only supposed to do that for the damn test! Not all the time!"

The boys paled. "Oh," they whispered.

"Oh? Oh?" Kendrick threw his hands up. "Do you have any idea what could've happened if you lost control of that much power?" He walked away keeping his back to the room.

The boys let their heads hang. "We're sorry. We didn't think about the damage we could do to the city," Neil confessed.

Vivi knew that was the wrong thing to say when Kendrick whirled around and stalked over to the boys. She thought he was going to lay into them when suddenly he pulled them into a fierce hug. "To hell with the city! The two of you could have died! Gods above! That much power could have burned you up." He gave them one final squeeze then stepped back. "No more hiding your power. You're to work directly with me for as long as I'm here, and if I have my way I will strong-arm Magnus into letting you return with Meryn and me to Lycaonia."

The boys were reduced to tears they kept trying to manfully wipe away. They looked up at Kendrick, hope a living thing in their eyes. "We could go home with you?" Nigel whispered.

Kendrick nodded. "Absolutely. I'm not leaving you here to languish while being used to clean refuse tubes." His eyes narrowed when the boys' heads turned in opposite directions to look at anything but him. "Boys? You did check on the refuse tubes today, didn't you?"

They looked down and scuffed their feet. Neil looked up. "We meant to, but well." He exchanged shudders with his twin. "It's nasty."

Kendrick's eyes rolled toward the ceiling before he pinned the boys with a glare. "That's why they are called refuse tubes. Tomorrow morning, no later."

Their heads bobbed. "We will."

Kendrick pointed at the door. "Go directly to bed and tomorrow a full breakfast. After using that much power your bodies will soon be feeling the effects. Make sure you're in bed before it hits."

They beamed at him. "Yes, sir!" They ran out of the room much in the same manner they had entered it, recklessly.

Once the door shut, Kendrick pulled out a stool, sat down and resumed rubbing his arms. "How in the hell did they go unnoticed?"

Rheia walked over looking concerned. "Are you well?"

Kendrick nodded and sighed. "I'm angry at myself for not seeing their abilities sooner. When I think of what could have happened." He scrubbed his hands over his face.

Rheia lay a comforting hand on his shoulder. "You're not a god Kendrick, no matter how much you like to act like one." When he looked up, she winked at him, and he relaxed.

"What do we do now?" Ellie asked in a small voice. "Seeing the virus was the only ray of light from Clara's death." She wiped at her eyes.

Vivi wrapped an arm around her. "You're forgetting my other specialty, hematology. I've studied blood since the invention of the microscope."

Ellie looked confused. "What good will studying their blood do if we can't see the virus to work on a cure?"

"I didn't just study human blood to improve it for my people. I also studied using vampire blood as a healing agent for others," Vivi informed her.

Rheia frowned. "We thought of using vampire

blood, but decided against it because of the bonding that would occur."

Vivi looked at the human doctor. "What if you could use vampire blood without worrying about the patient bonding with the vampire donor?"

Rheia stared. "Then we could cure just about anything." Her eyes widened. "That's what you've been working on?"

Vivi nodded. "I've been very secretive about the procedure since it's still being tested among humans, but yes, I believe I found a combination of science and magic that may work."

"I thought you said you didn't have much experience with magic," Kendrick pointed out.

Vivi shrugged. "I personally don't, not really. What I use as part of my procedure was created by a witch years ago. I use it in the same manner as I would use a microscope or centrifuge."

"What exactly are you talking about?" Kendrick asked.

"It's a flat stone the size of dinner plate that was bespelled to sever bonds. In the wrong hands, it could be placed under a bottle of wine to break up a marriage or under a coffee carafe to destroy friendships. I use a combination of three different strains of vampire blood, then set the bags of blood on the stone before infusion. It can take eight to twelve hours. The time varies depending on the age of the blood. By using different donors and the stone, so far, it's prevented a bond from forming in trials," she explained.

"Trials?" Rheia asked. "Wait, you've been using this on humans?"

Vivi nodded and smiled at Ellie. "Like my friend,

I have a soft spot for children. I have a small net-work of vampire donors who work with me to treat childhood cancer patients. The vampires have to be willing to move to the child's town for the first year of treatment in case a bond does form. If a bond forms, those vampires will stay close to the child for the rest of their lives."

"Good gods," Ellie whispered.

Vivi nodded. "Now you see why progress has been so slow. In the beginning before I figured out that using more than one strain of blood helped, we had two cases where the patient formed a bond." She chuckled at the memory. "Fate has a wonder-ful sense of humor because in both instances, the little girl ended up being the mate of one of the donors, so they, in essence, saved their own mates."

Rheia smiled. "That's amazing. Have you had any cases of bonding since?"

Vivi shook her head. "No. After the second case, we started using multiple donors and the bonding stone. So far, we cured an additional eight patients without a single bond forming." She turned to look at the microscope. "Though, I have no idea what parameters should be used with shifter patients."

"It's something," Ellie began bouncing on her feet excitedly. "We had to space out the antivirals because they are losing their effectiveness. This could be the breakthrough we need." She laughed. "If this works, we won't even need to see the virus. The vampire blood will give the shifters the boost they need to cure them altogether."

Kendrick stood. "I think we need to work and save as many lives as possible," he paused. "That being said, I also think we need to identify this virus and trace it back to its source." He looked around. "If the ferals, or reapers, or whoever is out there now working against us, can cook up this virus, they can make more. I'd rather kill them all and destroy any trace of their methodology before more death and chaos can spread."

Rheia chuckled at Ellie's shocked expression. She turned to Kendrick. "We'll leave the magic, killing and destruction to you. We'll work on keeping people alive," she said in a sardonic tone.

Kendrick shrugged a shoulder. "We all have our strengths."

Ellie turned to Vivi. "What do you need to get started?"

"You're lucky I don't go anywhere without my stone. It's the one component that would be almost impossible to replace." She looked around. "If you can find me three different vampires to donate, I can start tonight. I just need a flat surface in a refrigerated unit for the bags of blood to sit on. Preferably, the plate and the blood will be the only items in the unit."

Ellie turned to Kendrick. "Can you call some warriors down? Rheia and I can clear out one of the smaller refrigeration units we have."

Kendrick gave them an evil grin. "I'd love to." He unclipped the walkie-talkie again. "Tree Beard, come in."

Whoever Tree Beard was, he took longer than the twins to respond. "Do you have any idea what time it is?" A surly voice responded.

"I need you, Godard and Viktor to report to the lab as soon as possible," Kendrick ordered.

"Bloody fucking hell."

"Careful, women are present," Kendrick barked. He gave them a shit-eating grin that belied his anger.

"My apologies. We will be right down."

Kendrick was humming as he reattached the walkie-talkie.

Vivi stared. "Why did you derive so much pleasure from torturing him?"

Kendrick just gave her a sly smile. "Godard and Dimitri were in charge of Nigel and Neil before I got here. From what I heard they let the twins practically overdose on cookies then used them to create the hospital. Turnabout is fair play."

Vivi couldn't argue with that. "Good for you." She started looking around the lab until she saw a familiar silver and red case with her tags on it. Her lab equipment arrived before she did. She walked over and using her thumb, unlocked the case. "What the hell?" Kendrick exclaimed leaning away from the case. Carefully she lifted the stone from its custom-made foam insert.

"May I?" Kendrick asked. He held out his hand.

She gently set it down on his palm. He swallowed hard looking a bit ill. Frowning he turned the innocuous gray stone over in his hands before passing it back to her. "Nasty piece of magic that. Who did you say created it for you?"

"I didn't." She held up a hand when he went to continue his questioning.

"Don't bother grilling me, I have no idea who it was. It was literally a back-alley transaction at the turn of the century. I never even saw their face."

"Damn," he muttered.

"Look at it this way, we know that this stone is

used to help and heal people, not harm anyone," she pointed out.

"True," he said and straightened when a knock sounded at the door. Ellie was walking over to open it when Emeric moved between her and the door. "Why don't you let me open that chér?" He blew her a kiss and went to the door. "Who is it?"

"Godard, Dimitri and Viktor here to see Kendrick Ashwood," a male voice answered. Emeric opened the door and let the three warriors enter.

Vivi stared at the tall silver-haired warrior, when he smiled at her, she noticed he had violet eyes. "Are those contacts?" she asked.

He shook his head. "No, they run in the family." He looked her up and down. "It is rare to see red hair that deep on a vampire. You are a true beauty." His words were polite, but his eyes were flirting.

Kendrick cleared his throat from where he sat on his stool. "Dr. Vivian Mercy, this is Godard Kipling, Kappa's unit leader. The pretty boy with the freaky eyes is Viktor BelleRose, Iota's unit leader and Dimitri Romanov, Theta's unit leader. Gentlemen, this is Vivian Mercy, Etain Vi'Aerlin's mate." Kendrick stressed the word mate.

Viktor's eyes widened and he involuntarily stepped back. "My apologies doctor, I had no idea you found your mate."

She smiled. "It's no problem."

Kendrick snorted. "Maybe for you, but I bet Etain would find it interesting to know that Viktor found his mate to be a rare beauty."

Viktor swallowed hard. "I do not see any reason to share that little piece of information with him."

Vivi laughed. "Etain is gentle and kind. I know

he won't hold it against you."

Viktor, Dimitri and Godard stared before Dimitri shook his head. "Gentle and kind with you of course, you are his mate. However, he is one of the fiercest warriors the fae have ever produced. I would rather face down raging, bloodied berserkers than your mate when angered," he admitted.

"Etain? My Etain? You must be wrong." Vivi shook her head.

Godard chuckled. "He is not the fae warrior for the ranking unit in the city for no reason. His polite and detached fighting style is haunting."

Dimitri turned to Kendrick. "Why exactly are we here, besides to get Viktor killed?"

"I need your blood," Kendrick said simply.

At once, the three warriors began to scowl. Viktor shook his head. "Vampire blood is nothing to be played with, especially mine. Being of a Founding Family our blood is potent and in the wrong hands, can be used against us."

Ellie stepped in front of the three men. Her eyes were wide and tear filled. "Oh please! We can use it to save the children. I swear to you it will be treated with the reverence and respect it deserves."

Immediately they began rolling up their sleeves. Godard glared at Kendrick. "Why did you not just say it was for the children?"

"It was more fun my way," Kendrick admitted.

Ellie, Rheia and Vivi collected close to a pint of blood from each vampire. Vivi eyed their donations. "This should get us started." She placed the blood on the plate and set it in the refrigerator Ellie and Rheia cleared.

"Do we want to know?" Dimitri asked.

Kendrick shook his head. "Honestly? Probably not, stay dumb and happy."

Viktor gave Kendrick a dirty look. "Are you always like this or do you have something against vampires?"

Kendrick thought about it a moment. "No, I'm pretty much always like this, no offense," he smiled at them brightly. The warriors scowled at his flippant response.

Godard eyed Kendrick. "Since you are a member of the Alpha Unit, maybe you should come train with us tomorrow. That is, if your soft archivist hands can stand getting a little dirty," he teased.

Kendrick gave him an evil smile and rose to his full height. He stood nearly half a foot over them. "You will find that I am not as easy to manipulate as a certain pair of innocent witches. I look forward to seeing you first thing in the morning."

Godard's eyes widened. "Gods you are as tall as Warrick! I did not know witches could grow that big." His eyes narrowed. "It is not magic is it?"

Kendrick laughed. "No, I don't need it," he bragged.

Dimitri was chuckling as he dragged his friend toward the door. "Well it was nice knowing you Godard. Let us go fill out your will."

"I wonder whether Adriel will let me run both Iota and Kappa," Viktor teased.

Dimitri snorted. "I do not know why you think you are in the clear. I have a feeling our tall witch friend here will ensure Etain is at morning drills. I am certain he will have much to discuss with you for flirting with Vivian."

Viktor paled and trudged behind his friends.

When the door shut Kendrick was smirking. "Did you see their faces?"

Ellie looked worried. "Will you really hurt him? All of the warriors have been so wonderful with the children," she fretted.

Kendrick leaned down and kissed her forehead. "Your kindness shines out in front of you like a beacon." He sighed. "No, I won't kill them...much. Just impress upon them what it feels like to be at a disadvantage. The twins have assured me that no one here has been cruel, but some of the friendly big brother treatment of them gets my back up."

Rheia sighed. "That's because you spoil them. Don't hold that against the other warriors."

Kendrick sniffed and stuck his nose in the air dramatically. "I can and I will." He turned to Vivi. "I may not kill them, but that may not hold true for Etain."

Vivi winked at him. "Who's to say Etain will even be able to walk in the morning?"

"Vivi!" Ellie exclaimed blushing.

Rheia bumped her shoulder. "Good point."

Vivi looked around the lab. "Speaking of mates, it's about time I go and claim mine."

She had waited her entire life to find her mate. Now that she found him, she was going to tie him to her in every way possible.

Vivi stared down at her mate. He was lying half on and half off the bed, pants on, and his shirt wrapped around his head. She was shocked he hadn't suffocated. The entire suite reeked of whiskey.

"Dammit Hal!" she muttered. "This wasn't why I wanted him to be unable to walk in the morning," she griped.

She should have known she was going to find her mate like this when she passed her squire out cold on the floor next to the coffee table in the family room snoring like a freight train.

She struggled to remove Etain's boots. "At least they weren't kidding about the soundproofing otherwise Hal would keep me up all night." The second boot flew off with the third tug, and she landed on her tailbone. "Sonofabitch!"

She lifted his feet up onto the bed and made sure he was lying straight with no limbs contorted at weird angles. She stared then smiled. "Maybe I should take off his clothes. I mean, to get comfortable." Vivi said out loud to convince herself.

It took her another fifteen minutes to work him out of his clothes, but the effort was worth it. Lying in only his boxer briefs she could stare at his body all she wanted.

She was going to remove his boxers, but decided against it. It would be like opening a Christmas gift early. She tilted her head and sighed. Her mate was absolutely, freaking perfect.

Like most fae his skin was a honeyed golden color. His white-blond hair contrasted against the warm tones of his skin. He wasn't bulky but everywhere she looked seemed to be taut skin pulled over toned muscles. Her mouth was literally watering at the thought of licking his neck and drinking from him.

She pulled up the expensive duvet and covered him gently. Shaking her head at her own misfortune she decided against a shower. What was the point? She hadn't done anything to get dirty and there would obviously be no claiming tonight.

She stripped out of her clothes down to her panties and put her undershirt back on. After everything she had been told today concerning the virus, she was simply tired and didn't feel like unpacking. She turned off the light and climbed into bed next to her mate.

To her surprise, he flipped over on to his side and pulled her into the curve of his body. When he buried his nose against her neck and sighed happily she found she couldn't stay mad at him. Closing her eyes she enjoyed being warm for the first time, in a long time.

CHAPTER FOUR

WHEN ETAIN WOKE HE HONESTLY thought he was dying. It was a physical effort to peel one eye open. The other one was beyond him. He looked down and froze. Where were his clothes? What happened with his mate last night? He had to suppress a groan. Though he was still in the process of waking up, his body was raring to go, he was harder than he had ever been in his entire life, and his mate's rounded backside was pressed against his overly enthusiastic groin sending shockwaves of pleasure through him.

His traitorous arm was wrapped around her waist, a hand cupping one of her full breasts. He closed his eye and rested his cheek against the back of her head.

"I'm awake you know." He pried both eyelids open as his mate turned in his arms to face him. "You alive?" she asked grinning.

"I am not quite sure." He turned his head sharply to one side and sighed in relief when it cracked.

There was a knock at the door. "Wake up! Rise and shine kiddos! If you don't hurry you won't get any of my cinnamon rolls."

"Your squire is a sadist," he grunted.

She snuggled in under his chin, and he kissed the top of her head.

"Did you try to keep up with him?" she asked.

"Yes, though I do not believe I did a very good job. There was drinking, singing and..." He winced. "I think I may have promised to name our first child Hal."

She giggled. "Have you seen my squire? What on earth made you think you could keep up?"

"I could not say no." Even to his own ears his explanation sounded pathetic. "I am sorry about ruining our first night together. I assure you I usually never overindulge like this," he whispered his apology feeling as though he ruined their mating.

She pulled back to look up at him. "You took the first steps toward building a relationship with a man who has been like a father to me all these years. I could never hold that against you. I know you made an impression. He doesn't make cinnamon rolls for just anyone." She kissed his chest.

He felt a renewed sense of hope. Maybe he had a chance after all.

"How did things go in the lab?" he asked, forcing his eyes to focus. He could have sworn he had perfect vision before the whiskey.

She frowned. "The virus is no longer visible, so we will be trying a method I developed using vampire blood to help treat the sick."

"You found a way around the bonding?"

"Yes, though I've never tried it on shifters." There was trepidation in her eyes.

He kissed the tip of her nose. "If anyone can figure it out it is you. I have the utmost faith in your abilities."

"You have no idea what the process entails, and you believe in me?" she asked.

"Of course I do. Even without Broderick and Ellie singing your praises, your dedication to helping to eradicate this sickness was proven last night when, before resting, you insisted on seeing the lab. Ellie called, and you got here eight hours later. That speaks volumes to me, and I am sure to others," he explained.

There was another banging on the door. "Ten minutes! Breakfast is in the prince's quarters, in the dining room."

Etain felt his heart begin to race at the heated look in his mate's eyes.

"Ten minutes is plenty of time," she said huskily.

His hangover was immediately forgotten. "What did you have in mind?"

She pushed him on to his back and straddled his waist. Smiling seductively she easily pulled her shirt off over her head tossing it to the floor. "I'm hungry."

Etain stared up at the siren above him. Her gorgeous red hair seemed to float about her shoulders to drape over her pale breasts. Her normally stormy grey eyes were edging a ruby red that matched her hair beautifully.

He wrapped his hands about her rounded hips. "I am all yours. From this moment forward I will be all you need. I am your mate. It is my right and my duty to feed you. I offer all of myself to you." He recited the words he had learned upon moving to the city; the words that would allow a vampire to truly relax and get the most of their feeding from their mate.

The hungry look in her eyes softened at his declaration before she bent over him slowly. "Thank you, my mate," she whispered. Slowly, as the tips of her nipples teased his chest he felt her lean in toward his neck. He thought he had been hard before, he was wrong. Her slow seduction had him feeling like his cock would shatter.

She licked and teased his neck until he was panting heavily and gripping at their covers. "You're killing me," he gasped.

He heard her chuckle before her fangs sunk deep. "Gods above!" he shouted as pleasure so intense rocked him to his core. Every time she swallowed it felt as if she were milking his cock.

Without thought he bucked his hips desperate for any type of friction. She continued to feed, but one hand snaked down his body. When her soft fingers wrapped around him, he detonated.

He shouted from the intensity of the orgasm as it reduced him to a shuddering mass. When she finished she daintily licked his neck and sat back looking like the cat that ate the canary. There was a slight hint of red at the corner of her mouth. Where her mound rested against him, her liquid satisfaction seeped onto his body telling him exactly how much she had enjoyed her feeding as well.

Etain was still trying to remember how to breathe when she hopped down and padded toward the bathroom. She looked back and smiled. "That was one of the most pleasurable moments of my life." She gave him an evil look. "You have six minutes to recover, shower and dress." Chuckling she made her way to the bathroom.

"Of course she is a sadist. She was raised by that damn squire," he muttered as his heart remembered how to beat. Inside the bathroom he heard her laugh. Smiling, he stretched his body reveling in how good he felt. As far as hangover cures went, that had to be the best one he had ever experienced.

Vivi watched in fascination as the tiny human ate one cinnamon roll after another. Where was she putting them?

Hal assisted Ryuu and Sebastian in serving breakfast. There was a satisfied smile on her squire's face as Meryn whimpered and groaned over his cinnamon rolls. He met Vivi's eye. "This is the first new food she has indulged in since arriving in the city. Evidently, she's been living off of pudding, meat pies and meat kebobs," he preened.

Meryn swayed back and forth in her seat eyes closed engrossed in her foodgasm. Between Meryn and Aiden, her favorite breakfast treat was disappearing quickly.

Hal set a platter of fresh rolls in front of her. He smiled at her. "I know they're your favorite."

"You spoil me," she breathed and reached for the platter. She piled her plate high with six rolls. When she looked over at her mate he was watching her with a surprised look on his face. "Are they that good?"

She took a bite and paused. They were better than usual. She chewed quickly. "Hal, why are they different?"

Hal gave her a sly smile. "Good different? Or bad different?"

"Definitely good different. Damn, Hal, these are amazing!" she quickly polished off her six and reached for more.

She glanced over at her mate's plate, which was still empty. Frowning she picked it up and stacked the fresh rolls one on top of the other. She handed it back to him. "I am sharing these with you because you are my mate."

Etain looked down at his plate. "I don't think I can eat all these."

Moans from the other end of the table had both her and her mate turning. Declan and Colton looked to be in the midst of convulsions. Etain looked down at his plate and picked up a roll. He took a healthy bite and his eyes rolled back in his head. Vivi snickered. She had seen that expression not twenty minutes ago.

Etain would chew, then take another bite, then chew. Somewhere in that process he swallowed and reached for more rolls. He looked over at Hal. "I forgive you for trying to kill me last night." He chewed slowly. "Is this that Ceylon fae cinnamon Ryuu has been using?"

Hal nodded. "When I saw it in the kitchen, I had to try it. It's impossible to get in the human world."

"It's exactly what Meryn needs as well," Marjoram added. She turned to Vivi. "I knew it was only a matter of time before the two of you showed up."

"You've worked wonders here Marjoram, but I

expected nothing less when I heard you and Ellie were here," Vivi said giving the woman a warm smile. Marjoram was her adopted grandmother, and she couldn't help mothering her whenever she visited Ellie. Vivi soaked up the attention like a flower reaching for the sun.

Vivi looked around. "Where is Ellie?"

Marjoram placed a single roll on her plate. "She and Rheia are upstairs doing a morning sweep of the hospital. They should be here any moment."

"I want to live off of pudding and cinnamon rolls and coffee," Meryn leaned back in her chair patting her distended stomach.

Ryuu smiled fondly at his charge. "I am sure that we can add a few more things to that list *denka*."

"I think I hurt myself," a dark-haired young man groaned. "It was worth it though." He looked at her and gave her a goofy smile. "Not the best way to present myself as an Alpha is it?" he joked.

She smiled her reassurance. "I think under the circumstances it's understandable."

"I'm Stefan Bolivar, the Alpha of the Wolftown pack. I've been spoiled by being able to come down here for some meals when we do updates. I swear I've gained five pounds in a week." He looked over at Meryn. "By the way. I spoke to my brother Cristo about you, how I couldn't place your scent. He's very curious, not much gets past a wolf's sense of smell. He said he would swing by to meet you." He frowned. "I'll wait until he's here to update him on some of the more complicated details regarding this sickness."

Meryn shrugged. "Whatever floats your boat."

"Speaking of updates," Kendrick began. He

spoke softly a change in air pressure the only evidence he was soundproofing the room. He stood and looked around the table. "We ran into a bit of a snag last night."

"Snag?" Magnus asked leaning forward.

Kendrick nodded. "For some reason all traces of the virus have disappeared from our prepared samples." He held up a hand as he saw Adriel and Aiden gearing up for questions. "They were not tampered with, all traces of magic are gone."

Stefan sat back looking pale. "What are we going to do? Nearly a quarter of my pack are ill."

Vivi mimicked Kendrick and stood. "That is where I come in. In an effort to improve upon my people's food source, I have been studying human blood and disease for as far back as science allowed. I think I may have a way to use vampire blood to help heal the sick, without the typical bonding taking place."

Gavriel blinked. "How?"

"By using the best of science and magic, though, in an effort to keep everything transparent, I have never used this method on shifters before, only humans."

"Success rate?" Magnus asked looking hopeful.

"Once I was able to figure out the correct balance of methods using a bespelled stone and a mixture of different donors for vampire blood, one hundred percent."

Magnus sat back exhaling. "Thank the gods!"

Vivi shook her head. "Don't thank them yet. Shifters metabolize much faster than humans. Last night, we prepared donations from three warriors. They should be about ready for trial runs. I am confident this method will help, but I cannot guarantee any results."

Magnus shook his head. "You have given us hope, that means more than any guarantee." He looked at her then Kendrick. "When can we start administering?"

Kendrick was about to respond when Colton's walkie-talkie crackled startling everyone. "Colton! I need you, Aiden, Gavriel, and Beth up here now! We just had three vampires show up sick! I also need Anne desperately! Shit just hit the fan!" Rheia's voice called out frantically.

Vivi didn't know the woman well, but she didn't seem the type to get hysterical. Judging from the way the men practically leapt to their feet she knew she was right in her assumption.

Colton, Anne, Kendrick, Aiden, Gavriel, Beth, Adriel, Eva and Stefan bolted from the room. Declan hurried out with Grant and Micah. He was speaking into his walkie talkie to the other unit warriors coordinating their efforts to station men on different levels to prevent mass panic. Magnus along with Rex, Kari, Caspian and Broderick headed to his office to start fielding questions. Vivi stood unsure of what to do. She was medically trained, but she didn't have much experience in hospitals working directly with the sick. She was much more comfortable behind the scenes, sequestered in her lab.

Marjoram wrapped an arm around her shoulder. "Get to the lab and start the first batches of the treatment. When they are ready, call out directly to me on those walkie-talkies, I will be listening for you. I will come down here and take them to Level

Six to be administered."

Vivi sagged in relief. "Thank you."

Marjoram kissed her temple. "You are our best bet in beating this thing. Your place is in the lab dear heart." She turned to Sebastian, Ryuu and Hal. "Okay gentlemen, we will need a lot of easy to eat foods of two varieties for our loved ones. Spicy dishes to pique their tastebuds and get them hungry and blander food that will sit well."

Sebastian nodded and turned to the other two squires. "I have a few ideas if you are able to help."

Hal had already started to clean up after breakfast. "You just try to keep me out of that kitchen. I have a few dishes I need to make for my Vivi too. They will help with eye fatigue and anxiety."

"You're too good to me," Vivi blew him a kiss.

She looked at Meryn who was still munching away on a cinnamon roll. When the room got silent Meryn looked up. "What?"

Vivi frowned. Shouldn't the small human be doing something? "What are you going to do?" she asked.

Meryn laid out a cloth napkin in an empty basket and started placing cinnamon rolls in its center before folding the sides up. "I'm going to my bat cave to give the twins some cinnamon rolls and let them know their morning lessons with Kendrick are cancelled. He can swing by to get them later for lab work." She scrunched up her nose. "Then I'm going to see what I can do to create a PA system. I'm sure Magnus will want to put out some sort of general announcement fibbing about how everything is 'under control'. Those pin message boards they use now on each level suck."

Vivi blinked. She hadn't expected for her to have thought that far ahead. "You're doing very well in staying so calm."

Ryuu coughed and Meryn snorted before giving her a droll look. "I'm not really a people person. I don't know anyone who is sick, so why would I be upset?"

Vivi had no idea what to say to that. Usually, people weren't so blunt about not caring about their fellow man. She found it surprisingly refreshing. "Good luck," she finally said. Meryn waved and headed out the door.

Ryuu turned to Sebastian. "As long as Meryn stays in her bat cave, as it were, you can count on me in the kitchen. I need to prepare her a more healthy snack for later to balance out the obscene amount of sugar she ingested for breakfast."

Vivi turned to Etain. "Can you stay with Meryn on guard duty? If Kendrick makes his way back to the lab he may need Law."

Her mate frowned. "I would rather stay with you, but, unfortunately what you suggest is the best course of action." He turned to Law. "Nothing better happen to my mate under your watch."

Law gave Etain a flat look. "You mean I shouldn't hand her over to the ferals with a bow wrapped around her neck?" he asked sarcastically.

Vivi smiled as her mate's expression darkened. When he moved toward the witch, she intercepted him. Wrapping her arms about his waist, she stepped up on tip toe to kiss him. His arms tightened around her, and she enjoyed his embrace for a moment before stepping back. "I'll be perfectly safe in the lab," she paused. "Though I can't say the same for you with the little human. If she throws anything...duck."

Behind her Law chuckled as Etain leaned down to kiss her forehead. "I will do my best to stay out of her way." Reluctantly, she stepped away from her mate and headed toward the lab.

Once in the lab, she went immediately to the refrigeration unit where she placed the previous night's donations. When she opened the door, she was disappointed to see that the stone was only a dark gray. The blood would be ready when the stone turned pitch black. After the stone was finished processing she would remove the bags, and it would need to recharge. They would have to wait until it lightened from black to light gray for it to be used again.

She turned to Law. "We still have some time. By the look of the stone maybe another hour or so. Then we'll have to slowly bring the blood up to temperature."

"Does it normally take this long for the blood to be processed on the stone?" he asked.

"No, at least it has never taken this long before. I can only assume it's because we are using older blood. There's a lot more potency to it."

"So, what do we do in the mean time?"

"We can prep the injectors. I use jet injectors because they are needle-free, so we should be able to administer quickly once the blood is finished processing."

"Sounds like a plan."

When she checked the blood a half an hour later, the stone was ink black. "We're good." She pulled both the bags of blood and the stone from the refrigerator. She carefully returned the stone back to its case to recharge.

She placed the bags of blood into a water bath unit and set the temperature to one hundred degrees, hotter than a human, but just about right for a shifter. It would cool in a bit in transit, but should still be warm enough to be used.

Placing a sample of each donor on a slide, she observed them carefully under the microscope. In vampire blood, older red blood cells were slightly larger than their younger counterparts, but not by much. In fact, she discovered that it was nearly impossible to measure the differences from a scientific stand point. She was simply going by decades of experience to ensure that no one blood strain overpowered the other causing a bond to form. It was a tedious process, but a necessary one.

Together with Law she filled the long cylinders of six injector guns. When they were done she stepped back. "Time to call Marjoram."

Law handed her his walkie-talkie. She looked at it. "Do I just press the button?"

He shrugged. "The little genius gave us call names and said we should use proper walkie-talkie etiquette, but I think you'll be fine if you just call out for Marjoram."

Vivi pressed the side button. "Um Marjoram?"

Moments later, she had a response. "Is it ready?" she asked, with no preamble.

"Yes, I have six injector guns here ready for distribution."

"Injector guns? Really? My, aren't we fancy? That should make this entire process, quick and painless. Thank the gods you were called in. I'll be right down."

"Hey guys, are you heading up to Level Six?"

Vivi turned around and was surprised to see her mate with Meryn coming through the door. "We hadn't planned on it why?"

Meryn held up a bag. "I need these installed on Level Six. They are bluetooth compliant speakers. I should be able to get them set up using an iPad, but they kinda have to be in place. I figured we would need to make announcements there first."

Vivi reached for the walkie talkie. "Never mind Marjoram, we're heading up."

"Okay dear, see you soon."

Meryn frowned at her. "You didn't use her call sign."

"That's because I don't know it."

"Oh. Yeah. I should make a list or something."

"Come along Tiny, we'll go with you up to Level Six."

"I know you are but what am I?" Meryn retorted.

Vivi reached out and ruffled Meryn's hair making it stick up in every direction. "Let's go Frodo."

"I swear I will glue your eyelids shut. I have practice!" Meryn threatened.

Etain wrapped an arm around Vivi's waist. "Please do not antagonize the genius." Meryn half turned and stuck her tongue out at her.

"I can't help it. She's like a bratty kid sister. It's fun."

Law stayed next to Meryn as they floated up the tunnel.

"I am not a brat," Meryn protested as they reached Level Six.

"Whatever Frodo." Vivi grinned when Meryn

glared at her through narrow slitted eyes. "I have lash glue, and I'm not afraid to use it."

"Bring it on. I have needles at my disposal."

Meryn pursed her lips. "Good point." She turned in the direction of the hospital and groaned. "Not you again."

The tunnel escort glared at her. "I hope you are happy. I hear vampires are sick now. You and your human ideals have brought us nothing but trouble. It is not enough that you are an embarrassment to your mate, but you have also somehow put our prince under your spell."

Vivi watched as all the color drained from Meryn's face. "I'm a what?"

The tunnel escort turned his nose up at her. "You are too stupid to know what a laughingstock you are. Everyone feels sorry for your mate. The once great Unit Commander brought low by a worthless female. He would be better off without you."

Vivi felt an icy calm spread through her body. Before either her mate or Law could react, she was standing in front of the tunnel escort. He blinked once before she drove the tips of her fingers into his throat.

"Didn't your mother ever tell you that if you didn't have anything nice to say, to not say anything at all?"

The escort dropped to his knees gasping. Behind her she heard Law speaking to Etain. "I never even saw her move."

"Neither did I," Etain admitted, sounding astonished.

"You...you... feel as I do. I heard you calling her names," the escort choked out the words.

Vivi stared down at the insignificant man. "My mate adores her. My best friend trusts her, and my squire has been enchanted by her. That makes her like family. I can call her a bratty little hobbit. *You* can't." She kicked the escort in the face sending him sprawling on his back. She casually walked over and placed her foot on his throat. She smiled when his eyes began to bulge.

A sense of calm washed over her. The detachment she felt as his lips began to turn blue was almost liberating. "You would do well to remember to never, ever cross me."

There was stark terror in the escort's eyes as he tried to nod with her shoe under his chin.

Warm arms encircled her from behind pulling her against a muscled body. "I think he understands now my love," her mate whispered into her ear.

His spoken words seemed to sift down over her like a golden mist, chasing away the cold darkness. "Good." She managed to keep her voice even as she removed her foot and watched him scramble on all fours. He crawled to the tunnel and pitched forward out of sight.

Vivi turned to look at Meryn. She was shocked to see the small human somehow diminished. She seemed even smaller than before.

"Are you okay?" she asked.

When Meryn looked up, her eyes were without light or personality. "Yes. I am fine." She looked up at Law. "I can show you where to put the speakers."

Law turned to them as if unsure of what to do. Etain stepped beside Vivi and took her hand. "Help her install the speakers then take her directly downstairs to her squire. We will drop off the injectors and join you later."

Law nodded, concern still clearly written on his face. "I am yours to command Red Queen, show me where you want me to float your speakers." He followed Meryn when she turned and left without another word.

Etain looked down at Vivi. "I am worried about her," he sighed. "Ryuu will probably slow roast me over a spit for letting this happen. I assured him I would keep her safe when we let him know we were coming up here to install those bloody speakers." His eyes searched hers. "Are you well? You didn't seem like yourself for a moment," he asked rubbing his thumb over her lips.

"I would be lying if I said yes. I don't think I've ever been that mad before in my life. I do care for Meryn, but it was more than that. His words echoed a thousand different men over the years. 'You're just a woman.' 'You're worthless.' 'Give up.' 'You'll never get a man acting like one.'." She swallowed hard. "I think seeing the devastation on her face was just the last straw."

Etain cleared his throat. "Would it be entirely inappropriate if I told you how incredibly sexy you looked with your foot on his throat like that?"

Vivi felt the protective ice that formed during the altercation begin to melt. Her lips twitched as she tried not to smile. "Is that right?"

He leaned down and began to nibble on the side of her neck. "How about after we drop off the treatment, I escort you down to the Unit Level and show you my home."

Vivi tilted her head to give him more access to her neck. "You mean where there aren't any squires to interrupt?"

"Exactly," he breathed into her ear sending shivers down her spine.

"Lead the way my love," she pointed toward the hospital.

Etain pulled back and met her eyes. "Love?"

"I meant it, did you?"

His golden eyes darkened to a burnt amber color. "Once we are alone, I will show you how much I meant it."

"Deal."

She hadn't grown up around mated couples, so she had no idea if the flood of emotions she felt for this warrior were true, but, she found she didn't care. She was going to dig her fingers into the swirling mass of desires and outright need and never, ever let him go.

CHAPTER FIVE

VIVI MADE HER WAY TO the hospital with her mate at her side. When they walked through the doors, she was shocked to the core by the number of beds occupied. In her mind, she knew the numbers, but before seeing the tiny bodies it had been just that, a number. Never in her life had she seen so many paranormals ill. It was as frightening as it was surreal. Sights like this were common in human hospitals, but never among her own people.

Marjoram rushed up to her. "The injectors?"

"Here." Vivi handed her the small box. "Any questions on how to use?"

Marjoram gave her a grim smile. "Point and shoot."

Vivi nodded. "You got it."

The older woman tucked the box under her arm. "You head down. It won't take us long to administer this batch. We'll document any changes and later we'll bring you down new samples, for what they're worth."

Vivi looked around the room. "Are you sure

there's nothing I can do?"

"There are plenty of doctors and nurses here to take care of our patients. Let's keep you fresh for what you were brought to the city to do. I have a feeling this will be a marathon, not a sprint, so relax while you can," Marjoram turned her around to face the door. "Now scoot."

"Call me if you need anything, or if you have any questions," Vivi called out as she left with Etain.

"We will," Marjoram promised.

Vivi was anxious about leaving, but knew there was nothing more she could do. It could be hours before they saw any marked improvement. She allowed Etain to steer her toward the transport tunnel and instead of going down to Level One, he had them stopping halfway. She looked around. "What level is this?"

"This is the Unit Level. I want to show you my home." He took her hand and together they walked along the stone street.

They were just passing a large building when a small explosion surprised them both. Vivi's heart was in her throat until she heard male laughter. Seconds later, the twins ran from the building at breakneck speed heading toward the tunnel.

Etain was smiling as they watched the twins dive down the tunnel heading toward Level One. "They have certainly come out of their shell now that they have Kendrick and Meryn's support."

Vivi eyed the smoke coming from the large building. "Do you think anyone is hurt?"

Etain shrugged. "I'm sure any burns or missing limbs will be seen to," he pointed down the road. "Shall we?"

Missing limbs?

"Are you normally this cavalier about your fellow unit warriors' injuries or is it because you want to get me to the privacy of your home?" she teased.

Etain's eyes flicked back to the smoking building. "It's the unit house where some of the most trained witches, fae and vampires in our world like to relax. If something happens there they can't handle, then I'll get concerned."

"And you want to show off your house."

"And I want to show off my house."

They kept walking to the end of the long street. Vivi started laughing when she saw the castle. "Who on earth lives there?"

"Declan. Though in his defense, I think he was half joking when he requested a castle. Of course, the witches had to show off."

He stopped in front of what looked like a large tree house.

"It looks like the house was swallowed by the tree."

"Most of the fae warriors' houses look something like this. We got together and assisted each other when they were being built. It reminds us of home."

Vivi started to get excited. She had always wanted to play in a treehouse, but as she was especially susceptible to the sun, Hal never built one for her. She did, however, have an amazing basement playroom growing up.

She looked up at him. "Can we go inside?"

His eyes were dancing as he nodded. "Of course. You're excited aren't you?"

Vivi walked past him toward the door. "Well,

yeah. I've never been inside a tree house before."

Etain placed a hand on the small of her back and walked with her up the carved wooden stairs. "It's not a tree house."

Vivi stopped and looked up at him. "It's a house in a tree. Or a tree in a house. It's one of the most perfect examples of a tree house I have ever seen. How can this not be a tree house?"

Etain frowned. "Tree house sounds like it should be a tiny shed stuck on a branch for children."

"I am not changing my vernacular because you are insecure about your treehouse." She looked at the door. "Open says me!"

"It's 'Open Sesame'."

Vivi sighed. "Do you want to have sex or correct my grammar?"

Etain reached out and swung the door open. "After you my lady."

"That's what I thought." She walked in and couldn't stop looking around. "This is amazing!"

Behind them above the door, a huge stained glass mural cast colorful shadows of a forest scene on the floor. Crystal lanterns were hung from the ceiling to create floating lighting. All of the furniture built with a mix of woods; it was a warm kaleidoscope of walnuts, oak, maple and ebony.

He took her hand and gently led her up the stairs. "This way."

Still turning her head about, she followed him. Smiling she ran her hand along the polished wood. It was so well worn that the surface felt like silk. Her mate led her to a door and opened it. "The master suite."

When she walked in she was struck by how dark

it was. There was no natural light nor any form of lighting. "Um, Etain, it's kinda dark in here."

"One moment." He closed the door, and she heard his sure foot steps walk across the room. She realized that he must have done this hundreds, if not thousands of times to know exactly where to step.

After a few seconds, she heard a soft click before the room was flooded with light. She stared in amazement. One entire wall was created to be a fireplace. Reflected light danced across the room through crystals flanking the massive hearth.

She watched as he walked back over to her, his form outlined by red and gold flames. "Do you like it?"

Vivi swallowed hard. She felt like she spent her entire life shivering. Only her mate's warmth provided any relief. She couldn't help the tears that fell onto her cheeks. "I feel like I am in the sun, but it doesn't burn. It's just warm and comforting."

Etain pulled her into the circle of his arms. "I tried to recreate the sun-filled environment of Éire Danu. After leaving, I found that I not only craved the warmth but also the light." He paused. "I wasn't sure if you would like it. Adriel hates it, he says that he feels like it's a beast waiting to consume the room."

Vivi shook her head. "No, it's not like that at all. It feels like it's stretching out, wanting to erase my darkness and bathe it in light."

Etain tipped her head back. "What darkness could you possibly have?"

Vivi moved her face out of his hand, and rested her cheek on his chest. "More than I can bear at times."

Etain wrapped his arms around her and eased her to the floor. Vivi sighed and sank her hands into the soft floor covering. "This isn't a rug," she said inspecting it closer.

Etain shook his head. "No, it is a modern blend of cashmere and wool over a layer of memory foam eight inches deep that has been recessed into the floor. It was dreadfully expensive," he said pointing to the vast amount of floor it covered. "But worth it."

"My shoes!" Vivi pulled her foot up to remove her shoes when Etain laughed.

"It's been spelled by Micah to stay clean. You don't have to worry."

He got comfortable on his side and patted the space next to him. "I think you have a story to tell me."

She scooted over until she was next to him and lay back. "And what makes you think there is a story?"

He raised a brow but remained silent.

"Damn Hal and your male bonding." She met his eyes. "What did he tell you?"

"Nothing."

"Nothing?"

He shook his head. "He said that it was your story to tell, and you would share with me when you were ready."

She closed her eyes. She really didn't want to talk about her family, to do so she felt would bring shadows to his place of light and warmth.

Her eyes opened when she felt him begin to rub between her eyebrows. "You don't have to tell me anything you do not wish to."

Vivi took a deep breath. If she couldn't trust her mate, then there would be no one on this earth she could trust. "My father murdered my mother," she said simply. She heard his quick inhale before his arms pulled her close to his body.

"I am so sorry my love."

She shrugged. "I didn't really know either of them. This all happened when I was a baby. Hal took over the duties of raising me when I was one."

"Gods! What happened?"

"My mother was chosen for my father, they were a good match because of their bloodlines. She never really questioned it, especially after she was able to conceive and have me." She rubbed her nose on his chest. "All that changed when she took a trip to the closest paranormal town. Hal told me she confessed to him she began to feel restless, as if there was something she had to do. So she packed me up, told my father she would be visiting friends and left the city. After a few days of traveling at night because of me, we arrived at a small wolf-shifter town. There she met her true mate." She looked up. "That's also where she met Hal. Her mate called him in to interview for a squire position. My mother knew that if we left the city, we would need the extra help."

"Right before my first birthday my mother returned to the city and packed up her few precious belongings. She left my father a letter explaining everything and left in the middle of the night."

"My father was furious. He and his family tracked us down to the shifter town and began to kill anyone who stood in his way. He refused to be humiliated by having his mate leave him for a shifter."

Etain inhaled. "By the gods! You're referring to Armand DuSang. This was what started the skirmish that led to so many people being killed and Magnus taking over the city." He pulled back and stared down at her. "You're a DuSang?" he whispered.

She sat up scowling. "No. I am Vivian Mercy and before that I was Vivian Bergson. I am not like him."

Etain sat up quickly. "I didn't say you were, but darling, you are the last of a royal bloodline."

"Two," she said softly.

"Two what?"

"Two royal bloodlines. My mother was the last of her line, DuCoeur. It was why she was chosen to be my father's mate."

Etain shook his head. "I was in the city when you were born." He smiled at her. "I wish I could have seen you as a baby. But unlike Prince Magnus, no one but royals were able to step foot on Level One." He blinked as understanding filled his eyes. "That's what Hal meant when he said you have a past that could come back to haunt you." He rubbed the back of his neck. "I thought it might have been a past lover here in the city." Vivi snorted. Etain's eyes widened. "You're not a...? I mean you've been with other men right?"

Vivi put on a vapid expression and clasped her hands in front of her. "Oh no, I am a virgin. All females are hormoneless robots waiting for their one true love before indulging in carnal pleasures." Etain looked at her in shock. She rolled her eyes in an exaggerated manner. "Of course I'm not a virgin! I'm over seven hundred years old. A girl has needs."

Etain slumped forward a bit. "Oh thank the gods!"

"You're relieved?"

He looked at her incredulously. "Absolutely! Can you imagine if you truly had waited? No man could live up to those expectations. No matter what I did, it would be a let down." He shuddered. "No. Thank. You. I do not wish to hear details about previous lovers, but I do understand you having them." His eyes turned serious. "What happened to your mother?" he asked gently.

"Father caught up with her and her mate and ripped them apart. I was with Hal at the time. We were just returning from the market. He had taken me on an outing to give my mother and her mate some time alone. He said as we neared the house you could smell the blood. He waited until my father stormed out looking for me before running into the house. He grabbed what my mother packed for us, whatever valuables he could sell and ran."

"He later heard that when my father returned to Noctem Falls he was challenged by Magnus with the backing of the other families. He was killed, and Magnus was confirmed as the new Elder and ruler of Noctem Falls."

Etain frowned. "I was there when your father lost what was left of his mind and turned on his own family for backing Magnus. When Magnus killed him he was like a rabid animal. Javier BelleRose as the ranking Founding Family member was the one who confirmed Magnus as prince."

"It takes four royals to confirm a new prince, otherwise anyone strong enough would just take over." She scooted down, and Etain got comfortable beside her. "My mother knowing she was leaving the city for good left her recommendation for Magnus signed with her blood for authentication. I think that's what drove him to murder. My mother inadvertently started the end of his reign."

Etain rubbed his head over her hair. "I don't think it was her. DuSang started to unravel years before your mother ever left. I think her leaving a letter proved to the others the reality of his instability. By the time he massacred the shifter town and turned on his family it was too late to simply bring him before the other families."

Vivi's heart was in her throat. "Does that change how you feel about me?"

Etain looked down at her. "How would that change things between us? You are no more your father than I am the Queen of the Fae."

She felt her eyes fill with tears. "All my life I felt as if his darkness weighed down my heart. Knowing what he did, the people he murdered, the lives he destroyed, made me want to help people; to somehow atone for his sins."

"My darling, they are not your sins to atone for." He placed a hand over her heart. "Let my light protect your heart. You are free of him."

Vivi thought that what he said was simply a gesture until a soft light began to glow under his palm. Moments later, she felt his warmth seep into her very soul. The guilt and sorrow she had carried all her life began to dissolve and float away. When the light dimmed she felt better than she had in centuries. She hadn't felt so carefree since she was a child and ignorant of the havoc her father caused.

"Thank you," she sighed as the bands of guilt relaxed allowing her to breathe easier.

"You are my mate, there is nothing I wouldn't do for you, no matter your name."

"Maybe I could be Vivian Vi'Aerlin instead," Vivi whispered lowly almost afraid of his reaction.

He rolled them until she was pinned under him. His eyes were shining as he stared down at her. "You would do that? You would take my name?" he asked breathlessly.

"Rheia, Anne and Meryn have all taken their mate's names," she pointed out.

"But they are human and very, very young. You're a paranormal and have built a life for yourself in your own right under your own name. Not many older females take their mate's names."

She smiled shyly up at him. "I don't think my mother would mind if I changed my name from Mercy to Vi'Aerlin."

He cocked his head to one side. "Your mother?"

"Her name was Mercia. When it came time to choose my own name, I chose Mercy in her honor."

He smiled. "I thought it was because you became an angel of mercy."

"If anyone here is an angel it's you. Have you looked in a mirror lately? You're all sun-kissed hair and golden skin." She leered up at him. "Maybe a fallen angel, because you are tempting me to do some wicked things."

He leaned down on his forearms and ground his

hardened bulge between her legs. "And what sort of wicked things were you thinking of?"

She fought for breath. "The kind that involves being naked, sweaty and screaming out to the gods."

"I think that can be arranged." He pushed himself up and sat back. Standing he slowly began to unbutton his uniform jacket.

As she watched his long fingers work each button, she was busy peeling off her clothes in a haphazard manner. She flung her clothes away from her in her rush to touch his skin.

He gracefully let his clothes fall to the floor, his eyes locked on her. She leaned back on her elbows as naked as the day she was born. She smiled up at him. "I don't think I will ever tire of looking at you."

He gave her a wicked grin and dropped to his knees. She watched his muscles glide under his skin as he made his way to her. "I cannot wait to see where your lights are."

"My lights?"

He didn't reply. He simply leaned down and began to kiss up her inner leg. His blond hair created a golden curtain so she couldn't see what he was doing. He bypassed her mound and began to nibble on her hip bone. She moaned as darts of pleasure raced through her.

"Light yellow. Pleasurable but not exactly what I was looking for," he said then resumed his leisurely exploration of her body. He teased her not only with his lips and tongue but also with his fingertips. His touch was never more than a graze, a fleeting tantalization before he moved on.

By the time he wrapped his lips around her nipple, she gasped and arched her back. "Gods!" she exhaled. She was strung out by his torturous expedition. She wanted him to fill her, to give her the pleasure that seemed just out of reach.

"Burnt orange. I'm glad, because I could feast on your breasts for years." He nuzzled between her breasts and moved up her neck.

Growling low in her throat, she wrapped her legs around his waist and raised her lower body up to contact his. Like a cat in heat, she rubbed herself against him, desperate for them to become one.

"I will give you what you need." He reached between them and guided himself between her folds. A moment later, he was thrusting deep and finally reaching that one spot that promised to send her soaring.

"Yes! Gods, yes!" She kept her legs wrapped as he kept up a steady pace.

He pulled back and looked her in the eyes. "Will you complete my soul? Will you allow me to join us together to face eternity as one?"

She reached up and pulled his head down capturing his lips. She sucked on his tongue and allowed him to dominate the kiss. When she wrapped her hands in his hair and tugged his head back gently he went wild. His hips began to piston as he plunged deep. She was congratulating herself on having found one of his hot spots when he found her biggest one.

When his teeth clamped down on the sensitive part of her neck, she screamed as her body exploded. Her mate shouted his release. A moment later he pushed himself up to watch their souls

claim each other. Between their bodies, two play-
ful balls of light lifted from their chests. His was a
soft amber color, hers a silvery blue. They darted
around each other before swirling into one pulsing
light. When the two spheres separated their colors
reflected the joining of their souls.

Etain's warm light completely surrounded her
silver core. The little balls returned to their chests
and disappeared again. When the light faded she
could feel Etain as a part of her, as surely as if he
were a physical piece of her body.

Groaning he pulled completely from her body
and slumped down to one side. "Your neck is definitely a fiery red light."

Gasping for air she swatted at him. "You think?"
She rubbed her chest. "Your light feels like warm
honey."

"Your's feels calming. The way moonlight seems
to gently guide those at night."

"It's not cold?"

"No, it almost feels like a balm on a sunburn."
He pulled her close. "You are my solace. Only in
your arms do my cares fall away. Now that my soul
has been soothed by yours, I do not think I could
face the world alone."

She kissed his chest. "You will never have to. I
will never let you go. As I have soothed you, you
have warmed me. I feel like I stepped into the sun
after a lifetime of living in the shadows."

"We will have to return to Level One eventually," he said sighing.

"But we will return together." She closed her
eyes. "Let's rest for a bit then head down. I'm worried about our little midget."

He chuckled. "I think she could weather any-thing."

Vivi pulled back and looked up at him. "Not this time. His words hurt her. Words can be more devastating than any injury."

His features softened. "You speak from experience."

She scrunched up her nose. "Because I couldn't go outside much as a child, the other kids used to call me a blood-sucking vampire."

Etain frowned. "But you are a blood-sucking vampire."

She sniffed haughtily. "But those little bastards didn't know that."

He buried his face between her shoulder and her neck laughing. "I adore you."

"You're lucky I adore you too, or I would be very upset at you laughing over my childhood trauma."

When he licked where he had bitten her, she exhaled softly. "No fair."

"Rest love, when we get up, I may show you exactly how unfair I can be."

She wiggled closer and yawned. "I could get used to this."

"That's the idea," he whispered cradling her gently.

She couldn't fight the wave of exhaustion that swamped her, smiling, she fell asleep in her mate's arms.

They swung by the lab to see that Marjoram dropped off new blood samples, and Ellie had already prepped the slides. She pulled them out of the refrigerator to look at them under the microscope.

"Well?" Etain asked.

"I bet Ellie is dancing a jig." She moved the slide to the left. She could clearly see evidence of the virus now as it seemed to be under attack by the vampire blood. Flashes of magic were making it hard to see.

"Why?"

"Take a look." She stepped back and allowed him to look into the eyepiece.

He straightened. "It looks like a tiny battle."

"Because that's what it is. From the number of inert cells, I'm going out on a limb and saying that the warrior blood is about sixty percent effective in eradicating this thing."

His face brightened. "That's amazing news!"

Vivi couldn't help the blooming sense of hope. "We're dealing with a magic driven virus that shouldn't exist. I'll take any progress."

"Let's go share the good news," he held out his hand.

Together they made their way to Prince Magnus' quarters. When Sebastian opened the door, he was frowning.

They stepped inside. "What?" she asked.

Sebastian pursed his lips. "They were just about to call for you. I will let them explain." He led them to the dining room where everyone sat looking grim.

Magnus looked relieved at their arrival. "Good,

we were about to send someone to get you. Please sit down. Have the two of you eaten lunch yet?"

Vivi shook her head. "Not yet."

They sat down, and Sebastian brought in a fresh platter of sandwiches. As they helped themselves, Kari started. "Stefan got a call from his brother this morning. Cristo is in Albuquerque and was ready to complete the last leg of his travels to come visit when he discovered the fae portal at the Council Estate wouldn't open."

Etain froze with his sandwich halfway to his mouth. He set it down. "What?"

Magnus grimaced. "Exactly. Which is why we were waiting for you. Have you ever heard of such a thing occurring?"

Etain didn't reply instead, he reached for his phone. "Damn!"

"What?"

"My sister has been trying to reach me for hours. I have it on 'Do not disturb'. We always seem to be in the lab or in meetings, so it was easier to leave it silenced, especially since we have walkie-talkies now. I never even thought to check it." He pushed a button and started to rise.

Magnus shook his head. "Do not feel as if you have to leave on our account. Unless you desire privacy, you are more than welcome to stay. I think we are past formal manners at this point in time."

Etain sat back down looking relieved. "Allia what is..."

"Where in the hell have you been!" a female voice demanded.

"Baby sister, I am sitting at the Prince's dining table. Everyone can hear you," he informed her.

"Oh. In that case. Where in the hell have you been! I have been calling for hours Etain. Hours!" Allia continued.

Declan chuckled, and Grant covered his mouth with his hand to hide his smile. Etain glared at them. "My mate found her way to me. We have been getting to know one another."

"Next time you have sex leave the damn ringer on. Do you have any idea what's happening? No one can open a portal to Noctem Falls," his baby sister ranted.

Vivi leaned in listening avidly. Her mate's sister sounded like a firecracker.

Etain turned to her, his cheeks pink. "She's normally much more collected."

"I think she sounds amazing," Vivi admitted.

"Is that her?" Allia asked.

"Yes, I'm here. My name is Vivian Vi'Aerlin, or it will be as soon as I file the paperwork with the council to change my name."

A soft gasp was heard. "Oh! Oh! Oh!" Allia repeated.

"Here, let me." A male voice said. "Etain, congratulations on finding your mate."

"Ailain, thank you. Is our sister well?" Etain asked looking worried.

"She's crying she's so happy. We feared the worst when she shared your earlier concerns with us in regard to your mate's safety. I cannot tell you how relieved we are to hear both of you are well," Ailain answered.

Etain turned to Vivi. "Allia and Ailain are twins. They are my younger siblings by nearly a thousand years. Both serve directly under the queen. Allia acts as her lady in waiting or a more modern term would be her personal assistant, and Ailain fulfills the same role for the Queen's consort Brennus Vi'Eirlea," he explained.

"Brother, what is going on in Noctem Falls? Allia nearly skewered the poor guard who was supposed to open the portal to send you your requested support when he failed to establish a connection." Despite the seriousness of the situation, Ailain's voice sounded amused. Vivi could only imagine the amount of trouble the little spitfire caused.

"Ailain, I need you and Allia to go to the Queen's antechamber and have her cast a soundproofing spell," Etain requested. Beside him, Kendrick was securing the dining room.

"Hold." Gone was Ailain's mirth, he was all business now.

Everyone heard their footsteps as they walked down what sounded like a marble hallway. They heard a knock then a soft voice. "Enter."

"My Queen, I have my brother Etain on the phone. He is with Prince Magnus and is requesting that you soundproof this room before anything is discussed."

"Of course," was the reply. A moment later, the melodic voice returned. "Etain, the spell has been cast." There was a pause. "Prince Magnus, I offer greetings to the City of the Night from the Land of Eternal Sun. It has been too long since we last have spoke."

"I have been pining away since our last conversation Aleksandra," Magnus said in an amorous tone.

Over the phone, they heard a low growl. "Magnus! What have I told you about flirting with my mate!" a deep voice demanded.

"Oh, Brennus were you there? Sorry about that." Magnus didn't sound the least bit sorry. Behind him Sebastian had his face buried in his hands.

A soft tinkling laugh was heard before the queen came back on the line. "Etain, it has been so long since your last call. How have you been? I heard you found your mate! I am so excited for you. We have all missed you dreadfully here. Malcolm is doing a fine job as Captain of the Guard, but you were so much better at it. When can you come home for a visit? " the queen asked question after question.

Etain's face softened. "As I have missed all of you. And yes, I have found my mate. She is as beautiful as she is kind. As for visiting, I fear that the reason for this phone call prevents me from leaving the city any time soon."

"Could that be the reason why none of my children can establish a portal to Noctem Falls?"

"Yes." Etain paused before shooting a glance to Magnus who nodded. He continued. "We seem to have something of an anomaly here."

"Sounds interesting. What type of an anomaly?"

"A virus that affects both shifters and vampires."

"There is no such thing," the queen refuted.

"There is now your majesty," Rheia replied.

"Who is that?"

Rheia blushed. "My name is Dr. Rheia Albright."

"Perhaps some introductions are in order," Magnus suggested.

It took a few moments, but they worked their way around the table.

"Dr. Albright, Dr. Kimball, what can you tell me

about this virus?" the queen asked.

"Please, call me Rheia," Rheia started.

"And me Ellie. We haven't been too formal here," Ellie replied.

"Not formal? At Noctem Falls? Did Sebastian stop starching Magnus?" Aleksandra asked playfully.

Magnus opened his mouth.

"If you make one comment about being stiff, I will find a way to thrash you over this phone," Brennus warned.

Magnus closed his mouth sighing. "Having young people about has greatly improved my outlook."

"I know what you mean. Speaking of young ones, I noticed that Meryn McKenzie was not one of those introduced. Is she there?"

Aiden turned to Ryuu with a puzzled look on his face. "Where *is* Meryn?"

Ryuu's features were drawn tight. "I sent her to bed. Someone said something to her that hurt her terribly. It felt like someone raked claws along her soul."

Aiden's expression shut down. "I see."

"Aiden as soon as this call is over, I will tell you what happened," Etain offered.

Aiden just nodded, but Vivi noticed that a faint outline began to appear around the Unit Commander.

"By all means, let us quickly conclude this call so that our Unit Commander can comfort his precious mate. I have to admit. I have a soft spot for that little human. I am *most* displeased to hear she was hurt," the queen's melodic voice became frosty.

"I will see it set to rights My Queen," Etain

promised.

"Good. Now what is this about a virus?"

Nervously Ellie began to go over what was happening in the city. Vivi's mind wandered back to Meryn. To her, it seemed as if he was just being a Grade-A dick, but the tunnel escort must have hit on a painful issue for Meryn to be affected so greatly.

Ellie's voice brought her back to the conversation at hand. "And this morning we started a trial run from the blood gathered from the warriors. Not even an hour later, we began to get notifications that the city's portal wouldn't open," Ellie concluded looking a bit winded.

"I also issued an edict that the doors to the city shall remain sealed until we can figure out what is going on. If the fae portals are refusing to open to prevent this from spreading, we must do our part and keep the city locked down," Magnus added.

"It must be the virus," Aleksandra concluded. "The portals wouldn't recognize shifters getting sick as they are not the majority race in the city. However, with vampires now sick, the portal shut down to protect the fae. I'm afraid we won't be able to reestablish a connection until the sickness is gone from the city."

"We're working on it." Vivi replied. "Just before coming here I checked in on the results of the blood work from this morning. Tentatively, we're looking at a sixty percent success rate," she shared.

"Thank the gods!" Magnus whispered.

"Indeed," Aleksandra echoed. "Now, on to our other pressing issue," she continued.

Everyone shared confused looks with one

another.

"Is there anything I can do to help cheer up that adorable little human?" she asked.

"One of the things she really wants is a bag like Kendrick's," Anne volunteered softly.

"Do you still have that silly thing?" the queen asked laughing.

"As if the fae ever created anything that could be silly?" Kendrick refuted playfully.

"There's the other flirty bastard. Though I heard he mated. Good." Brennus groused.

"I flirt with Aleksandra because you wouldn't give me the time of day you stud," Kendrick bantered back winking at Anne. She shook her head grinning.

Vivi glanced around. She wasn't the only one shocked by Kendrick's urbane teasing of the Queen's consort.

"He has you there Brennus," the queen giggled.

"Tricky witch," Brennus muttered.

The queen laughed again. "Tell Meryn that I will get one started just for her. I have been meaning to send her something anyway. Her Facebook posts had me laughing harder than I have in a very long time." The queen chuckled.

"It is true. One of the happiest days of my life was the afternoon I watched my love roll around on the bed snort laughing," Brennus admitted.

"Brennus! I do not snort!" the queen said indignantly.

"Of course not darling. What I meant to say, was when you breathed through your nose while laughing and convulsing on the bed," he corrected.

"Oh you!" The queen laughed. "On that note,

I will let you all go. But Etain, Magnus, keep me abreast of any and all progress." Her voice was pleasant, but an order was an order.

Magnus grinned cheekily at the phone. "Any excuse to speak to you again," he teased.

"Etain you may call our queen with any updates. Magnus you call me directly," Brennus corrected.

"Of course sire," Etain said and ended the call. He leaned back in the chair before turning to Magnus. "What was with the flirting?"

Magnus shrugged one shoulder. "There are days when I feel as if people forget I am a person as well as the Prince. After so many millennia being in charge, I think maybe your queen likes to be treated like a woman now and then."

Vivi looked at Magnus with new respect. He seemed to go out of his way to make sure people were taken care of. Their people couldn't have asked for a better leader.

Cracking wood had everyone turning to Aiden. He looked at Etain. "What the hell happened to my mate?" he demanded.

CHAPTER SIX

ETAIN'S EXPRESSION DARKENED. "EAR-LIER THIS afternoon when Vivi and I took the injectors up to Level Six, Meryn joined us. She wanted to install speakers there for her new PA system. One of the tunnel escorts said some things to Meryn that hurt her feelings."

Vivi rolled her eyes. "Men." She turned to Aiden. "From what I heard Meryn has had run-ins with this particular escort before because she said, 'Not you again.'. The tunnel escort said people were talking about Meryn, saying she was an embarrassment to you and how people felt sorry for you."

Rheia sucked in her breath, and Aiden snarled. Vivi looked down the table at Rheia. "What?"

Rheia's eyes were misty. "Meryn had a very difficult childhood. We're still getting details as she's not one to share, but one thing has become extremely clear. She must have been told on an almost daily basis how worthless she is. Her grandmother ignored her to the point of neglect and put her down often. Meryn has been walking around for the past couple months waiting for Aiden to announce that he changed his mind and would never be with someone like her."

"Oh gods! Hearing that from the tunnel escort must have been like her worst nightmare coming true," Ellie said sniffling.

Aiden stood chest heaving. He looked over to Etain. "You're with me."

Etain stood. "Yes, sir."

"Aiden," Magnus called out as the Unit Commander stalked from the room.

Aiden spun a dark-brown muzzle semi-imposed on his face. "Yes," he snarled.

"Whatever you do. You have my blessing." There was a dark look in the prince's eyes.

Aiden simply nodded and headed for the door. Etain dropped a kiss on the top of her head.

"Have fun storming the castle," she called out after him.

Etain frowned. "What castle?"

Vivi shook her head. "Never mind. Give em hell."

"That I can do," he promised, grinning evilly.

Etain had to almost jog to catch up to the commander by the transport tunnel. Etain held out his arm. "What level, sir?"

"Give me a second. If we go up there now, I will kill someone." Aiden put his hands on his hips and took a few deep breaths.

Etain noticed that when Aiden rested his hand

on his arm, his claws were out despite trying to calm down. "Level Five first," Aiden said.

First?

Once on the level, Aiden walked up to the door of the first set of quarters. Etain inwardly groaned. The quarters next to the tunnel were always those of the highest ranking family, in this case. DeLaFontaine.

Aiden raised his hand, but instead of knocking, he beat on the door so hard it split down the middle. A moment later, a frightened looking squire opened the door. "Y-y-yes?"

"Tell DeLaFontaine he has two minutes to assemble his people before I start pulling people out of their houses and considering how pissed I am. They may not make it out in one piece."

"Yes, sir!" the squire left the open door at a run.

Less than a minute later DeLaFontaine was standing in front of him. He opened his mouth to speak, a sneer on his face. When he saw the state Aiden was in, he swallowed hard. "Unit Commander, what can my people do for you?"

"With Etain Vi'Aerlin as my witness, I am challenging anyone on the level who feels they have a right to hurt my mate. Once I leave this level any future insult will be seen as a direct challenge to me, and I will respond in kind with a fight to the death," Aiden announced in a quiet tone.

DeLaFontaine's face drained of color. "Gods, what has that idiot escort done now?"

"Five minutes I will wait. After that I will assume everyone on this level has nothing to say. After I leave this level all bets are off," Aiden looked at his watch. "Four minutes and thirty seconds."

DeLaFontaine scrambled away from the door and a moment later runners were heading in every direction.

Aiden cracked his knuckles. "While we wait, fetch your mouthy tunnel escort, I am challenging him directly."

DeLaFontaine nodded. "Of course."

Etain had never been more proud to call himself a unit warrior. Aiden McKenzie through action and deed had proven over and over again through the centuries how deserving he was of his rank. It was moments like this, not his bloodline, that earned him the respect and admiration of every unit warrior across the country.

Etain knew he would never forget this moment for as long as he lived. He knew he was witnessing something that would live as legend throughout his long lifetime. He would do anything and every-thing possible to ensure Aiden saw this through to the end.

DeLaFontaine dropped a struggling man at their feet. "Commander, he is all yours. I hope this small show of support on my part helps to prove I do not share this worm's feelings."

Aiden simply nodded before kicking the escort in the teeth, much in the same way Vivi had earlier that afternoon. "Get up you sack of shit. I am going to remove my mate's name from your mouth phys-ically. When I am done with you, you will never again look in her direction. You won't even stand in the same proximity as her, stealing her air."

Etain stood feet spread, hands clasped behind his back and watched as Aiden McKenzie beat the liv-ing hell out of the man who hurt his small mate.

Now he understood what he meant by Level Five first. The commander was only getting started.

"Do you think they're okay?" Vivi asked for the third time.

Anne snorted. "I think *they* are just fine. I would hate to be anyone standing in their way."

Ellie's eyes were huge. "I've never seen a shifter that close to third form before. He was hanging on by a thread."

Anne sighed happily. "That's how much he loves her."

"I would tear apart continents for you my love," Kendrick interjected.

The three women looked over at him, and Anne nodded. "Of course you would." They exchanged looks and laughed.

"I am feeling very left out over here," Kendrick said pouting.

Anne popped up off her stool. "My poor mate." She walked over and kissed his face repeatedly.

Vivi relaxed against the lab counter. Rheia and Marjoram were doing another sweep at the hospital seeing if there were any major changes with the children. So far, the children were doing well. According to Ellie, they looked better than she had ever seen them.

Rheia was also responsible for securing three new donations for further trials. Per Magnus' request, the second batch of donated blood would be coming from the citizens on Level Six. He didn't want the warriors contributing to the point of being pulled from their normal duties. His reasoning was there was plenty of vampire blood in a city of vampires.

Vivi watched as Anne placated her mate when the book he was holding caught her attention. It was black with blood-red lettering. "Kendrick, what's that book?"

Kendrick held up the heavy volume. "A gift from our little midget. She saw it in Magnus' treasure trove and picked it up for me. She said and I quote, 'It's black and looks like it's written in blood, I thought of you.'" He glanced down at the book. "I am very glad she brought it to me. I hate to think what this could do in the wrong hands."

"Black magic?" Vivi asked.

He nodded gravely. "It makes your stone look like a fidget spinner."

Vivi winced. "I wonder what else she got."

Kendrick's answering grin was terrifying. "Something for Felix."

"I don't even want to know," Anne admitted.

"Did she get anything for herself?" Ellie wondered out loud.

Anne nodded. "She got this little necklace. It's very simple, but she said she liked it."

"So she got a free pass to pick out any three things from Prince Magnus' vault, and she only got one thing for herself?" Vivi was impressed.

Kendrick shrugged and turned back to his book. "That's just Meryn. If she didn't see anything she wanted she would have just walked away. She never would have taken something just to take it."

Behind Vivi the door opened and Rheia walked in smiling. "Getting donations was a breeze. Though, we are starting to get questions from the vendors about a possible treatment for the vampires." She walked over and handed Vivi the bags of blood.

Using her thumb, she unlocked her biometric case. Kendrick shuddered. He was the first witch she'd met who showed such a sensitivity to black magic. Carefully, she lifted the stone out the case and carried it over to the refrigerator. She set everything inside before shutting the door and looking up at the clock. It was already time for dinner.

"I don't know about you all, but I'm starved." Vivi stretched her arms over her head.

"I know I am. I want to check on Meryn too. She hasn't been out of her room all day," Rheia said, looking worried.

"Let's get ready and meet in the antechamber. We can check on her together," Ellie suggested.

"Sounds like a plan," Anne agreed.

Vivi followed the women out of the room and headed toward her quarters. She wondered if she would see her mate before dinner.

"Did I tell you about how he picked up the tunnel escort and used him to beat one of the Noble Family's sons?" Etain asked.

Vivi hid a smile. He had, in fact, twice, since arriving in the suite an hour ago. "Yes, but you can tell me again."

Etain laughed, his eyes shining. "I wish I recorded it, for posterity of course."

"Of course," she murmured as she applied the last of her make up.

When she turned around she could only stare. Etain was in full fae dress. His long robe was a cream color that draped over his body beautifully. The full body overvest that hung to the floor was a burnt orange accented in embroidered gold. She sighed. "You are so beautiful."

He sauntered up to her and nuzzled her neck. "If I hadn't just watched you perfect your make up for the past half hour, I would kiss you senseless."

"You're too good to me," she teased and leaned her head away, giving him better access to her neck.

He gave her one final quick bite that had her knees threatening to buckle before he stood back and offered her his arm. "Shall we?"

They left her quarters and headed to the ante-chamber. When they walked in she was struck by how very quiet it was. She glanced around, everyone stood looking grim. Under her hand, she felt Etain's body tense. She followed his gaze and saw Meryn, or at least, she believed it was Meryn.

The small human sat on the edge of the chair her back ramrod straight. Instead of her normal tee and sweatpants she was dressed immaculately in a stylish black cocktail dress. Her hair was perfectly coifed, and jewels dripped from her neck, ears and wrists.

"Who's that?" Vivi whispered.

Meryn gave her a short smile. "Don't be silly. It is just me."

Ryuu stood off to one side. His face was an unreadable mask, but his rage seemed to simmer just below the surface. Waves of anger radiated from him like heat off asphalt.

Aiden just looked confused. "Are you comfortable baby?" he asked.

"I am very well, thank you," she replied.

Beth, Anne and Rheia exchanged worried glances, which had their mates frowning, their concern doubled, both for their mates and for Meryn.

Sebastian cleared his throat looking anxious. "Dinner is ready," he announced to the subdued room.

Meryn turned to Aiden and waited for him to stand before offering him her gloved hand. He instinctively helped her to rise and escorted her to the dining room. When the door shut behind them, Rheia turned to Kendrick. "What the actual hell?" she growled.

Kendrick shrugged. "I scanned her. She's not under any influence; drug, magic or otherwise. This is all her."

"Come on, we don't want them thinking we are talking about her," Anne said pulling Kendrick toward the door. He frowned. "But we are." Rolling her eyes she walked beside him through the doorway.

Colton looked down at Rheia his eyes shiny. "I want *our* Meryn back. Fix her," he pleaded.

Rheia bit her lip. "This may not be something I can fix, my love." Growling under his breath, he escorted his mate to dinner.

One by one, the couples made their way into the dining room. No one spoke. The silence was overwhelmingly oppressive. Everyone grasped for something to say and all efforts at small talk fell flat, creating an awkward miasma. As the courses were served everyone ate quietly. No one was laughing at some silly prank or story.

Across the table, Vivi watched Meryn closely. When she wasn't eating she sat with her hands folded in her lap. Her manners were impeccable to the point of being too proper.

"Uh... We've made some progress today," Ellie started, unable to take the silence anymore.

Magnus turned to Vivi. "Yes, please update us on the results of your trials." Even Vivi could tell he was trying to get a conversation going based on Ellie's cue.

Vivi cleared her throat. "We chose to inoculate half the children with the first batch of donated blood from the warriors. Under the microscope, we are now able to see reactions from the virus as it fights off the vampire blood. I am estimating that the blood is able to destroy at least sixty percent of the virus before it begins to replicate itself."

"Sixty percent on the first trial? That is wonderful news." Magnus exclaimed sounding overly enthusiastic. He turned to Meryn. "Is that not joyous news Meryn?" he asked.

She nodded primly. "Yes, Your Highness, that seems to be felicitous news indeed."

"That is it!" Law growled. "Meryn, what in the hell is wrong with you?"

She gave him a frosty look. "I don't know what you mean."

Law waved at her. "You, all of you. It's not you," he fumbled.

Kendrick patted his shoulder. "Good job."

"He's just worried about you baby," Aiden said. He reached over to pull Meryn into his lap as usual when she slapped at his hands. "Don't act childish, it's embarrassing," she snapped.

Aiden recoiled back in shock looking sick. "What?" he whispered.

Suddenly, everything made sense. Meryn was acting the way she thought she should, so she wouldn't cause problems for her mate. Something in the way she said the words 'childish' and 'embarrassing' sounded as though she were channeling someone else.

"Etain, my love. Why don't you tell Meryn what Aiden spent the afternoon doing," she suggested.

Frowning he looked down at her. She saw the moment of realization dawn in his eyes when he figured out what was going on. He nodded and squeezed her hand under the table. "Today I was privileged enough to witness something that will become legend. The retelling of this afternoon's events will be passed on from generation to generation for thousands of years to come."

Meryn looked at him. "What did you see?"

"Your mate, the Unit Commander, Aiden McKenzie challenging every level of Noctem Falls."

Meryn's head spun around to Aiden. "Why on earth did you do something like that?" she asked sounding more like herself and less like the wooden doll she was trying to be.

Aiden looked down at her, his wounded soul shining in his eyes. "Because I was tired of the people in this city hurting the most important person in my world."

Meryn's mouth dropped. "You fought an entire city... for me? Why! They're just gonna hate you now, and it's all my fault!" she buried her face in her hands.

Aiden couldn't bear it a second more and scooped her into his lap. She thrashed around, but he didn't let her go. "What makes you think I care if they hate me? They're a city of douchebags right?" he asked.

She stopped wiggling and looked up at him her eyes narrowing. "Are you seriously quoting me back at me?"

"I'll do whatever it takes to protect you," he growled. "You are mine, made perfect just for me! What makes you think I want a mini version of Daphne Bowers?" he asked shuddering. "I want my tiny, mouthy, crazy, quirky, brilliant mate to throw things at me, accidentally shoot me and beat me with my toilet!" he roared breathing heavily.

Meryn's mouth twitched and a moment later the air around her shimmered until she was wearing her *Cheeto* stained *Pikachu* pajamas. "I knew you were a mannequin."

Aiden rolled his eyes. "Masochist baby. The word is masochist."

Someone snorted out loud and the entire room erupted into laughter. Colton banged on the table. "I knew you were a glutton for punishment!"

Aiden gave his best friend a flat look. "It's easier to just roll with what she says than to argue."

"He likes it," Meryn said grinning.

"Thank the everloving gods!" Kendrick muttered sitting back in his chair.

Beth glared at Meryn. "If you ever scare me like

that again I will... I will..."

"Yeah?" Meryn challenged grinning.

"I will block all your streaming accounts and super glue your laptop shut!" Beth threatened.

Meryn's eyes widened. "You wouldn't!"

"Try me," Beth crossed her arms over her chest.

Meryn looked down at the table. "I thought I was helping Aiden. I didn't want to embarrass him."

Rheia laughed. "You're only now worrying about that?"

Meryn looked up concern on her face. "I do embarrass him?"

The men were all shaking their heads, but Anne and Rheia were nodding and laughing. "Of course you do, but he doesn't care," Rheia replied.

"Rheia..." Colton started.

Rheia held up a hand to head off her mate before focusing on Meryn. "You ignored protocol and moved into the Alpha Estate. You called René Evreux a douchebag in the council chambers. You beat Aiden with a toilet, set his car on fire, took over trainee assignments, somehow managed to get an article printed that Daphne Bowers had vaginoplasty, covered the entire Lycaonia town square in flour glue, flew a drone into Noctem Falls' detention cells to bewitch Gerard Dubois into calling himself a douchebag while under oath..." Rheia gasped for breath. "Do I need to go on?"

Meryn looked up at her mate. "Was that embarrassing?"

Aiden's mouth opened and closed. He looked around then back down at his mate. "I'm not quite sure how to answer this."

Most of the men around the table at this point

could barely breathe including Etain. Prior to this, Vivi had no idea the woman in front of her was so wonderfully nuts. She rubbed her mate's back as he gasped for air.

Beth wiped her eyes from laughing. "I think Rheia's point is, if you can do all that and Aiden still thinks you are adorable, what made you believe the way you dressed or spoke made a difference?"

Meryn shrugged and stared down at the table.

Vivi took a deep breath and went out on a limb. "Don't act childish! It's embarrassing!" she barked. Meryn turned to Aiden, visibly shrinking against her mate.

"Vivi!" Ellie gasped.

"Meryn, who used to say that to you?" Vivi asked in a softer tone.

"My grandmother," Meryn whispered.

"Where is she now?"

"Dead."

"Good. She sounds like a hateful bitch."

Meryn looked up smiling a bit. "She was. My Aunt Lily said we may be able to get her grave moved closer so we can desecrate it easier."

Law, who had just taken a huge gulp of wine, began to choke. His face turned red as he struggled to breathe. "Gods Meryn, don't do that!" he fussed.

Meryn turned in Aiden's lap and looked at Ryuu who was visibly fighting his emotions. "I'm sorry."

Ryuu walked over and knelt beside Aiden's chair taking both her hands in his. "Please don't ever change. I would rather take on the entire world than to see you become something terrible."

"You mean a douchebag?" Meryn asked.

He shook his head. "No, normal. You are not

normal Meryn, that is what makes you so unique and special. When people conform, they make themselves fit a cookie cutter mold and when that happens, they become interchangeable and replaceable. You my dearest heart are so perfectly imperfect that others fear who and what you are, because you reflect back at them how ordinary and small minded they are. Do you understand?" he asked keeping eye contact.

She gave him a wobbly smile, fighting back tears. "Basically, I'm a *Fruit Loop* in a bowl of *Cheerios*."

Ryuu raised both of her hands to his lips before pressing them to his forehead. He brought them down between them. "Yes. Yes, you are."

"You're our *Fruit Loop* Meryn and don't forget it," Colton said wagging a finger at her.

Etain looked down at Vivi. "How did you know about her grandmother?"

"I didn't. I was much older when I attended university. I may have looked like a twenty-year old, but I had several centuries under my belt. My roommate used to put down others, but when she did, her voice became harsher. I didn't understand it until the first Christmas when her family visited. Her father would bark at her in the exact same tone. I knew when I heard Meryn's voice they weren't her own words, she was just parroting back something she heard repeatedly," Vivi explained.

"What happened to your roommate?" Meryn asked turning back around to face the table. Ryuu took a step back but didn't move far away from his charge.

Vivi smiled. "She fell in love with a local farmer much to her father's dismay, moved far away and lived long enough to have great-great grandchil-dren running around her kitchen."

Meryn gave a decisive nod. "Good." She looked up at her mate. "Did you really fight everyone?"

Aiden grinned and held up his knuckles, that despite shifter healing, were still red and swollen. Meryn peppered his hand with kisses. She looked up her eyes sparkling. "Didja kill anyone?" she asked brightly.

"Oh yeah, she's feeling better," Rheia com-mented, sipping her water.

Aiden shook his head. "No baby I didn't."

"I bet if he went against the offending tunnel escort after Meryn slapped his hand, that would not be true," Gavriel commented.

Aiden's eyes darkened. "More than likely."

Etain cleared his throat. "He didn't just beat them Meryn."

"Oh? What else?" she asked.

"He declared, if anyone else moving forward hurt you through word or deed it would be seen as a direct challenge to him, and he would fight them to the death," Etain explained.

"Holy shit," Colton whispered then frowned at Aiden. "If you were going to go all out you should have invited me. I think I'm pissed."

Aiden rolled his eyes. "I needed city's warrior who witnessed the transgression for which I was basing my challenge on." He gave Colton a sour look. "You would have complicated matters."

Gavriel chuckled. "That is putting it mildly. There would have been a number of disembowel-ments and our lovely doctors and nurses are busy enough as it is. They did not need to spend the afternoon stitching up bigoted bootlickers."

Declan sat back. "Etain gets all the fun," he griped.

Colton eyed his new friend. "Maybe we could meander through the levels to see if anyone else needs a reminder on how to treat our midget."

"I am not a fucking midget Colton," Meryn threw a roll at him.

Adriel and Aiden pinched the bridges of their noses before Adriel turned to Aiden. "That is *your* second in command."

Aiden pointed to Declan. "And he's yours."

Kendrick looked over at Etain. "That reminds me. We need to attend morning drills with Goddard and Viktor. I owe Goddard a bit of sparring and I told Viktor you would be interested in training with him after I told you how he flirted with Vivi."

Etain's eyes hardened. "Oh, he did, did he?" He gave a menacing smile. "Just let me know when you are available," he offered. Kendrick gave him a mock salute.

"Now *that*, I have to see," Meryn said eagerly. "It will be better than watching an MMA match."

Magnus sat back in his chair looking relieved. "Now that is more like it. This is what I have come to look forward to," he raised his goblet then stared, as it began to shake. He looked around confused. "Something is wrong with the glass," he announced before his eyes rolled up into the back of his head, and he collapsed to one side.

"Uncle!" Beth screamed.

Vivi stood as chaos erupted.

CHAPTER SEVEN

MARJORAM PUSHED HER WAY TO the end of the table to get to Magnus. Beth was pulled back by Gavriel. He held her close moving them off to one side as she wept hysterically.

The older nurse knelt beside the prince. "I saw this coming a mile away." She looked up. "He's in no immediate danger so everyone calm down. Adriel, Aiden clear the room. Rheia, Ellie you're with me. Broderick prep the infirmary," Marjoram said barking her orders. Everyone began moving, grateful for direction. Vivi and Etain hung back. Vivi wasn't sure if Marjoram would need her help in devising a treatment for the prince.

"Beth honey, come here," Marjoram said in a motherly tone.

Sniffling Beth moved forward until she was beside her uncle. Marjoram took her hand and placed it on his chest. "See, he's breathing. He's just unconscious at the moment."

"What's wrong with him?" Beth asked gently running a hand over his hair.

"I believe he somehow contracted the virus.

He's probably had it for some time," Marjoram said sighing.

"How?" Beth looked up horrified.

"That I don't know. But he's been too weak and exhausted lately for it to simply be stress." She held his wrist between her fingers.

"Beth if he reacts like the other vampires, he will be unconscious until we can work out a treatment. The adult shifters react in a similar fashion, but they wake up now and then. So far, the vampires haven't," Rheia explained.

Broderick and Caspian ran up to where they knelt. "We're ready."

Marjoram stood as Caspian easily lifted his brother and carried him from the room, Sebastian following close behind them. She turned to Vivi. "The timetable for the trials may need to be moved up a bit. Be thinking about how to treat an older vampire."

Vivi nodded. "I'll start immediately."

Marjoram turned to Ellie. "I will be taking over Magnus' care personally so you will need someone else assisting on Level Six."

"Don't worry about us," Ellie protested.

Marjoram kissed her granddaughter's cheek and rubbed Beth's shoulder comfortingly before looking around the room. "You girls stay close to one another. I don't believe Fate brought you together for no reason. If you need me, I will be in the infirmary, with the prince." She gave Beth's shoulder a final squeeze then hurried after Broderick and Caspian.

When Vivi and the others walked out of the dining room, she noticed that no one had left. Micah stood from the love seat where he was sitting and motioned for Gavriel and Beth to sit down. They were decidedly more cramped in the antechamber, but no one seemed to want to return to the dining room.

"Ladies and gentlemen, if you would give Ryuu and myself some time, we will clear the dinner table and bring out refreshments," Hal announced.

Adriel nodded. "Take your time."

"What do we do now?" Beth asked in a small voice.

Kari paced behind the sofa. "Did not Magnus make Gavriel and Beth his heirs?"

Gavriel shook his head. "That only goes into effect in the event of Magnus' death. If we try to enforce that, we will have pitched battles on each level. Even our allies within the Founding Families would have a hard time backing us."

"What's the difference?" Meryn asked.

Vivi turned to the small human. She knew it would be difficult for her to understand the intricacies of vampire politics. "Because power once bestowed is hard to take back."

"Exactly," Gavriel agreed. "Magnus was able to get away with naming us his heirs because everyone knows how young he his. He has centuries to find a mate and have children of his own. No one thought Beth and I would have to take over, not really," Gavriel's eyebrows were pulled together as he scowled.

"What if we were to confirm Gavriel as the interim prince?" Adriel suggested.

"Gavriel? Not Caspian?" Aiden asked.

Adriel shook his head. "Caspian has never been

a leader. He said so himself on many occasions. His place for now, is at Magnus' side helping him recover." He sighed. "Besides you need four royals to confirm a new prince, even an interim one." He looked to Kendrick, who nodded. A moment later, the room was soundproofed. Adriel continued. "Some of you may not know, but I am of Gavriel's bloodline, an Ambrosios. I have chosen not to claim it, I am happy as I am, as unit leader."

Gavriel leaned forward his elbows on his knees. "Now that I have the Ambrosios Book of Life, we can easily prove our claim."

"Caspian is a Rioux, that makes three." Ellie pointed out. "What about Broderick, Beth and Eva as mates? Do they count?"

Adriel shook his head. "No, only those who carry royal blood can confirm a new prince. Magnus was only able to be confirmed with the support of Caspian and the last DuCoeur. When the remaining members of the DuSang family saw that DuSang's own mate supported Magnus, they threw their lot in with them."

"I thought the DuSangs died in that skirmish thing?" Meryn said frowning.

Adriel nodded. "Nearly all of them did. Only a handful returned to the city with DuSang. He was later challenged by Magnus. When his own family turned against him, he slaughtered them right there in the council room before the Elders."

"I bet that's why the skirmish got left out of the history books, Magnus laying the smack down probably seemed more important," Meryn mused.

Vivi sat very still barely breathing. She clutched at her mate's hand tightly. He gave her hand a squeeze and when she looked up, she saw nothing but support. Without words, she knew what he was trying to say. He would back her, no matter what she decided to do. Movement by the door caught her eye. Hal stood quietly watching her closely. He smiled and nodded giving her his blessing as well.

"Since Beth's pregnant with a royal can't she just cast a vote for little Jack?" Meryn asked.

Beth sniffled then laughed. "Stop calling my baby Jack."

Gavriel blinked. "I never would have thought of that." He looked over at Meryn. "I love the way your brain works."

Meryn shrugged. "Made sense to me."

Adriel rubbed his chin. "I do not think that will work either. The Families could just as easily claim the child would vote against confirming Gavriel."

Kari leaned against the sofa. "If we do not figure out something soon, this could turn ugly very quickly. Some of the Founding and Noble Families have been positioning for power for years according to Magnus' past reports. Short of an outright coup there has not been much they could do, so they have been held in check, this could be the opening they need to begin a takeover."

"So we have an unknown virus spreading, the city is locked down, fae portals don't work, the city's leader is incapacitated, the council elders are in a different city and to top it all off, we could be facing a civil war?" Meryn asked.

"To be put it succinctly, yes." Aiden confirmed sourly.

Vivi swallowed hard. "If there was a fourth royal, how likely is it that the Founding and Royal Families would capitulate and follow Gavriel's lead. Couldn't they just ignore the confirmation?"

Kari tapped her lips. "I believe they would fall in line. As long as we are able to prove that Gavriel is a true royal and can confirm him using established vampire law, there is nothing they can do to block us. It would be the single rare occasion where them following tradition to the point of idiocy would work in our favor. Confirming a prince is one of our oldest established rituals, they would never overturn it." She looked at Vivi. "Why ask?"

Vivi's throat turned sand dry. She looked between Etain and Hal. Her squire walked over and stood behind her, placing a hand on her shoulder as Etain took her one hand in both of his.

"I could be the fourth. I could confirm him." She spoke softly almost as if by not saying it louder she would be able to call her words back. No one said a word.

Gavriel's eyebrows were nearly to his hairline. "You are a royal?" He really looked at her. "Gods! You are a DuSang. I should have guessed. The DuSangs were known for their blood-red hair." He shook his head. "Of course so many dye their hair nowadays."

Adriel looked shell shocked. "Why hide? Why not step forward and claim your heritage?"

Vivi raised an eyebrow then pointed to him and Gavriel. "Like you, I am perfectly happy as I am. You have an honorable past to embrace. Mine is littered with bodies and filled with bloodshed."

Adriel winced at her response. "How did you escape? It was months before we got an accurate count of the dead." His face tightened. "My own parents were killed in the crossfire returning to Noctem Falls." He paused. "Gods! You were just a baby, an infant!"

Vivi pointed to Hal. "My mother's mate chose him for me. He raised me and kept me safe."

Kendrick chuckled. "I love being right."

Vivi scowled at him. "You are annoying, has anyone ever told you that?"

He nodded. "On multiple occasions in different languages."

Kari leaned over the sofa. "Can you prove you are royal?"

Gavriel turned to her. "Do you have your family's Book of Life?"

She nodded. "Both of them."

Adriel's eyes bugged out. "Both?" he collapsed back in his chair. "You have your mother's book? Magnus and I looked everywhere for it. You had it all this time?"

She smiled. "I never leave home without them. Where I go, they go."

"Whoa, whoa, whoa. For those of us not older than dirt, some inside info please," Meryn complained.

Vivi turned to Meryn. "My mother was Mercia DuCoeur, and my father was Armand DuSang."

"The crazy one?" Meryn asked.

Vivi sighed. "Yes Meryn, the crazy one."

Meryn winced. "Sorry."

Gavriel buried his face in his hands. Concerned Beth wrapped an arm around him. "What's wrong my love?"

When he looked up, his eyes were bright. "I thought they were extinct. For the first time in centuries, we have all four royal bloodlines." He took a shuddering breath.

"Which means we can confirm you as prince," Kari said pulling out her iPad.

Gavriel looked around his eyes wild. "I never wanted this," he started.

"Which is why you are perfect for the job." Kari retorted. "It is only temporary. No offense but I almost have Magnus broken in. I do not want to start over with you."

"Besides you are coming home with us when this is over. I couldn't do without my second in command," Aiden said gruffly. "Lycaonia is your home."

Gavriel sat back dazed. "Right. Just temporary."

"My PA system is looking pretty sweet about now isn't it," Meryn gloated.

Kari shook her head. "If we made a general announcement like this, we would have mass chaos on our hands." She paused. "No, we need to call a meeting with all the heads of the Noble and Founding Families first. Apprise them of the situation and prove Gavriel, Adriel and Vivi's bloodlines. Then we can let them make announcements to the citizens on their levels. That way they can field most of the questions and concerns, not us. We are too busy as it is."

"Too bad we can't just put Kari in charge," Meryn pointed out.

"Bite your tongue! I could never lead," Kari exclaimed.

Around the room suppressed laughter tittered through hand-covered mouths to fill the ante-chamber.

Kari looked around. "What?"

Her indignation set off gales of laughter that acted as a release from the mounting stress of Magnus' sudden collapse. Declan stood and wrapped his arms around his mate. "Kari my love, you could run this city with one hand tied behind your back and blindfolded."

"Pish Posh! I will leave that headache to Magnus and now Gavriel." She brought her cell phone up to her ear. "Avery darling, I need a massive favor. Could you along with your huge mate go to every level and tell all the ranking heads of the Founding and Noble families to meet on Level One in one hour?"

From where she sat Vivi heard an adorable squeak followed by reassurances that he would have everyone assembled in the meeting room in an hour.

Kari, however, wasn't done. She dialed again and brought the phone back to her ear. "Rachelle, hi. I need a favor. Can you hit up the vendors for me? I need refreshments put together and brought down to Level One. I need enough for a large meeting with the Founding and Noble families and in less than an hour."

"Of course Kari, they would walk through fire for you. Is there anything I can help with?" Rachelle asked.

"Unofficially can you put a few sets of friendly ears on each level? I will need feedback later."

"Gods above it must be something huge. Not to worry I still have my contacts from living on Level Five with DuBois. Will there be some sort of announcement?"

"More than likely first thing tomorrow," Kari

answered.

"Pencil me in for a late-afternoon meeting. I will have them report to me first then I will update you with the pertinent information. I have time to wade through those reports, something tells me you do not," Rachelle huffed.

"You are a miracle," Kari gushed.

"Just for that I will bring you some of that peanut butter pie you love so much. See you tomorrow," Rachelle said before hanging up.

Meryn looked around. "Why can't we put her in charge again?"

Gavriel shook his head ruefully. "That, is a very good question Meryn."

Vivi felt like she was going to be sick. She sat between Caspian and Adriel on a platform at the front of the room. The heads of the eight Noble Families and four Founding Families were seated in rows before them. As the distinguished vampires entered the meeting room Caspian whispered their names in her ear so if called upon she could address them correctly. It would go a long way to present the image that she belonged here. At the podium, Kari stood between Beth and Gavriel.

"Ladies and gentlemen, if I could have your attention? We are ready to begin," Kari announced. The low murmur that had been buzzing since people started arriving quieted. "Thank you. Now, I am sure you are all wondering why we requested our ranking families assemble here tonight." Kari paused and took a deep breath. "It is with great sadness that I report that our prince has been laid low by the mysterious sickness plaguing our city." Immediately everyone began speaking at once.

Looking irritated at the lack of self-control of his neighbors Javier BelleRose, the highest ranking Founding Family member stood and raised a hand. Begrudgingly those around him nudged each other until it was quiet again. "Ms. Kari, how is his condition?"

Kari smiled warmly at Javier. "He is resting easily in his quarters." She smiled. "He is probably getting more sleep now than he has in the past few weeks," she said jokingly.

Javier looked relieved. "I take it; we were called here to establish who will lead the city while Prince Magnus... recuperates?"

Kari nodded. "Yes..." Before she could continue Ivan DeLaFontaine stood. "Guiding our city will take someone with experience in leading a large amount of people. As we are in a time of crisis, I will throw modesty to the winds and volunteer my time to direct the city in her time of need."

Javier rolled his eyes. "You are the lowest ranked among us. What makes you think you are capable?"

Ivan looked down his nose at Javier. "Everyone knows my level has the most citizens. Level Five makes up nearly thirty percent of the city's population."

Simon Géroux stood. "Duly noted. Personally, I feel that either Aiden McKenzie, Rex Lionhart or Gavriel Ambrosios should be called upon to lead." Furious whispers erupted at his declaration.

DeLaFontaine's cheek flushed. "We are a city of vampires, why would you suggest two shifters?"

Simon gave Ivan a droll look. "Not only is Rex Lionhart an Elder and already in a position of leadership in the city, but he has more political experience in his baby toe than you do in your entire body. He was raised by Jedrek Lionhart, the most brilliant tactician our world has ever known." He pointed to Aiden. "Aiden McKenzie has commanded our unit warriors from the tender age of one hundred and has done so with maturity and honor. He is the future Elder of Lycaonia. As a Founding Family member himself, he was also raised to lead." He eyed Gavriel. "Gavriel Ambrosios bears the name of one of our Royal Families and has been named as co-heir with his mate Elizabeth by Prince Magnus himself." He smiled woodenly at Ivan. "And he is a vampire, since it seems to be so important to you."

Jervasius Régis stood smiling ingratiatingly to Javier. "I would like to point out that we, as a people, have never been presented with such a scenario. We have only confirmed a new prince after burying an old one. Might we take this opportunity to create a new chapter in our history?" He exchanged looks with Ivan. "I would rather we have a leader who knows the city than outsiders." Vivi's heart skipped a beat at the number of supporting nods he was getting.

Kari cleared her throat. "Since I am new to city politics, let me ask for clarification. The preferred method of selecting a new leader, that everyone here would support completely, would be to follow the traditions set forth by our ancestors?"

Damn she's good.

Everyone looked around the room nodding. There wasn't a single person who denied that, given the choice, they would rather do things the way they always have.

Kari smiled and gave an exaggerated sigh. "You have no idea how much it relieves me to hear you all say that." She turned to them and nodded. Vivi stood and reached into the large canvas bag hiding her families' Books of Life. She walked to the center of the stage and set her books down on the wooden table. She followed Gavriel, Adriel, and Caspian behind the table to prop up their books.

"I take it all of you know what these are?" Kari continued as if they hadn't just revealed four of the most precious treasures of their race. "Some of you may have seen the Rioux Book of Life during Prince Magnus' confirmation, thus you know that Caspian is a royal. We are here to validate the other three."

Javier's hand trembled as he brought it up to his mouth. "Gods!" he whispered.

"This is impossible!" DeLaFontaine railed. "Do you not find it convenient that as Magnus is laid low these imposters show up to swoop in and steal his title? Why come forward now?" he demanded.

"Maybe because they didn't want to deal with a dipshit like you on a daily basis. *Prince* Magnus has more patience," Meryn drawled. It wasn't lost on the room that Meryn remembered Magnus' proper form of address. Aiden covered her mouth with his hand as he fought a smile.

Hugo Evreux guffawed loudly not even bothering to hide his amusement. "You really did call

René a douchebag!" Around him, people smiled, but their eyes were locked on the four books.

Simon turned to Kari. "May we authenticate their books?"

Kari smiled. "Yes, please do."

Simon and Javier exchanged looks and stepped forward eagerly.

Ivan pushed his way to the front. "It requires three ranking family members' blood to authenticate. I insist on being the third."

Javier gave him an impatient look from the stage. "Then get up here."

Together the three used their own sharp fingernails to draw blood and allowed the drops to fall on the cover of each book. One by one, each book glowed with a brilliant golden light. Around the room, everyone pointed. Vivi could hear their exclamations of wonder.

Simon and Javier stood on either side of Ivan and practically manhandled him off the stage when he reached for one of the books.

Kari looked over her shoulder at them. "Go ahead." She turned back to the room. "From my understanding, now that the books have been proven to be authentic, each person who wishes to claim a royal title need only place a single drop of blood on the last page of their book. If their claim is true, it will glow silver. If they are not of that particular bloodline it will glow red."

Vivi watched as the others opened their books to the last page and pulled out their prepared daggers. She followed suit and cut her palm, letting it drip onto the bespelled page. All four books began to glow with a soft silver light. Gasps were heard throughout the room.

"Princes Gavriel, Caspian and Adriel. Princess Vivian. Do you have a name you would like to put forward as royals to be confirmed as our interim Prince or Princess while Prince Magnus recovers?" Kari asked in a clear voice.

Caspian nodded. "We would like to confirm Prince Gavriel to act as our leader and prince, until Prince Magnus is able to return to his duties."

"I demand to see Gavriel's name in the book!" Ivan screeched. "He was a no-name upstart who appeared out of nowhere six hundred years ago. He takes orders from a shifter as second in command. No one of royal blood would do such a thing!"

Vivi watched as an evil grin appeared at Gavriel's lips. He picked up his book and walked in front of the table for the entire room to see. In a dramatic fashion, he started at the back of the book where the younger members of his family were listed. Page by page he continued to flip. One by one, as the pages were turned Ivan grew more and more gray. Gavriel took his time, treating each page gently.

It took him a full three minutes to reach the very beginning of the book. When page one appeared, his name glowed as if written with a silver ink. Vivi wasn't the only one who felt as if the air in the room was suddenly sucked out the door.

Javier and Simon fell to their knees, and the entire room followed their example. More than one person was moved to tears. Caspian and Adriel walked around to the front of the table and knelt down on one knee in reverence. Vivi stood frozen, unsure of what to do. Gavriel turned his head so the room couldn't see his face and winked at her.

His comforting action allowed her to breathe again. She carefully set her books down and walked around the table to kneel beside Adriel and Caspian. The only ones standing were the shifters, fae and witches of the Alpha and Eta units. Every single vampire in the room offered Gavriel their neck with their hands over their hearts.

"Please stand, this is not needed," Gavriel said in a firm but gentle voice.

No one moved, like Vivi they were overwhelmed by his very presence. Gavriel Ambrosios, the one from history and legend. The Dark Prince himself, come to life from their childhood stories and dreams. Every vampire in the world knew his name and owed them their very lives. Vivi had assumed the gentle vampire she was introduced to had been named for his illustrious ancestor, not that he was the Dark Prince himself.

From the floor Javier looked up, tears streaming down his face. "Why did you leave us?" he asked brokenly. His eyes held a vulnerability that one didn't see often in older vampires. For once Javier and the other ranking family members weren't the oldest ones in the room. Javier was looking to Gavriel the way a child looked to a parent.

Gavriel gracefully jumped from the stage and knelt down between Javier and Simon and placed a comforting hand on their backs. "Because you no longer needed me. You all learned how to stand on your own. You came together and built this city and established the laws that allowed our people to thrive." He pulled the two men to their feet, and they unabashedly leaned into his strength. "I am the past, but you all are the future. When this crisis is over Prince Magnus will resume his position with my full support. I will return to Lycaonia and continue down the path Fate has set before me."

"But you are our prince," Simon said choking on the emotion in his words.

Gavriel smiled. "I will always be watching over you, never doubt that. But you already have a prince, and right now he needs our support."

Simon stood a little straighter. "What can we do?"

"Tomorrow I will need for you all to make a general announcement on your levels that Prince Magnus is feeling a bit under the weather and in the meantime I have been confirmed to help him while he recovers. The last thing we need is chaos and panic," Gavriel said.

"Yes, sire," the room spoke as one.

Gavriel blinked. "That will take some getting used to."

Javier turned to him. "Do you really have to return to Lycaonia? As the highest ranking member of our race, there is nothing that would be denied you." He looked over to Aiden. "I mean no offense," he turned back to Gavriel. "Why would you take orders from anyone?"

Gavriel met Aiden's eyes and smiled. "Because he protects everyone." He looked around the room. "And I protect him."

CHAPTER EIGHT

"HE IS OVER TEN THOUSAND years old! Can you even imagine?" Vivi exclaimed flinging herself on Etain's high four-poster bed.

Etain nodded. "Our queen is just as old. It isn't unheard of for the fae to live thousands of years."

She was already undressed and was freezing. She hurriedly pulled back the covers and dove in. "Well, not all of us are fae," she said scrunching her nose at him.

"No, you in particular, are a sexy vampire that tempts this poor fae warrior to distraction," Etain admitted removing his boxers and climbing in beside her.

She immediately snuggled in close to him. His skin was so warm. Being in her mate's arms reminded her of how it felt when she would toss her favorite blanket in the dryer. "So warm."

Etain began to kiss the back of her neck before moving to the side. Groaning she wiggled her bottom against his hardness. "And what am I tempting you to do now?" she asked breathlessly.

"I need to make love to my mate," he replied in a

low voice sending shivers down her spine.

She rolled onto her back. "And I need to feel you. Surround me and hold me. After revealing who I am, I feel exposed, and I don't like it."

Etain moved until he was between her legs nearly covering her from head to toe. "I will always be your shield."

Vivi giggled and shifted her hips. "Right now, you're feeling more like a sword."

Etain grinned. "I love that we can smile and joke as we make love. You make my heart soar."

Vivi reached up and traced his cheekbones, then his lips. "I couldn't have done tonight without you. I wouldn't have had the courage."

Etain lowered himself until his cock was teasing her entrance. He latched onto her neck and slowly bit down.

"Gods!" she cried out as her body lit on fire. Never before had any man learned her body so quickly. He was playing her like an instrument. She bucked her hips so that the length of him slid along her folds causing them both to moan.

His lips moved, and he kissed her temple. "You sell yourself short. You would have stepped forward had I not been there because you would have never put the city in danger."

Unable to take their mutual torture a second longer he reached down and eased into her. Both of them sighed in relief. Hooking her legs on his forearms, he opened her wide to him.

On the third thrust, he hit the perfect angle. "Don't you dare move!" she threatened. His masculine chuckle and deeper thrust was his only response. Vivi closed her eyes as he worked that elusive spot inside of her.

"Vivian," Etain groaned and she knew he was close. She reached down and had barely touched her clit when her own orgasm swept her away. Her shouts lifted with his until they were both a sweaty tangled mess. He pulled from her and literally collapsed to her side. When their eyes met they both laughed at the sheer joy of their union.

"Does your bed self clean too?" she asked.

Grimacing Etain shook his head. "I will change the sheets tomorrow," he promised.

"Put self-cleaning sheets on our wish list," she murmured her eyes drooping.

"Whatever you say my love," he agreed and pulled her close.

Love it when he says that.

The first thing they did the next morning was check on the new donations and prep them for treatment. She was somewhat surprised to see that not only had the blood finished processing already, but the stone was back to grey. That meant the blood had finished sometime in the night, and the stone had hours to reset.

It didn't take her long to find the correct ratio for the three donations. Carefully she filled the cartridges, and they ran them up to Level Six. She smiled when she saw Ellie was already doing her morning check-ins.

"Is that the next batch?" she asked when Vivi

handed her the new injector cartridges.

"Yes. So if you could do the same as before and just document any changes that would be great."

"I'll send down a new blood sample sometime this afternoon." She looked around when she heard a child crying. She turned back to her. "See you at breakfast?"

Vivi nodded before Ellie hurried to the child's side. As much as Vivi loved helping others, she was definitely not a hands on person. To her, Ellie was a goddess.

When she and Etain walked into the prince's quarters, Vivi was shocked at what she saw. The antechamber was filled with gift baskets and intricate arrangements of flowers. To her delight Sebastian greeted them with a smile. With his hand over his heart, he bowed low to her.

She scowled and shook her head. "Don't do that, at least, not you." Personally, Ivan DeLaFontaine could stay bent over for all she cared, but Sebastian was different.

"Prince Magnus?" she asked.

Sebastian's straightened, his eyes clouding a bit. "Still sleeping." He perked up. "But that is probably for the best. He has been going non-stop for weeks." He pointed around the room. "Half of these are baskets for Prince Gavriel, and the other half are for you. I have taken the liberty of separating the two." He indicated how the baskets lined opposite walls. "I have also wrote down the names of everyone who sent something and forwarded them to Kari to deal with proper replies."

Vivi exhaled. "Thank you! To be honest, I'm not too sure about this princess thing. Thank the gods for Kari, because I have no idea how to respond."

Sebastian nodded. "You all are too busy to be dealing with trivial things like this anyway." He smiled softly. "You also have a guest waiting for you in the dining room."

Vivi looked at Etain, who shrugged. She looked at Sebastian. "Who?"

"Leana Géroux. She arrived an hour ago."

"You should have reached out to me," Vivi said feeling terrible.

Sebastian shook his head. "She said to let you sleep, that you had had an eventful evening, and she knew you would be busy this morning." He blushed. "She said it was worth coming early to partake in my waffles."

Vivi brightened. "We're having waffles?"

Sebastian chuckled. "This way," he opened the dining room door for them.

When they walked in the men stood. She sat down next to Leana, and the men resumed their seats. She turned to the elegantly dressed woman. "Have we met?" she asked.

Leana's eyes were bright. "Yes, a long, long time ago. I was your mother's best friend. I was there the day you were born."

Vivi couldn't help but smile. "I have so many questions." A flood of things she wanted to know flooded her mind. She started with the most important. "What was my mother like?"

Leana laughed. "Dutiful, but stubborn. She said you were the only good thing to come from her association with DuSang."

"How did she end up with that jerk?" Vivi always wanted to know why her mother hadn't waited for her mate.

Leana's face became thoughtful. "Things were different before Magnus. It was a different era. Your mother lost her parents in the Great War and was the last of her bloodline. She put off mating for thousands of years until she finally caved under the Founding Families' pressure to produce an heir."

"Then why didn't she choose Magnus? He was a royal too," Vivi pointed out.

Leana shook her head. "Because Armand was older and he outranked Magnus."

"Outranked?" Vivi asked.

"Yes. After the Great War, Houses Rioux and Ambrosios were elevated to royal standing by the joint councils for their work in preserving life. DuCoeur and DuSang were the original royal families. When it came time for her to choose a mate, House Ambrosios had all but disappeared so it made sense that between Magnus and Armand she would end up with DuSang." She gave Gavriel a sly look. "Though, had Gavriel been around, she probably would have chosen him."

Gavriel choked on his orange juice. Beth laughed and handed him a napkin. She smiled at Leana. "That wasn't nice."

Leana laughed. "A little pay back for last night. I almost swallowed my tongue when I saw how old he is." She wagged a finger at him. "My poor Simon went all to pieces."

Beth winked at Leana. "Men."

"Truly," Leana agreed, then turned back to Vivi. "Your hair must have changed color as you grew older, though that is the only trait of him I see in you. You have your father's red hair, but you look just like your mother. I knew who you were the moment I laid eyes on you." She wiped the tears from her eyes. "It was like Mercia had returned to us." She smiled. "I guess in a way she has. She would have loved the fact you took the last name of Mercy." She reached out and cupped Vivi's cheek. "I was devastated when they reported your mother's death. I asked about you of course, but no one could find you. It was assumed you wandered off and died." She let her hand fall and placed it back in her lap. "For all his sins, your father never would have hurt you. You were his heir, so I knew you had not shared your mother's fate, but as days became weeks, then months, then years without any clues, I gave up hope." She shook her head. "Magnus was inconsolable for months."

Vivi tilted her head. "Why?"

Leana's eyes widened. "Of course you would not know." Her eyes twinkled mischievously. "Your father hated Magnus with a deep-seated passion that knew no reason. However, Magnus and Caspian were the only other living royals, so he chose the eldest Rioux to be your *athair*. Your mother of course was tickled pink. She adored Magnus and knew him to be a good man." She giggled. "Magnus used to wait until your father left Level One, then sneak over to the DuSang quarters to visit with you. In fact, he is the one who gave you your first stuffed animal. It was a..."

"Pony," Vivi whispered.

"Oh my goodness. You remember?"

Hal chuckled as he walked in from the kitchen with a large platter of waffles. "Remember? She still has that ratty little pony. I never knew Prince Magnus gifted it to her. When I met her, she refused to be parted with it. I thought she was the first vampire fabric hybrid and it grew from her chest. She would scream bloody murder if you tried to take it. I had to wait until she was sleeping to patch the poor wretched thing."

"Hal!" Vivi felt her face heat with embarrassment.

Leana beamed. "Magnus would be so pleased if he knew. Do you remember what you used to call it?"

"Her name is Maggie." Vivi ducked her head. "I don't think there is an original stitch of fabric left on her. Hal has done so many repairs over the centuries, she's more a patchwork pony now."

Leana nodded. "Maggie. You could not say Magnus as a baby."

Vivi felt her mouth drop open. "My stuffy is named after Prince Magnus?"

"Unlike your father, Magnus would spoil you with his time. He knew when your naps were. He was there for your first steps and your first word."

Etain leaned in. "What was her first word?"

Leana's mouth twitched. "Maggie."

Vivi covered her mouth with both hands. "No!"

"Your father was furious, especially since your second word was 'Mama'."

Vivi sat back stunned as Hal piled her plate high with waffles. "Prince Magnus is my *athair*."

Sebastian practically danced around the table. "He is going to burst his buttons with pride when he wakes up. A godsdaughter!"

Leana sighed as she took a bite and chewed daintily. "This is amazing. Simon will be jealous when he hears Sebastian was serving waffles. I invited him to come along, but Gavriel made quite the impression last night. Simon and Javier have been walking through our levels personally answering questions and speaking to the citizens. Everyone was thrilled to hear that the three previously lost royal houses had been restored. They are singing Magnus' praises saying he has led us into a 'Golden Era'." She cut up her waffle. "Will you be moving into the DuSang or DuCoeur quarters?" she asked.

Vivi dropped her fork. "What?"

"Oh dear. Please tell me I did not upset you." Leana asked looking worried.

Vivi waved her hands. "No, no you didn't. But what?" She looked up at Hal who shrugged. "I figured that would come next," he admitted.

"What next? I don't understand." Vivi asked feeling lost.

Etain gently turned her in her chair. "My love, you have reclaimed your heritage. Both royal families of DuSang and DuCoeur have established quarters here on Level One along with family vaults." He rubbed up and down her arms. "I did not assume prior to your announcement that you would stay here simply because I was a unit warrior for the city. Had you wanted to leave, that's what we would have done. But things are different now," he explained.

"We're moving here?" Vivi asked looking around the room for confirmation.

Everyone was nodding including Hal. "Vivi darlin' you belong here. I have never seen you happier, and we don't have to worry about you getting burned all the time." He shrugged. "Just choose which set of quarters you want, and I'll get Ryuu and Sebastian to help me get it cleaned and set up for use."

Beth turned to Gavriel, her eyes a bit frantic. "Do we have to move?"

Gavriel shook his head. "We will clean up the Ambrosios quarters, but I imagine Adriel will be the primary resident along with Eva." Beth looked like she was two seconds away from hyperventilating. Gavriel rubbed her back. "Look at it this way *zain'ka moya,* Magnus will not have to worry about running out of guest quarters now. Everyone will have their own living space down here on Level One."

"But this is my home. I grew up here," Beth protested.

"And we will be just a few hundred yards away. We can easily walk over here for breakfast," Gavriel said before leaning in to kiss her forehead.

Sebastian ran a hand over her hair. "We can turn your room into a nursery! That way, you do not have to worry about carrying around things for the little one."

Vivi concentrated on Etain's hands because Beth was simply echoing her own panic.

"Vivi." Etain lifted her chin with his finger. "If you do not want to stay here we do not have to. If you tell me you want to leave here when this virus is cured, I will follow you anywhere you want to go." His handsome face was filled with worry.

Vivi took a deep breath. She looked over at Hal. "It's not as if we can go to Éire Danu, I'd end up a crispy critter." She turned back to Etain. "What if you had never come here? We could never have found one another."

Etain blinked then smiled slowly. "Maybe you are my reward for all of the long centuries I spent serving here."

Hal snorted. "It's a good thing you've been here so long, you don't have to adjust to the city."

Vivi looked around the table. "I wonder exactly how long the threads of Fate are."

Gavriel eyed his mate. "Truly."

Vivi winked at Sebastian. "Can I come here for breakfast sometimes too?"

He nodded enthusiastically. "Of course! The more the merrier."

Vivi turned the issue over in her mind. The only thing she hated was how close she would be to her father's residence. She couldn't find any reason not to stay.

"If we have any children, and they're like me, I won't have to worry about them getting burned," she thought out loud.

Hal ruffled her hair. "As much as I hate to admit it, you're a perfect fit here kiddo," he said begrudgingly.

"Good morning," Aiden said walking into the room. In his arms, he carried a small blanket wrapped person.

"Is that Meryn?" Vivi asked. "And is she okay?"

Aiden nodded. "Oh yeah, this is normal. She really isn't a morning person." He set his burrito mate in her chair and carefully laid her head on the table. He sat down and simply scooted the waffle platter in front of him before dousing it in syrup.

Ryuu emerged from the kitchen with a cup and set it down by Meryn's head. He reached into his vest pocket and pulled out an odd-shaped straw. He placed one end in the cup and guided the other end between Meryn's lips.

"You created a straw she can use face down?" she asked.

Ryuu nodded. "It quickly became a life necessity."

"You have no idea," Colton added walking through the door with Rheia.

Slowly, the dining room filled as everyone began waking up.

Adriel sat down and pulled out his iPad. "I take it from the number of baskets in the antechamber our announcement went over well?"

Leana sipped her coffee. "If anyone has anything negative to say they are keeping it to themselves. Magnus' popularity is at an all-time high. Our people see the return of the four Royal Houses as a sign from the gods that great things are coming to Noctem Falls."

"The children even made 'Get Well' cards for Magnus." Sebastian said excitedly. "They are the most adorable things! I am getting them framed for the antechamber."

"We were also discussing the new living quarters," Vivi added slyly. She wasn't disappointed by Adriel's reaction.

He frowned. "What new living quarters?"

Vivi sat back with her cup of coffee as Gavriel explained how they were reopening the Ambrosios royal quarters and since he would eventually be returning to Lycaonia, Adriel would be the primary resident.

The more Gavriel spoke the paler Adriel got.

"But I cannot leave the men!" he protested.

"I am sure we'll get along fine with you down here," Declan said reassuringly.

"Fine? Fine! We almost lost Godard yesterday when the twins accidentally blew up the kitchen!" Adriel looked like he was on the verge of a panic attack.

Eva chuckled. "Time to let your baby chicks fall out of the nest."

Rheia looked at her. "Don't you mean fly from the nest?"

Eva gave her a pointed stare. "Have you met the men?"

"Good point."

"They will die." Adriel said simply.

Kendrick leaned forward looking amused. "What did the twins do?"

Adriel waved a hand at him. "Something about increasing the gas pressure of the oven."

Eva shrugged before sliding half the platter of bacon onto her plate. "It might be safer for us to move down here."

"If it makes you feel any better I had a bit of a meltdown myself," Vivi said encouragingly.

Adriel sat back in his chair. "I think it is just now sinking in. Last night, it was simply the next step to take to prevent chaos, but this morning it seems more real." He met her eyes. "Everything has changed."

She nodded. "Trust me, I understand."

Adriel eyed Declan. "My first decision as a Royal is to make Declan attend all future council meetings in my stead."

"Whaaa?" Declan choked out through a mouthful of bacon and waffles

Gavriel rubbed a hand over his chin. "That sounds like an excellent idea. He can act as my proxy when I leave as well."

Declan who had just taken a huge gulp of milk to clear his airways inhaled and began to choke again. Frantic Kari began beating on his back. "If you die, I swear I will kill you," she threatened.

Declan's face was beet red as he pounded on his chest. When he was finally able to breathe, he glared at the two new royals. "That was not funny. Don't even joke like that."

Gavriel and Adriel exchanged looks. Adriel looked at his second in command. "What makes you think we were joking? We are taking a page from Aiden's book and putting you in charge. It will do you good."

Aiden grinned around the table his cheeks puffed out like a chipmunk from stuffing his mouth with three waffles. He gave Declan a thumbs up.

Declan rested his face on the table. "Shoot me now. Save me the misery!" he moaned.

"Don't be such a crybaby Declan. You are per-fectly capable of attending meetings," Rex chided. He eyed Adriel slyly. "Of course since he will be doing so much work for Prince Adriel, I fully expect him to set up living quarters for you on Level One."

Declan's head perked up. "Level One?" He turned to Adriel with wide eyes. "I could eat Sebastian's cooking everyday?"

Sebastian smiled as he refilled Declan's plate. "I love cooking for hearty appetites."

Adriel nodded slowly smiling. "Since so many

of the Eta warriors' mates work in the lab, or with Prince Magnus, maybe the entire unit should move down here."

Eva smiled at Vivi when she caught her staring. Adriel didn't want to leave the Unit Level because he would have missed his friends.

"Isn't he just the sweetest thing?" Eva asked to no one in particular.

"I think that is a wonderful idea!" Beth exclaimed. "That way when we visit it will be easier to see Ellie, Eva, Kari and Vivi!"

"And I will be able to visit Declan, Kari and Baby Lionhart whenever I wish since the council quarters are on Level One as well." Rex was grinning from ear to ear.

"Sorry I'm late everyone! The children are feeling better and are wanting to get out of their hospital beds and play. It's making them irritable," Ellie said breezing through the door with Grant, who carried Benji on his chest in a papoose. They sat down and started reaching for food.

Vivi turned to their new prince. "Gavriel, I've been thinking."

He raised an eyebrow. "Yes?"

"The second batch that is going out today only took a few hours to process. I think it's the age of the blood. The older it is, the longer it takes to break any bonds." She looked down at Ellie. "If this theory is correct, then we may see a slight decrease in effectiveness with the second batch."

Ellie frowned. "We drew blood for testing at the six-hour mark last time. I'll have new samples down in the lab around noon. I hope you're wrong."

Vivi strummed her fingers on the table. "I do too,

but I don't think I am." She turned back to Gavriel. "That being said, I don't think warrior blood will be very effective for Prince Magnus."

"You wish for me to donate?" he asked sitting back in his chair.

Vivi nodded. "I do. The method I came up with to treat the vampires is to mix a known compatible vampire blood strain with a donation from an older vampire. It is my hope the older blood will give sick vampires a boost in much the same way as vampire blood helps shifters. The stone will reduce the need to have an exact blood match." She looked around the table. "This is all experimental. I have no idea if it will work or not, but it's the best idea I have."

Beth faced her mate. "Please," she whispered.

Gavriel cupped the back of her head and pulled her close to kiss her gently. "You need not even ask my love. He means much to you, of course I will help in any way I can." He looked over to Vivi. "I must make two requests, however."

"Of course," she agreed.

"First is that you only take what is absolutely needed. If there is any blood left over, it is to be destroyed immediately. Secondly, I wish to be there to see it administered."

"Those requests are more than reasonable. We can start this afternoon drawing your blood, if you are free." Vivi couldn't help but feel excited. She would be able to see the oldest vampire blood in the world under a microscope.

"I will make time. The sooner Magnus is on his feet, the better," Gavriel answered.

Rheia leaned forward. "Do you want me to

gather some older vampire blood from among the vendors just in case? We can have it processing while we're waiting."

Vivi nodded. "That is an excellent idea. While you do that, I'll get donations from Caspian and Gavriel. We'll put all five bags on the stone first thing so that it can start processing. Something tells me it will take longer than even the warrior's blood to finish. I'm thinking if we get it started this morning, we could start administering the third batch the day after tomorrow."

Beth gasped. "That long?"

Ellie turned to Beth. "The warrior's blood took over twelve hours, and they are nowhere near as old as Gavriel. If Vivi is right about age playing a factor, then Gavriel's blood will need the extra time."

Beth slumped down in her chair. "I just want Uncle well."

Rheia gave Beth a sympathetic look. "We all do honey."

Sebastian cleared his throat, and everyone looked to where he stood by the door leading out to the antechamber. "Prince Gavriel, Princess Vivian, you have a guest waiting for you in the next room. Founding Family head, Ivan DeLaFontaine wishes to speak to you regarding Prince Magnus." Sebastian's voice was neutral, even pleasant, but the irritation on his face spoke volumes.

Vivi looked over to Gavriel, who stood. "Please tell him we will be with him momentarily Sebastian."

"At once, Prince Gavriel," Sebastian responded laying it on thick.

Vivi opened her mouth but was brought up short by Gavriel raising a finger sharply. A second later the air in the room flexed.

"We have maybe two minutes before he realizes he no longer hears normal dining room sounds, like silverware and glassware clinking," Kendrick advised.

Gavriel turned to her. "If you feel more comfortable, I will do most of the talking. I will try to keep everything vague and hurry him out the door." He turned to Aiden. "If he is still here in five minutes announce you need my assistance with a concern from Lycaonia. He will not be able to ask about that." He turned to Kendrick. "The same for you. In five minutes remind Vivi she is needed in the lab." He looked around. "Any questions?"

Meryn raised her head for the first time. She looked around, her eyes barely open. "Huh?"

Gavriel stared at Meryn a moment then nodded. "Right. Let us go deal with that prat."

Meryn scowled. "Huh?"

Vivi watched in amusement as Aiden helped Meryn out of her chair and away from her coffee cup. Colton made a huge production to walk on the other side of the room, far from the barely conscious human.

"Surely that isn't necessary?" Vivi asked her mate as Colton steered Rheia in the opposite direction to walk the long way about.

Etain leaned in. "I heard from Gamma that Meryn threatened to castrate Colton the first morning she spent at the Alpha estate. I don't think he's taking any chances."

"That's silly," Vivi scoffed.

Etain pointed to the other end of the table. "You notice that Rheia isn't protesting."

"Should Meryn be allowed in the same room as DeLaFontaine? She hasn't even finished her first cup of coffee?" Eva whispered to Adriel.

Adriel flashed them a rare boyish grin. "Why do you think we are all heading to the antechamber?"

Vivi shrugged. "Let's go watch the midget in action."

Etain bowed regally and held out his arm. "After you Princess Vivian."

She accepted his arm and headed to the ante-chamber.

CHAPTER NINE

IVAN DELAFONTAINE STOOD AS THEY entered the room. There were a thousand other places Vivi wished she could be, mainly the lab. But instead she found herself forcing a smile as Ivan walked up to her. "Thank you for seeing me. I have a few questions concerning Prince Magnus."

"I'm not sure how much I will be able to tell you that wasn't shared last night," Vivi said.

Ivan reached out and took her hand in his. He bent over slightly raising it to his lips when out of the corner of Vivi's eyes, she saw a dart of light. Moments later, Ivan was jumping back cursing, holding his bleeding hand to his chest.

"Restrain him!" Gavriel ordered, moving Beth behind him.

Tarak, in one fluid motion, swept Ivan's feet from under him and slammed his face into the floor. "Yes, sire." He replied as he pushed his knee into the back of Ivan's neck.

"What is the meaning of this!" DeLaFontaine screamed. "I demand you release me at once!"

Gavriel turned to Meryn. "Was that Felix?"

She nodded. "Yes." She turned her head to her shoulder. "What's the matter?"

Seconds later, a tiny sprite shimmered into view holding a bloody little sword. "He tried to hurt Vivi!" Felix exclaimed as his wings fluttered in an aggravated staccato. Vivi had never seen a sprite before, but she was pretty sure they were passive flower lovers, not sword wielding warriors.

Gavriel leaned down so that he was eye level with Felix on Meryn's shoulder. "He looked like he was simply going to kiss her hand in greeting."

Felix shook his head causing his auburn curls to bounce. He took flight and landed on the floor next to DeLaFontaine's wrist. "He was going to stab her!" he pointed to DeLaFontaine's cuff. Etain swept Vivi behind him. Vivi held onto the back of his shirt. She stepped to one side, so she could see what was happening in the room.

Gavriel stepped on DeLaFontaine's arm before it slipped under his body. "What have we here?" he asked. Kneeling down he carefully removed Ivan's cufflink. He turned it over in his hands. The more he examined it, the more his eyes changed, turning from a bright ruby red to a deep crimson.

He held it out to Vivi. "Be careful."

Vivi hurried forward, with Etain at her side. She took it and held it up. On the other side of the sharp cuff, a small dram vial was filled with a clear liquid. "I'll have to test it to be sure, but I think we may have the source of our virus." She was impressed at the miniaturization of the delivery system. "This cost a small fortune."

Gavriel pulled out his walkie talkie. "Viktor, Dimitri I need you both on Level One."

Viktor's reply was almost instantaneous. "At once, sire."

Aiden walked over and placed his foot on DeLaFontaine's arm so Gavriel could move. "Why Viktor and Dimitri?"

"Because I trust Viktor's loyalty as the son of a Founding Family head. BelleRose has always been a supporter of Magnus." He gave Aiden an evil grin. "And Dimitri, because he is the most creative when it comes to 'Advanced Questioning Techniques'."

Aiden's answering smile was no less wicked. "Perfect."

Gavriel turned to Kari. "As soon as this traitor is moved to the detention cells we will need to have a meeting with just the Founding Family heads." He looked at Meryn. "You've already cleared Simon and Javier, but we need to check out Jervasius Régis."

Meryn glanced up from cuddling Felix. "Sure."

There was knock on the door which Sebastian quickly answered. Viktor and Dimitri walked in and looked down. Their eyes widened. "Did we miss something?"

"Your word that what I say will go no further?" Gavriel asked.

Both men nodded. Viktor looked to Dimitri then back to Gavriel. "You have our word."

Gavriel pointed to the floor. "Ivan DeLaFontaine just tried to use his cuff link to inject an unknown substance into Vivi." Vivi held up the small cuff, and he continued. "We think this may be the source of the virus." He looked from one warrior to the other. "I would like for Viktor to stay here on Level

One for a Founding Family meeting, Dimitri, I would like for you to escort DeLaFontaine to our detention cells and see if you can get him to share any information about his cuff links."

Dimitri's face hardened as his fangs lengthened. He knelt down and pulled DeLaFontaine's head up by his hair until his neck was at an odd angle. "I have two small, precious friends among the shifter children on Level Six who are sick. If I find out you are the reason why, not even the gods will be able to hold back my anger," he growled.

DeLaFontaine began to struggle at that point. "I demand to be interviewed by the council!"

Dimitri slammed Ivan's face into the floor. "Too bad, they're stuck at the Council Estate since the city is on lock down due to the virus."

Meryn edged closer her eyes bright. "He's so cool."

Aiden pulled her against him. "You just like violent people."

Meryn turned to Dimitri with puppy-dog eyes. "Hit him again?" she asked pouting.

Dimitri gave her a wolfish grin and reached for DeLaFontaine. Gavriel shook his head. "Save it for later."

Dimitri stood and winked at Meryn. "He will get what is coming to him."

Meryn gave a short nod. "Good, because he upset Felix and that's not acceptable."

Vivi frowned. "Where did he go?"

Meryn pointed down her hoodie. "He's still shaking." She pulled the hoodie away from her chest. "That was totally badass though Felix. We need to get a picture of you with your bloody sword, that was awesome."

Aiden peeked down Meryn's shirt. "Where did he learn how to use a sword?"

"YouTube," Meryn replied glibly.

Gavriel pointed to the door. "Dimitri, if you would?"

Dimitri placed a hand over his heart and bowed. "My Prince, it would be an honor." He bent down and pulled a thrashing DeLaFontaine to his feet. He looked around the room until he spotted Kendrick. "Air shackles?"

Kendrick spoke low staring at DeLaFontaine. A moment later, he exhaled. "That should do it." DeLaFontaine's hands were now lying on top of each other seemingly pinned to his tailbone.

"My thanks," Dimitri said and dragged DeLaFontaine from the room.

Gavriel turned to Kari. "Kari if you…"

She held up a hand. "Five steps ahead of you. They'll be here in ten minutes."

Gavriel grinned. "Of course you are."

Rheia, Anne and Ellie walked over with Colton, Law and Grant. Rheia jerked her head toward the door. "You don't need us for this. We're heading to Level Six to start a blood drive of older blood for the next set of trials and to check on the children."

Gavriel waved Micah over. "Can you go with them as an additional guard?"

Micah wrapped an arm around each woman's shoulders despite the low growls coming from their mates. "I would love to spend more time with these heavenly creatures." He steered them toward the door, their irate mates in tow.

"Kendrick, a soundproof spell please?" Gavriel

asked.

"Five steps ahead of you," Kendrick teased as the air flexed.

Gavriel pinched the bridge of his nose. "I am surrounded by comedians."

Aiden clapped him on the back. "Welcome to my world."

The rest of their group sat down and got comfortable. Vivi was ensconced in the love seat with her mate. She kept turning the cuff link over in her hand. Etain reached over and took it from her.

"Here," Kari said handing Etain something small and red.

Vivi looked at her. "What's that?"

Kari held up a pencil. "The eraser. We do not want anyone dosed accidentally." Etain affixed the eraser to the cuff and dropped it in his front pocket.

It didn't take long for the Founding Family heads to arrive. Javier and Simon were all smiles until they saw the grim expressions around the room. Javier paled. "Magnus?"

Gavriel shook his head. "He is the same. No, this is regarding something else, please have a seat."

The three couples sat down looking worried. Gavriel eyed each one in an appearance to be neutral. "I will ask a single question and require an immediate answer." They nodded, and he continued. "Do you have any knowledge regarding Ivan DeLaFontaine distributing the virus around the city?"

The BelleRose and Géroux couples answered immediate. "No, sire."

Jervasius Régis turned a deathly shade of gray. His mate shook her head and meekly whispered.

"No, sire."

Gavriel walked over until he stood in front of the Régis Founding Family head. "Well Jervasius?"

Jervasius shook his head and covered his mouth with a trembling hand. "No, sire."

Gavriel looked over to Meryn, she was watching the distraught man closely. Finally, she gave a firm shake of her head. "He's a complete asshole, but he's not lying." She turned and looked at his mate. "She needs help though. I think she lied when she told Kari that she was with her mate willingly."

The woman looked up sharply, fear in her eyes. "No, I am."

Meryn in an uncharacteristic show of empathy, walked over and took her hand. Using all her weight, she pulled the woman to the other side of the room and sat her down in an empty love seat. "No, you're not. But that's okay. You're safe now."

Jervasius went to stand and Gavriel simply pushed him back into his seat. "You stay there until I tell you otherwise." Gavriel told him his voice devoid of emotion. The man began to shake when faced with the prince's anger.

Gavriel walked over and knelt in front of the woman who had buried her face in her hands. "Bree is it not?" he asked gently. She nodded without looking up. "Bree, do you know who I am?" Bree lowered her hands slowly and looked at him before shaking her head. "My name is Prince Gavriel. I am in charge of the city until Magnus is feeling better." Bree covered her mouth with both hands and swayed in her seat. "Now, I need you to answer me truthfully. Are you mated to Jervasius against your will?" When her eyes cut to the mate in question, Gavriel very lightly turned her head until she was facing him. "You need not fear any reprisals. If you wish to leave him you will be protected, no harm will come to you for speaking the truth."

Tears began to spill down her cheeks. "Will you protect my mate as well?"

Gavriel frowned. "Jervasius?"

She shook her head causing her shiny curls to bounce around. "No, my real mate."

"He is not your mate! I am!" Jervasius screamed.

Gavriel stood and turned so that Bree did not see his anger. His eyes were blood-red and his fangs extended past his chin. "You kept her against her will knowing she had a mate?" he asked in a low growl.

"Sire, we have been mated for centuries. We have three fine sons together." Jervasius protested.

"No, we do not," Bree said softly.

"Quiet woman!" Jervasius hissed. "Sire, she is very weak minded. She does not know what she says."

Bree stared down at her hands. "I may have been forced to endure your attentions over the centuries, but I was not the only one you lay with. Each time I declared I was pregnant you left me alone for months at a time, and you were never there for the birth of the child. Each one of your sons was born by a different woman. Their silence bought their child a life of ease as a legitimate son of a Founding Family head." When she looked up, there was a spark of defiance in her eyes. "They are *your* sons, not mine."

Jervasius flew out of his seat toward his mate

only to be brought up short by Gavriel. The prince simply cold clocked him, sending him to the floor. Gavriel looked around. "We seem to be running out of escorts to the detention cells."

Declan rubbed his knuckles. "Oh, please. Let me," he begged.

Rex stood and cracked his neck. "This could be great for brotherly bonding. Plus, I can make sure DeLaFontaine is settling in."

Gavriel mockingly gave a half bow. "He is all yours gentlemen."

Declan walked over and kicked the man in the stomach before pulling him up by the back of his collar effectively choking the man. "Let's take the long way around, shall we?" Declan slammed the man into every wall as they walked toward the exit. Sebastian opened the door for them as Declan was describing exactly how long it would take them to reach the detention cells. Rex was laughing as he followed. Sebastian closed the door behind them.

Gavriel had to take a few calming breaths before he turned back to Bree. "Now, about your mate. If you tell us his name, we will call him down here for you."

Bree looked around shocked. "Just like that, it is over?"

Beth sat next to her and wrapped an arm around her shoulders. "Just like that. My mate does not tolerate bullies."

"His name is Pavil Desrosiers. He is the Régis squire," she replied demurely.

Vivi wasn't the only one who simply stared. The idea she had found her mate and was kept from him while living in the same household sounded like a form of hell.

Beth's eyes were filled with fire as she looked up at her mate. "A fine will not be enough this time."

Gavriel nodded. "Agreed." He turned to Etain. "Would you please go up to Level Three and retrieve Pavil?"

Etain stood and kissed Vivi on the top of her head. "I will return shortly."

Gavriel practically collapsed into Jervasius' empty chair. "We lost two Founding Family heads in less than an hour." He looked over at Kari, who was tapping away on her iPad. "Kari, please tell me you have an idea how we can salvage this."

Kari looked up frowning. "Of course I do, now hush. I am thinking."

Gavriel rolled his eyes and slumped down in his chair. "I cannot wait for Magnus to return."

Kari gave a final tap then looked at the room. "Okay I have an idea." She frowned at Gavriel. "I would tell you to act your age, but that may have you mummified in the corner." Beth giggled as Gavriel straightened glaring at his borrowed personal assistant. Kari continued. "We are giving Gavriel mystical powers."

Gavriel's mouth dropped. "We are what?"

Kari waved her hand about. "You are the Dark Prince. We could say DeLaFontaine and Régis looked at you wrong, therefore incurring your wrath and the people would cheer." She smirked at them. "But that would be a waste of a golden opportunity. Instead, we will make a huge general announcement that over time Gavriel has acquired the ability to detect evil in those around him. Now that he has stepped forward to lead the city and has the backing of the Founding and Noble Families, he is cleaning house for Magnus. We will simply say he is starting at the top and working his way down."

Leana clapped her hands together. "That pretty much gives us carte blanche to arrest anyone later with impunity."

Kari nodded. "Plus it will send all the other rats scurrying. We may find a pest or two we did not know about in the scramble."

Gavriel turned to Adriel. "Why is she not in charge again?"

Adriel sighed. "She is smart enough to avoid the responsibility."

Bree looked around eyes wide. "Is it always like this on Level One?"

Beth shook her head. "No, usually we are just sharing updates and eating pudding."

Vivi turned to Bree. "Do Jervasius' sons know you aren't their mother?"

Bree gave a short nod. "They kept quiet of course, to preserve their own way of life."

There was a knock at the door and Sebastian hurried to open it. Seconds later, Etain and a handsome vampire walked in. The man looked around the room before locking on Bree. He was at her side a moment later. "Lady Régis, how can I assist you?"

Vivi gave her mate a flat look. "You couldn't tell him?"

Etain shook his head and sat back down beside her. "There were too many people listening in."

Pavil's eyes narrowed in anger. "Tell me what? What have you done to my charge?"

Gavriel gave him a sly smile. "Your charge or your mate?"

Pavil sucked in his breath and looked down. Bree nodded, wiping her tears. "Prince Gavriel has arrested Jervasius. We are finally free of him." The announcement drove Pavil to his knees in shock. "What?" Bree held his face between her hands. "We can finally be together. The prince will protect us."

Pavil looked over at Gavriel and struggled to stand on shaky legs. He placed his fist over his heart and bowed low. "If I can serve you in any way, you need only to ask." Vivi found herself tearing up as the man choked the words out, he was that overwhelmed with emotion.

Gavriel looked at Adriel, who shot him a questioning look back. Gavriel then turned to Pavil. "How would you like to become the squire for House Ambrosios?"

Beth squealed her excitement. "My love, that is a perfect idea!"

When Pavil swayed Beth hopped up and had him sit down next to his mate. She walked over and sat in the chair closest to Gavriel. Leaning to one side she rested her head on his shoulder.

Gavriel continued. "It is a recently revived house, so there is much work to be done. The living quarters have not been attended to in centuries." He pointed to Adriel and Eva. "They will be the primary ones you will be serving after I return to Lycaonia."

Pavil clutched at his mate's hand tightly. "It would be an honor to serve House Ambrosios."

Adriel looked relieved. "When can you start?"

"Now?" Pavil blurted.

Eva simply shrugged. "Sounds about right." She stood and stretched. "Come on Pavil. Let's go snag a warrior or two along with some of my pack-mates, and we'll head to your old place to get your stuff."

Pavil's eyes widened, and he jumped to his feet. "Lady Ambrosios, please do not trouble yourself."

Eva waved him off. "I'm feeling kinda restless after hearing about the shit those two assholes have been up to. With any luck, some idiots on Level Three will try to stop us." She flexed her fingers together cracking her knuckles.

Adriel stood and clapped Pavil on the shoulder. "Lady Ambrosios is not like most women."

Bree looked up at Eva in awe. "She is amazing." Eva blushed at Bree's sincere praise. Pavil turned to his mate. "Is this something that you want? You are essentially going from being a Founding Family member to a squire's mate."

Bree stood and took his hand into hers. "I have wanted nothing else since the day we met." She looked over at Eva shyly. "If Lady Ambrosios is amiable to it. I can help maintain her schedule and guide her in navigating the politics amongst the other high-born ladies."

"She's your Yoda," Meryn whispered staring at Bree.

Eva laughed at Meryn's declaration and turned to Bree. "I would appreciate any and all help I can get." She turned to her mate. "While I go up and get their stuff, you wanna show Bree our new living quarters?"

Adriel turned to Gavriel. "Do you need us for

anything."

Gavriel waved them off. "No. You both go get House Ambrosios back in order."

When they left Gavriel exhaled. "I could kill Jervasius for what he put that woman through."

Beth patted him on the leg. "You showed great restraint. I am very proud of you."

Gavriel looked over at Meryn. "It is a scary day when I am leaning towards Meryn's version of politics. I swear it would be easier just to kill him and be done with it."

Meryn looked over at Javier and Simon. "Speaking of politics. What happens to the Régis and DeLaFontaine Houses now?"

Gavriel rubbed his chin. "To be honest I am not sure. I do not think we have ever had a situation where two Founding Family heads were arrested within thirty minutes of each other."

Simon leaned forward. "Jervasius has three sons who can take his place, each one horrendous in his own special way."

Javier grunted his agreement. "Thank the gods Viktor turned out so well," he turned in his chair to smile proudly at his son.

Without missing a beat Viktor smiled. "Must be the genes."

Marie laughed. "Yes, mine." Javier chuckled and brought her hand up to kiss. "Of course darling."

"What about DeLaFontaine?" Kendrick asked.

Simon shook his head. "He has no heir."

Leana frowned. "Does he have any relatives?"

Gavriel looked to the ceiling as his mouth moved. To Vivi, it looked like he was counting. When he looked around he looked surprised. "He is the last of his line."

"Might I make a suggestion?" Kari interjected.

Gavriel indicated the floor was hers. "By all means."

Kari scrolled on her iPad. "I will have to check our records, but I vaguely remember something like this happened before. A son was adopted into the bloodline from the highest ranking Noble Family."

Beth's face scrunched up. "That would be DuBois, they aren't much better."

Meryn waved her hand. Gavriel smiled at her. "Adriel has told you, that you do not have to raise your hand."

She shrugged. "It's kinda a habit now. Any who. What about Warrick? He's a DuBois we like. But instead of making him take that douchebag's last name, we change the Founding Family to his name. Only since he was just disowned from the DuBois family he can use his mom's name or something." When no one spoke she ducked her head. "It was just a suggestion."

Leana turned to Beth. "She is brilliant."

Beth preened. "I know. She shows so much promise."

Javier looked from Simon to Gavriel. "Can we get away with it?"

Gavriel smiled. "It will work out perfectly, especially considering who his mother was."

Beth thought about it for a moment this smiled. "You are right. It is perfect." She turned to Meryn. "Did you know about his parents?"

Meryn looked lost. "What about his parents?"

Leana turned to Meryn. "His father of course

was Gerald DuBois' older brother. But his mother was a Fortier." When Meryn just blinked at her, she continued. "After the Great War when the collective council elevated Ambrosios and Rioux, they offered to make the Fortier bloodline a Founding Family. The Fortiers are very altruistic. They believed they should only serve a higher purpose, so they declined the elevation."

Meryn started nodding. "Let me guess. DeLaFontaine was elevated instead."

"It's almost as if we are putting things the way they were meant to be," Beth said. Her words hung in the air.

Kendrick recovered first. "Either Fate has a more intricate weave than I can imagine, or she just likes to roll the dice."

Vivi couldn't shake Beth's words. Did that mean she was always meant to be here too? Across the room she met Meryn's eyes. The small human just shrugged as if to say 'what can ya do?'.

Vivi stood needing a break from the headache of politics. "I have hit my quota for royal stuff." She looked at Gavriel. "Whenever you're ready."

He looked confused for a moment then nodded. "Of course. Give me just a few minutes to set things up with Javier and Simon to get the ball rolling to elevate Warrick."

Kari clutched at her iPad. "You are serious?" She swallowed hard. "My baby brother. My innocent, sweet, baby brother will be a Founding Family head?"

Meryn winced. "Sucks to be him."

Kari grabbed at her chest. "He needs guards. Lots and lots of guards." She reached for her walkie talkie. "Law, I need you."

A moment later, Law answered. "I'm in the infirmary at the moment."

Kari's knuckles turned white from grasping the handheld. "I do not give a flying fuck where you are! I need you here now. There better be warriors heading your way now to relieve you or so help me gods!" Viktor ran from the room.

"Oh dear," Beth said watching her friend unravel.

Law strode into the room a minute later. The air around him pulsing with magic. "Who upset you?" he demanded.

Kari just stared at him from the center of the room her chest heaving. She pointed to Gavriel then Meryn. "They said...she suggested that they... and they are serious. He... he... Founding Family..."

Law was at her side in a moment rubbing her back. "Sweetheart, you're having a panic attack. Just concentrate on your breathing."

Law looked around the room. "The only thing that sets her off like this is if something happens to Avery. So will someone please tell me what the hell is wrong with my little brother and sister!" he roared.

Vivi waited for someone to speak up but everyone was simply looking at each other as if asking how they should respond. Vivi sighed. "Basically, we arrested DeLaFontaine for possibly being the one to distribute the virus." She paused. "I say possibly, but there's a ninety-nine percent chance he's guilty as hell. Anyway, since he doesn't have any heirs Warrick is being elevated to Founding Family head under his mother's name." She pointed to Kari. "She began to meltdown when she realized that Avery would be a new Founding Family head right along with him."

Law's mouth dropped. "Avery. Our Avery will be a Founding Family head in Noctem Falls?" Kari just pointed and waved as she tried to catch her breath.

A door slamming against the wall had everyone turning to see Declan and Rex snarling in the doorway. "Kari!" Declan shouted moving furniture to get to her side.

Law held up a hand. "She's fine. What upset her is a good thing but overwhelming. She just needs some time to process." Declan and Rex seemed to shrink in size as they began to calm down. They stayed close to Kari whispering encouragements and trying to get her breathing under control.

Meryn began to giggle. Declan glared at her. "What?"

"You and Rex puff up like house cats when you're mad."

Both brothers scowled at her. Behind them Kari began to laugh. She put both hands on her knees and bent over slightly. "She is right. You do." Rex and Declan exchanged hurt expressions.

There was a knock at the door and Sebastian chuckling to himself moved to answer it. After a moment an enormous warrior and small man rushed into the room.

"Kari! Are you okay? We heard you on the walkie-talkie, but I couldn't get off the phone with the Council Estate." The small blond threw himself at Kari.

"Oh, Avery honey, I am so sorry to worry you."

Vivi stared at Avery's slight build and delicate

features. No wonder Kari was having hysterics. The ranking vampires of the city were going to eat him alive. Vivi eyed the tall man at his side. Then again, maybe not.

"Warrick DuBois?" Vivi asked.

The large warrior turned and nodded. "Yes," he said his voice kind. "I am sorry I have not introduced myself yet Princess Vivian, but I was working with Avery answering questions from the Council Estate."

The more she looked at the pair, the better she felt. Warrick was a good choice to lead Level Five. Vivi gave Meryn a thumbs up. "Good job."

Meryn grinned. "I know right?"

Vivi reached down and took Etain's hand. She was amused at the rapt attention on his face. He was watching the scene unfold as if it were a favorite soap opera. Looking up he schooled his features when they made eye contact. Clearing his throat, he stood as well.

Vivi turned to Gavriel and pointed to the room. "You have your hands full, but I will need you in the lab within an hour to get the processing started."

Gavriel nodded then eagerly turned back to Avery, who was now in the process of completely melting down. It seemed her mate wasn't the only one entertained by the scene in front of them.

She tugged at Etain's hand. "Coming my love?"

"Of course."

As they left a loud screech bounced off the walls. Vivi smothered a chuckle. Little Avery had just found out he was going to be a Founding Family head.

CHAPTER TEN

WHILE GAVRIEL ORGANIZED THE NEW
Founding Family, Vivi stopped at the infirmary to gather Caspian's blood. His bedside vigil
continued while Broderick lent support from a
seat nearby. Both were hopeful as she explained
what she would be attempting in the form of a
cure.

When they got back to the lab she immediately
put the sample from DeLaFontaine's cuff under
the microscope. Little flashes of light confirmed
the presence of the virus. Using the walkie-talkie
she let Gavriel know the DeLaFontaine test came
back positive.

After that it was simply a waiting game. It ended
up taking Gavriel over an hour to get away. He,
Beth and Kendrick walked in fighting smiles.

Kendrick crossed the room to sit down on his
preferred stool in front of his long lab tables, where
he picked up a book to read as usual. His normal
routine consisted of him checking on the plates he
set up to test the magic within the virus. He told
her earlier they lucked out, because the process of

starting the magical tests put the virus in a type of stasis, so the magic that disappeared from the first slides was preserved for testing on his plates. He'd occasionally grumble to himself, write down some notes then resume reading. Today he simply sat down and pulled out the book Meryn gifted him.

Vivi turned from where she sat in front of the microscope. "Did they both live?"

Beth sat down on one of the stools as Gavriel stood at her side. "Yes, though it took us forever to calm Avery down. His one point of contention was that he didn't want to quit his job. He says it allows him to help Magnus and stay near Kari. If I had a little brother as adorable as Avery, I probably would have lost it too. He's just so darn cute!"

Gavriel clucked his tongue. "Meryn can be pretty adorable."

Beth shrugged. "Avery is adorable like a puppy. Meryn is adorable like a baby velociraptor. It's cute because it's small, but it's also kinda deadly and dangerous."

Gavriel looked at his mate impressed. "That has to be one of the most accurate descriptions of Meryn I have ever heard."

"She is my little sister. I know her best."

Vivi waved a needle at Gavriel. "Ready to get poked?"

Gavriel rolled up the sleeve of his elegant dress shirt. "I am your humble servant."

Vivi made sure only to take a single vial, not a bag like the others. It would probably take a gallon of Caspian's blood to cancel out the strain requirement if she used a full pint of Gavriel's blood.

As she was finishing the label, the door opened

to reveal Rheia and Colton. They walked in, three bags of blood in Colton's hands. He looked at them. "Is Kari okay? She sounded stressed."

Kendrick turned a page of his book. "Yes, though Avery is the one who is stressed now."

"Why?" Rheia asked sitting down next to Beth.

Kendrick got them caught up as Vivi placed the collected blood on the stone in the refrigeration unit. Her hands were itching to get Gavriel's blood under the microscope.

Etain walked up behind her and wrapped his arms around her waist. He leaned down and whispered in her ear. "You're grinning like a mad scientist."

She rested her head against his chest. "That's because I am a mad scientist."

"And you know your stuff," Rheia added. "You were right about that second trial. We don't even have to run a blood sample. The kids look awful. The younger blood was about as effective as the antivirals are becoming."

Etain turned their bodies so they faced the room. "How was the idea of a blood drive received?" he asked.

Rheia nodded slowly. "Good and bad. Nearly everyone over three thousand years old lined up to donate. But there were some grumbles about ensuring that no bonding would take place. Ellie and Anne are still up there drawing blood." She stretched her back. "I'd like to lie down for a bit in our room."

Colton began to rub her shoulders. "You should have said something earlier," he admonished.

Rheia sighed. "I'm used to being able to do a lot more. I had no idea being pregnant took so much out of you."

Colton paled. "It does," he agreed. His eyes glazed over, and he shivered.

Rheia glared at Kendrick. "If he passes out during delivery, I am going to use surgical glue and glue your dick to your leg."

Kendrick's eyes widened at her threat. "Seriously?"

"Dead serious." Rheia pointed to Colton, who was shuddering at his own memories. "This is your fault. You and that stupid video."

Kendrick held up his hand. "Can I use magic to ensure he doesn't pass out?"

Rheia laughed. "I don't care what you use as long as he is conscious."

Kendrick exhaled in relief. "He'll be fine. I promise."

Colton blinked. "What type of magic?"

Kendrick looked at him with a droll expression. "Something considerably less scary than a glued down dick that's for sure."

Colton nodded then his eyes narrowed. "Wait, that's pretty scary." Kendrick shrugged.

Etain looked between the two of them in horror. "How does the Alpha Unit function?"

"Meryn updates their routines, Anne and I patch them up. Amelia mothers them and Beth keeps them organized," Rheia replied.

Vivi enjoyed the feel of being in Etain's arms. She tilted her head back. "So I'm pretty much done in here. What did you want to do today?"

Etain unwrapped his arms and took her hand. "I have an idea."

Rheia stood. "I could use a nap." Colton looked

relieved. "Good idea. You and the baby need rest."

Gavriel leaned in to kiss Beth's temple. "How are you feeling?"

Beth went to answer then yawned. She looked surprised. "Actually, a nap sounds like a great idea." Gavriel was immediately all business. "Should we have Tarragon check you?"

Beth stood from her chair. "I'm fine, but I could close my eyes for a bit."

Gavriel and Colton exchanged looks and herded their mates toward the door. Vivi and Etain walked with them as far as the entrance to Magnus' quarters. Etain held her back when she went to follow.

"Hal should already be there."

"Where?"

Etain led her past the transport tunnel to the other side of the level. Vivi felt an odd sense of familiarity as Etain walked her up to a dingy looking wooden door. The poor thing had seen better days.

Vivi looked up at him. "Do we knock?"

Etain chuckled. "Welcome home Vivian DuCoeur."

Vivi frowned. "You mean Vivian Vi'Aerlin," she stopped sentence. "Home?"

The door creaked open and Hal filled the doorway. He had a handkerchief wrapped around his head and was wearing a full-length apron. "About time you two showed up. I was about to be carried off by spiders. Sebastian was able to unlock the quarters for us and added me to the hand sensor so I could get started. He said he would swing by and get the two of you added later."

"These are the DuCoeur quarters?" Vivi asked.

No wonder she kept wanting to turn right coming off the transport tunnel on Level One. How many times had she been carried down that hallway as a baby?

Etain nodded. "Hal and I figured you would choose this one over the DuSang home."

There was a loud bang before a billow of dust emerged from the open door across from theirs. Moments later, Adriel, Eva, Pavil and Bree ran out coughing.

Vivi stared at the four. "The Ambrosios quarters I assume?"

Etain nodded as he watched his fastidious unit leader pull cobwebs out of his hair. Without looking away he pointed to the left. "The DuSang quarters are next door." His eyes began to dance with mirth as Adriel spun in circles trying to get something off his back. Finally, the unit leader shed his jacket and threw it on the floor shuddering.

"Problems sir?" Etain asked jovially.

Adriel froze and looked up. When he saw the three of them his cheeks flushed. "There are an indecent amount of spiders in there."

Vivi pulled out her walkie-talkie. "Kendrick can I borrow you for a moment?"

"Sure. Where are you?"

"Come out of the lab and head toward the transport tunnel. Walk past the Rioux quarters and head right."

"Got it. Be right there."

Bree picked up Adriel's jacket and popped it out before folding it carefully.

Kendrick walked up to them waving the dust away from his face. "You rang Princess?"

Vivi jerked her thumb towards the open door of the DuCoeur living area. "Is there a spell that will get rid of dust bunnies and spiders." She paused and thought about it. "And maybe fix any damage due to neglect or age?"

Kendrick rolled up his sleeves. "My secret specialty. Having raised Keelan, I quickly mastered a myriad of mundane cleaning spells. The little devil could attract every speck of mud and grime within a five-mile radius. Give me about twenty minutes." He walked inside past a disgusted looking Hal, who threw his dust rag on the floor.

Adriel looked no less disgruntled. Etain was laughing his ass off, pointing at his unit leader. "Wait until I tell Declan about your spider dance."

Eva began to crack up. "Spider dance!" Adriel gave them both a frosty look, but his mouth twitched as he fought a smile.

Vivi turned to Hal. "Sorry about that."

Hal looked over at the others and shrugged. "At least I wasn't the only one who forgot we could ask the witches to help."

Vivi nudged Etain. "How will we set it up the way we want if the city is locked down? It's not like we can go shopping."

Eva turned to Adriel. "You remember when the pack was getting set up in their new houses, how the vendors all donated items? What if we let it be known we're moving in and looking for new stuff. I bet some of the older vampires would appreciate some of this antique, gold junk better than me. We could do a swap."

Adriel winced at her description of the Ambrosios quarters. "As long as we check with Gavriel to ensure we do not get rid of anything he may want to keep. I say that is a wonderful idea."

Vivi looked up at Hal. "How bad?"

Hal nodded. "There is a fair bit of gold overlay."

"We need to get in on that swap. Because as much as I love my golden mate, I don't want to live surrounded by the stuff." Vivi liked a more minimalist style. She and Hal had gotten used to moving every ten to fifteen years, which meant they tended to pack light.

Eva pointed to the large area in front of the three royal quarters. "What if we just set up stuff out here? We can put Sebastian in charge of making sure the swap is fair while we go through everything."

"Step up ladies and gentlemen! It's the deal of several lifetimes. Our trash could be your treasure," Vivi pretended to be speaking into a megaphone. Bree giggled, and Eva got in on it. "Is your toilet looking a bit drab? Why not upgrade to a new gold covered model? Guaranteed to impress your friend and freeze your ass."

Etain and Adriel leaned against one another laughing uproariously as Vivi continued. "Don't let your decor, bore, the neighbors. Everything is on the gold standard."

Kendrick walked from the DuCoeur quarters. "We have gold, silver and even jeweled mosaics! Literally blind your friends with a golden shower," he leered at them. "Pun intended."

Vivi wiped her eyes. "It's going to take us forever to make this a reasonable living area."

Adriel kissed his mate before he headed back into their home. He came back out carrying his iPad. "I will organize the swap. You ladies just tag anything you want gone," he paused. "On second thought, tag what you want to keep. It will probably turn out to be fewer items." He winked at Vivi. "I am calling in the cavalry. With our fae and witch warrior brothers, it should not take us long to gut both homes."

"Work smarter, not harder," she quipped.

Adriel looked at Kendrick. "Could I ask that you assist us as well?"

"Of course. We're all on a hiatus while we wait for the next batch of treatment to finish. Point me in the direction of your dust bunnies," Kendrick replied with a sweeping bow.

Eva nodded toward the open door. "That-a-way. Help yourself." Kendrick disappeared into the Ambrosios' quarters.

Adriel turned to Hal and Pavil. "Since most of the major cleaning is done. Could the two of you work with Sebastian to see if you can secure items we may actually use?" Hal and Pavil both nodded then together they walked back to the Rioux home to recruit Sebastian.

Vivi was dying to get inside and see where her mother grew up. She tugged at Etain's hand while walking toward their new home. "We'll be going through stuff," she called over her shoulder.

"Take your time," Eva replied. "We still have to get with Gavriel about the Ambrosios antiques."

Feeling like a kid at Christmas Vivi crossed the threshold and entered her mother's home for the first time in her adult life.

"This place looks like something out of museum," Vivi couldn't believe the ostentatious decor.

Etain stared at the large tapestry and shook his head. "Maybe we should start in your mother's bedroom where the more personal items may be? I have a feeling everything else can go."

"Good idea. Now, we just have to find it."

After opening several doors Vivi walked into the room she knew had been her mother's. "This is it."

"How do you know?" Etain asked.

Vivi felt her eyes fill. "Because it smells like her. Gods! I remember this smell! This is my momma," Vivi covered her face with her hands as a lifetime of yearning overwhelmed her. Etain was beside her in an instant, rocking her back and forth.

"Shush my love, it is okay."

"What if we get rid of things and I lose that smell? I can't lose it! It's the only thing I remember."

Etain pulled his walkie-talkie out. "Kendrick, can you come over here please?"

"On my way... again," Kendrick replied.

It didn't take long before there was a knock on the doorjamb to the room. "You rang?" he asked. He looked at Vivi, and his features softened. "This was your mother's room wasn't it?" She could only nod.

Kendrick's eyes became sad. "I know exactly how you feel. Is it her things or something else?"

"Her smell. It's going to go away," Vivi sobbed.

Kendrick walked over and rubbed the top of her

head. "Not if I can help it." He swallowed hard. "It was my mother's smell too, that got me when I returned to their home for the final time."

He turned to face the room and began to look around. He walked over to the bed and picked up a small, cream satin pillow and began to whisper softly. There was a rush of air then everything quieted. He handed her the pillow. "That will never lose her scent."

Etain clasped forearms with the witch. "Thank you. This means more than you know."

Kendrick opened the pouch at his waist and pulled out a small sachet. "Trust me, I know." He kissed it and tucked it back in his pouch. He looked around the room. "Good vibes in here. You should make this a nursery." Without saying another word he walked out.

Vivi clutched the pillow to her chest. "I don't even remember what she looked like, but I can remember this smell."

"You were very young when she was killed. Your whole world was probably centered around being held in her arms. It makes sense that you would recall her scent more clearly."

Vivi wiped her eyes on her sleeve. "Let's get started."

Etain kissed both of her eyelids. "Did you see anything walking through that you wanted to keep?"

"The books, the china, that amazing tapestry," she grinned when Etain shuddered. She knew he hated it, but she thought the attention to detail was mesmerizing. "Oh, and the dining room furniture. It looks custom-made for that space. I don't think we'll find much better." She nodded. "That's it for me. Be sure to ask Hal if there's anything he would like to keep. He'll be living here too." She looked around. "I want time to go through everything but to be honest there isn't much here I would change. My mother had amazing taste." It was true. The room looked almost utilitarian in comparison to the rest of the living quarters. It was decorated with a simple design that evoked a sense of calm. Everything about the space spoke of the owner's character from the creams and dusty pink colors to the small statues of horses. Evidently, her mother had been an equestrian. It made her patchwork pony doubly precious. She wondered if Magnus chose it with her mother in mind.

"I think that is an excellent idea. If you need me, I will be with Hal doing most of the heavy lifting." He kissed her again and headed toward the door.

Vivi was admiring the view as he walked away when an off thought struck her. "Etain?"

He turned. "Yes?"

"Both the DuCoeur and Ambrosios quarters haven't been used in centuries right?" He nodded. "Then they probably didn't run any electric or internet down here did they?" Etain cursed under his breath. Vivi looked around panicked. "Do we have running water?"

"I will find out and if not, I will get the witches to run new lines. You take your time here." He blew her a kiss and shut the door behind him.

Vivi took her time going through her mother's belongings. There wasn't much she would be get-ting rid of. Her dresses were works of art and to her delight, she fit into them perfectly. Had her mother lived, they would have been the same size. Vivi grinned when she realized she knew that much more about her mother.

Her jewelry was so intricate and jewel laden Vivi was scared to touch most of it. She could see empty spaces in the jewelry case where her mother had chosen her favorite pieces to take with her when she fled the city. Those pieces were currently tucked away in her luggage. She would bring them back and put them where they belonged.

She felt herself begin to tear up again when she came across a half-finished embroidery piece with her name on it. Her mother started it to give to her. Maybe she could learn how to embroider and finish it?

Overall, she would move the clothing and jewelry into whichever room they made the master, but everything else could stay here. Kendrick was right. This room had peaceful vibes, and it would be a shame to redecorate and disturb it. She closed the door behind her when she left to look for Etain feeling closer to her mother than she had in her entire life.

When she walked into what used to be an opulent parlor she was floored. It was nothing short of a miracle what the men accomplished in a few hours. "Is this the same room?" she asked her mate walking up behind him.

He turned, a smile brightening his face when he saw her. "Looks amazing doesn't it? We took down a few walls and opened up the space." He pointed to the cream-colored walls. "When the witches changed the wall color, the room looked twice as big." Everywhere she looked the space had been transformed from gaudy gold overlay and black lacquer to creams and neutrals. They went from museum relics to *Pottery Barn*. "How?" she kept spinning as she took in every detail.

Etain chuckled. "When the citizens found out we were getting rid of most of what was in here they flocked down to Level One. Poor Pavil, Hal and Sebastian were a bit overwhelmed until the warriors corralled everyone. What even Adriel hadn't realized when he made the announcement is that most families buy a surplus of home items to keep in storage since it can be difficult to run to the Council Estate to go shopping for as mundane as a set of sheets. It's easier to keep a few backups." He pointed to the room. "That includes furniture as well. We were able to get nearly everything we need." He showed her the new dining room. The long wooden table had been polished to a glass-like finish, and the bone thin china had been replaced by a simple white everyday dish. "Oh! I love that set," she exclaimed.

"We know. Hal said you picked this one out for your last home." Etain took her to the kitchen where they found Hal humming and putting things away. It struck Vivi that her squire was nesting.

Because she had so many issues about going in the sun, her 'illness' stayed in the minds of the humans they met, which meant they had to move more often than most paranormals. This was the first time since Hal met her where he could call a place home. "Oh, Hal," she whispered.

He looked up his easy grin disappearing at her distress. "What is it baby girl?" he asked walking around the expansive island.

"You gave up so much to take care of me. You could have found your mate and had children of your own, but you were stuck with me." She waved her hand about the kitchen. "You couldn't even get comfortable in your own kitchen knowing we would be moving."

Hal stared down at her frowning. He reached out and thumped her on the forehead with his middle finger.

"Oww! Dammit Hal, you know I hate it when you do that," she complained.

"Then don't say foolish things. If it came down to a choice between having granite countertops or you, I would choose you every time. Yes, I could have found a mate, but I didn't miss having children." He smiled down at her. "I had you."

She wrapped her arms around his waist. "I love you Hal."

He held her close. "I love you too baby girl. I don't regret raising you for a second."

Vivi used his shirt to wipe her eyes and nose. Hal looked down at her and raised an eyebrow. "Really? You know I hate it when you do that."

She giggled. "Then don't thump me." She ducked behind her mate and looked around the kitchen. "I take it we have running water?"

Hal nodded. "Thank the gods you mentioned something about having power. We probably would have realized it after all our volunteers left. I swear those witches were like little genies. I would no sooner ask if something could be done and I turned around and it was finished." He walked over to the stove. "Look Vivi, a gas range! I love cooking on gas." He beamed at Etain. "They said I have you to thank for it. Something about having to run a major gas line to the master suite for your fireplace."

Vivi looked up at her mate. "Master suite?"

Etain rubbed the back of his neck. "You were busy and I didn't wish to disturb you, so I kinda made an executive decision about which room would be ours."

She narrowed her eyes and he held up both hands defensively. "It's perfect, trust me. It looks like your mother kept her childhood bedroom after her parents were killed. When I walked to the end of the hallway, I found the master suite untouched since your grandparent's death. It's huge, which gave us plenty of space for our new master bathroom and closets."

"And your fireplace?"

"It fit perfectly. Once the gold was gone and we started putting up neutrals the grey stone floor began to pop. I have a collection of rugs and linens stacked up for you to go through."

"One question," she said holding up a finger.

"Of course," he nodded looking nervous.

"Self-cleaning floor and sheets?"

He grinned wickedly. "Absolutely."

"Thank the gods for those sheets. There are some things I don't need to see," Hal muttered putting away the stemware.

Vivi blushed furiously as Etain laughed. "Come on my love. I can show you our new room. If there's anything you need to change Micah said he would come back down and fix things for you." Etain steered her out of the kitchen toward the bedrooms.

He stopped her in front of a large set of wooden double doors. Vivi pointed. "A bit of an overkill isn't it?"

Etain pointed to the carvings in the door. "It was spelled for protection, yet another reason I wanted to stay in this room." He placed a hand on the wood, and the lock clicked.

Vivi's mouth dropped. "It's biometric?"

Etain brought her hand up, placed it beside his and whispered a phrase softly. She felt the wood warm under her palm, then cool. "Not science, magic. It isn't detecting your fingerprints, but your aura." He pushed the door open then swept her up in his arms. He carried her across the threshold and kicked the door shut with his foot.

He set her down. "Welcome to our new bedroom."

Vivi loved everything. "Is that the original furniture?" she asked pointing to the massive bed.

"Yes, though we swapped out the mattress. Luckily, Declan had an extra one in storage, only his bed came close to being this huge. It turned out to be almost a perfect fit."

Vivi couldn't find anything she would change. Etain kept the same ivory color predominant throughout the rest of their new living quarters, but here he chose to accent in navy blue. Vivi knew she would never have picked the color herself, thinking it to be a dark and masculine. However, the small ways in which he used it contrasted the cream in such a delicate manner that it created a truly harmonious space.

"Well?" he asked nervously.

"I don't like it." She glared up at him. His eyes

widened, and she laughed. "I love it! I never knew I loved blue until now." She walked around the room inspecting everything. Her favorite item was the navy cashmere throw at the foot of their bed.

She pointed to the bed and wagged her eyebrows. "Want to test those self-cleaning sheets?"

He groaned. "I wish we could." He held up his cell phone. It was already after six. "We're expected at dinner to discuss all the new changes and to get feedback regarding what is being said on different levels."

Vivi simply started stripping. "In that case I will break in our new bathroom."

His strangled moan was worth facing the cold air. She pointed to the huge fireplace. "Can you turn that on on your way out to get my clothes from Magnus'?"

"Yes, my love," he replied as he spun her around and pulled her against him. She could feel exactly how her little strip show had affected him. "It feels scandalous being naked while you're fully clothed," she grinned. "Can we do it again later when we christen those sheets?"

"Absolutely," he promised and took possession of her lips. There was nothing gentle about his onslaught. His tongue dueled with hers driving her need through the roof.

When he stepped away they were both breathing hard. He looked down and smiled. Her flush had worked its way down her body.

"Enjoy your bath," he said cheekily and headed toward the door.

She waited until the door closed behind him before she stuck out her tongue.

"Later!" he called out through the door.

Vivi covered her mouth with both hands. Damn man knew her so well already!

CHAPTER ELEVEN

VIVI STARED AT THE TINY sprite who was seated on a stack of coasters in front of a thick book at the end of the table where Magnus usually sat. Sebastian served him very carefully with small plates and cutlery as Ryuu and Hal served the others.

"Where did you get the serving pieces for him?" Etain asked.

Sebastian took his time as he gently placed the tiny platters heaped with sprite sized food around Felix. "One of the families had a small doll house that was no longer being used. They brought it down to donate to the shifter children, so I was able to secure some things for our hero here." Felix kept his face down looking entirely uncomfortable at the attention.

"He's my kind of hero, no spandex," Meryn shot Felix a thumbs up. The tiny sprite brightened and shyly began to eat from the huge selection Sebastian prepared for him.

Aiden turned to his mate. "What do you have against spandex?"

"Ball sweat," Meryn replied.

Everyone turned to face the small human.

Rex shook his head. "I'm sorry, did you say ball sweat?"

Meryn nodded. "I don't know why superheroes have an obsession with spandex costumes. That shit doesn't breathe. I bet Batman smells like that kid from gym class who went through a 'natural' phase and always smelled like funk and onions. Then in their movie the writers have the ditzy heroine smiling and willing to get down for sexy time after a huge battle scene," she shook her head. "Would not be me. He'd have to bathe in antiseptic first. No way would that shit be getting near my face with..." Aiden clapped a hand over her mouth looking mortified.

There was silence then Kendrick lost his composure. He rested his forehead on his folded arms on the table gasping for breath. Anne had her face buried in his back.

Meryn pushed Aiden's hand away. "What?"

Kendrick sat up. "I am so glad you're back to normal. I would have missed this if you had stayed a mini Daphne Bowers."

Meryn pointed to her sweats. "Definitely more comfortable this way."

Gavriel turned to Felix. "How did your sword work for you?" Felix gave him a thumbs up.

"Is that the sword from the vault?" Vivi asked still dabbing at her eyes with a napkin from laughing too hard.

Meryn nodded. "When I saw it, it was this huge fucking claymore. Magnus was trying to keep me away from it. I think he was scared I would cut myself in half." She grinned. "He tried to chase me away from it a few times, but I wore him down. Anyway, the second I touched it, it shrunk down to my size, and I was able to lift it. Then I wondered if Felix touched it, if it would shrink again, and it did. The scabbard changed size when the sword did, so we attached it to his belt."

"I heard you kept a necklace," Beth commented. Meryn lifted a small simple locket from under her hoodie. Beth gave her a strange look. "The Gown of Éire Danu can compliment each outfit with rare jewelry pieces, why did you choose something so plain as your reward from Magnus?"

Meryn shrugged. "I kinda felt sorry for it. It was all by itself looking out of place next to these fancy crowns and tiaras. Besides I like it." She stuffed it back under her hoodie.

Aiden looked down at his mate adoration in his eyes. "I think it suits you perfectly."

She smiled up at him. "Yeah?"

"Yes. I think you made a wonderful choice," he kissed the top of her head.

"Meryn you are an enigma," Law complimented.

Vivi picked up her wine glass and took a sip. When she set it down she noticed Rex's knuckles, which were still red. She grinned at him. "How did DeLaFontaine's interrogation go?"

Rex rubbed his knuckles with his other hand as Declan chuckled. Rex turned to her. "So far he's been very reticent concerning any information regarding the virus." He gave her a roguish smile. "But we're just getting started."

Meryn turned to Rex her eyes sparkling. "Can I watch tomorrow?"

Aiden pulled Meryn onto his lap. "You can spend the day resting and away from the Elder," he grumbled.

"I was just gonna watch. I bet Rex pounding on DeLaFontaine would be super hot!" Meryn exclaimed. "I mean look at those arms!"

Aiden nipped Meryn on the neck while trying to cover her eyes with his hand. Giggling she kept turning her head back and forth to avoid his hand.

Rex was sitting straighter in his chair. "She is a woman of impeccable tastes."

Law rested his arm over the back of Rex's chair. "When she's right, she's right."

Vivi watched the entire scene and brought up her napkin to hide her smile. Law was smirking. Rex was nodding. Declan was watching the pair his eyes narrowed and Kari was shaking her head. Law was most definitely fucking with Declan.

Vivi decided she needed to help stir the pot. She turned to Law. "You know, the two of you sitting together make a striking picture. There's an electricity about you that is enthralling. You should do couples modeling."

Declan's head snapped around. "Couples?"

Vivi nodded. "You know a couple of guys."

Rex smiled at her. "Modeling? Really?"

"Oh absolutely."

"Definitely shirtless," Meryn added.

Declan seemed slightly mollified as he continued to eat dinner a frown on his face. Law winked at her, and Vivi gave him a small salute.

Rheia leaned back to make eye contact with Vivi. "We administered a second dose of the first trial using the warrior blood. The results between the older warrior blood and the younger vendor blood was like night and day. I honestly feel we have a chance at beating this thing tomorrow using the collected blood from the older vendors. We specifically asked for anyone who was over three thousand years old."

Vivi felt a spurt of hope. "I should be able to start Magnus' treatment tomorrow as well."

Beth looked between them. "Wouldn't it be amazing if Uncle and the children recovered at the same time. He would be delighted to hear that, while he was taking his nap, the children were cured."

Gavriel wrapped an arm around his mate. "Let us not get ahead of ourselves."

Beth sighed. "I know I am being optimistic, but I feel like something should go our way after everything we've been through in the past few weeks."

"I bet you're right Beth," Anne said encouragingly.

Rex raised a glass. "To the health of our loved ones."

Around the table, glasses were raised in toast. Vivi ate quietly as the dinner progressed fueled by everyone's excitement. She refused to get her hopes up. She knew that sometimes it took months to formulate a proper treatment, but she wasn't about to rain on everyone's parade. They looked like they needed the good news, especially considering how they kept referring to Magnus' state as him taking a nap.

When Meryn yawned for the fourth time, Aiden put his hand to her forehead. "Are you feeling well?"

Meryn went to answer and yawned again. "Just tired."

Aiden shot a look to Rheia, who gave a one shoulder shrug. "We've all been through so much in the past few days. It's understandable that she would be worn down."

Aiden stood and scooped Meryn up in his arms. Instead of protesting Meryn simply rested her head on his chest looking sleepy. Aiden turned back to Rheia and Ellie. "Anything I should do?" Both women shook their heads looking amused.

Vivi put on a serious face. "You shouldn't feed her after midnight."

Aiden nodded. "Anything else?"

"Try not to get her wet," she advised fighting to keep her expression professional.

He blinked. "No sex?"

Vivi cracked up at his tragic expression. Meryn thumped him on the chest and glared at her. "No, she's calling me a gremlin, the heifer!"

"Meryn, she's a princess now," Beth admonished gently.

Meryn blinked her eyes innocently. "I'm sorry... Princess Heifer!"

Vivi just wiggled her fingers at her. "Night, night Gizmo."

Before she could respond Aiden carted her off toward their bedroom. Vivi couldn't help grinning. "I adore that little midget."

"I'm not a midget!" they heard Meryn yell from the hallway. Everyone cracked up.

Beth turned to Vivi. "Why do you agitate her?"

"Besides it being so easy? I don't know. It's weird. I feel like we're bonding over insults."

"I think Vivi found the quickest way to get Meryn to accept you," Kendrick mused. "It's kinda of sad, but considering Meryn's background, she is apt to distrust you if you're too nice. But Vivi's teasing makes her feel accepted, not bullied."

Law growled low in his throat. "Do we know for a fact that anyone who abused her is dead?" Kendrick just stared at him until Law held up his hands. "Just checking."

"As if I wouldn't follow up on something like that? I take a twisted delight in rationing out punishment to bullies." Kendrick admitted. Anne patted his arm. "At least you're honest about it."

Gavriel, Beth, Adriel and Eva also stood. Gavriel gave a half bow. "We will take our leave as well. It will be the first night we spend in the Ambrosios quarters, and Beth and Eva still have much to show us about our new home."

Law stretched in his chair before turning to Rex. "Come on, I will look at that hand for you in your quarters."

Rex's face brightened. "That would be appreciated. I'm pretty sure I broke something, it's taking forever to heal."

Law leaned in. "Don't worry, I'll take care of you."

Declan's eyes were practically bugging out of his head, but his lips remained sealed. Vivi felt bad for a moment for teasing him. He obviously cared for his brother and wouldn't interfere if he thought that it would hurt Rex. But that moment quickly passed as she realized that he was just too perfect of a target. No wonder Law loved teasing him. Declan's facial expressions broadcasted exactly what he was thinking.

"You might want to give him a full body scan. A floating bone fragment can wreck havoc if left unattended," Vivi suggested.

"What!" Declan exclaimed standing.

Law nodded with a serious expression. "Good point."

Rex shrugged. "Whatever you think is best."

Law stood with Rex, his back to the table. He gave her a hidden thumbs up and walked out with the Elder.

"But..." Declan looked around helplessly.

Kari took pity on her mate. "Let us turn in as well. Things will seem better in the morning."

"But..." Declan didn't know which way to turn.

Etain stood and rested a hand on her shoulder. "We will say goodnight too. There is one particular feature of our new home that I am dying to show Vivi."

Vivi sputtered in her wine as she was about to take another sip. She felt her cheeks heat up sure they were now crimson.

Adriel cleared his throat. "I hope you enjoy the first night in your new quarters," he said diplomatically.

Etain gave her shoulder a little squeeze. "Oh, we will." He looked down at her. "Ready darling?"

She rose to her feet and set her napkin beside her plate. She turned to Hal and Ryuu. "Thank you for a wonderful meal."

Hal stepped forward. "Get plenty of rest. Tomorrow will be a long day with the different formulas you'll be mixing."

"I will. Aren't you coming?" she asked.

Hal nodded. "I'll be along in a bit. I am going to help clean up here then go through my kitchen again to see if we need anything."

Vivi had a feeling she would have to pry him out of his kitchen in the future. "Goodnight everyone," she said walking out with her mate and the others.

When they got to their door Etain chuckled as they waved goodnight to Adriel, Eva, Beth and Gavriel from across the large alcove. "It feels like the Unit Level when we go inside our own houses at the end of the day."

When they shut their door behind them the first thing Vivi noticed was the quiet. In the Rioux quarters something was always happening. It's where people had meetings and where they ate their meals. To go from being surrounded by so many people to being alone with her mate felt strange.

"It's almost too quiet," Etain whispered.

"Why are you whispering?"

He shook his head ruefully. "No idea."

Vivi studied the room. "I really love it, what you've done to our home."

Etain walked over to a wooden side table and lifted a square looking box. Gently he lowered a small arm and moved it over. Soft jazz began playing in the room.

"Is that a record player?"

He nodded. "They produce the best quality of music." He held out his hand. "May I have the pleasure of this dance?"

She placed her hand in his, and he swept her up in his arms. They swayed together to the bluesy music of the past, letting the entire day drain from them.

"I had so much fun during Prohibition," Vivi murmured into his formal fae robe.

"Did you cause trouble? Were you a bootlegger?"

"Of course not. I was a singer at the Vamp Lounge."

He pulled back to gauge her expression carefully. "Are you joking?"

"No. I was stuck on a project and decided to head out among the humans for some fun. It had been awhile since I'd last gone out by myself. I was astounded by the clothes and music. Gods, the music! Since I was sensitive to sunlight, I usually went out after dark, which during that time meant I was just showing up as things were getting interesting. At first, I would hum along, but one night the bartender heard me and stuck me up on stage. I stammered and said I wasn't a singer, but no one cared. They said to give it my best shot, and the rest was history. I put my project on hold and delved into the nightlife of the Roaring Twenties."

Vivi smiled when a tune she was familiar with came on, so she began to sing for her mate. She stepped out of his arms and sashayed to the record player. She turned back to him and moved her hands down her dress. With her eyes, she told him how much she wanted him while she breathed the music. She felt exaltation race through her. She had forgotten how heady it was to sing for someone.

With every note, her mate's eyes grew darker until they were almost brown in color. He watched her every move. His breath subconsciously syncing up with hers. Through her, he lived each note. The song allowed her to weave the tale of a young man coming home from the war and the joy of being with his true love again, and how all the pain and suffering had been worth it because he had protected her.

When the song was over, he had tears in his eyes. "You have quite undone me, my love. Will you leave me in such a state or will you bring us both the pleasure we want in fitting our broken pieces together to make a single joyous whole?"

She walked over, simply took his hand and led him toward their bedroom. When she reached their door, she unlocked it with her hand and walked into the newly decorated master suite.

Still moving to the rhythm of the song in her heart, she began to strip out of her clothes. There was only one type of music she wanted to be making right now, the kind that involved low moans, breathy gasps and passionate shouts.

When she was naked, she turned to see his state of undress and was brought up short, he was still fully clothed. She stared at him confused, then remembered her earlier comment. Giving him a sultry smile she walked up and pressed her body against his.

"Your mate needs you," she said in a husky voice. She rubbed her nipples against the rough fabric of his robe. Each embroidered thread tantalized her body sending shockwaves of pleasure through her.

"Please," she whispered.

"Go get on the bed and wait," he said in a dangerous voice.

The edge in his voice sent shivers down her spine. She could tell he was hanging on by a thread. Making her way to the bed she crawled on slowly.

She positioned herself in the middle and spread her legs wide, letting him see how much she wanted him.

His nostrils flared as he stared at her. With deliberate steps he walked slowly up to the bed unbuttoning his robe, one button at a time. When he was done he simply let the robe fall. As he climbed up onto the bed, she saw that his cock was straining towards his belly button and already glistening with pre-cum. She wondered what part of her show drove him to this state, so she could do it again later.

"I cannot wait to taste you," he said before dipping his head down to lap at her folds. When he flattened his tongue and ran it from the bottom of her slit to her clit she dug her fingers into the covers.

He devoured her as if she were his new favorite dessert. Her mate was driving her mad with his slow method of love making. He was taking his time learning her, and it was going to cost her her sanity.

He didn't just lick. He sucked, nibbled, teased, and bit every inch of her exposed sex. He didn't stop at her clit. Everything was a feast to him. Her folds, her mound, her inner thighs and even her hip bones. He tasted everything, bringing her to the edge then soothing the tender skin only to start all over again.

"Please my love, I can't take it anymore. Please," she begged, tears streaming down her face from the sheer intensity.

"As I have told you, I will always give you what you need." Etain came up on his knees and eased his hips forward, impaling her slowly. Just when she thought he would plunge deep he stopped and lazily tortured her clit. When he filled her completely, he stopped again, lightly touching her hips before dragging his cock out of her. "If I could spend a lifetime watching the tears fall from your eyes as we made love not even an eternity would be long enough to live," he spoke the words in a low voice.

Vivi reached out and pulled him forward until he was holding himself above her. "More," she gasped snapping her own hips until he was moving in and out of her at the pace she wanted.

He leaned down and brushed his nose with hers. "So impatient," he said smiling.

"I need." She looked up giving him a sassy smile. "Think you're up to it?"

He smiled so congenially that she felt a bit disappointed. He had driven her to the brink, and as much as she loved his slow love making, she wanted to move.

When he shifted his weight and quickly grabbed both of her hands she blinked. She inhaled as he pinned them over her head. His expression never changed. He still looked oh, so pleasant. But his entire demeanor changed.

With his honey brown eyes he stared down at her. "Do you want me to fuck you?"

She shivered at his civil tone. There was something about his politeness that danced on the line between gentle and primal. She was starting to understand what Dimitri meant when he said that there was a haunting quality to her mate's detached savagery, and right now it was solely focused on her. She felt her fangs slip past her lips and he gave her a primitive grin.

"Make me feel it," she challenged.

He took her at her word and began to pound deep inside her. Using her vampiric speed, she met him thrust for thrust, making demands of her own. What may have started out as gentle love making was now an unrestrained, frenzied search for their pleasure.

She felt him hit her cervix and cried out. The pain melded into ecstasy and she threw her head back. "Gods!"

When he loosened one hand and wedged his face close to her neck, she knew what was coming. She knew, but was still unprepared for the sheer intensity of the orgasm that raced through her. She lost moments of time, all she knew was her mate, inside her in every way he could be.

When he moved back she struck sinking her fangs deep into the roped muscle of his neck. He thrust one last time and shouted his pleasure. His frantic cry reverberated through the room as she drank her fill. Satiated she retracted her fangs and licked the holes closed.

Still inside her, he collapsed as his arms gave out, causing them both to groan when her body reacted by clenching around him. Tiny shockwaves trembled through her.

Ever so slowly he pulled from her and fell to one side as they both fought for breath. "I don't think we'll ever be able to top that," she panted.

He chuckled and turned his head to look at her. "Mating heat between two paranormals only intensifies with time."

She closed her eyes. "We're going to die from fucking I know it." She giggled. "Hal will come in to get us for lunch because we missed breakfast and our corpses will have fiendish, macabre smiles on them and we'll scar him for life."

He tried to push himself up but fell back to the mattress. "As long as it's Hal, I don't think I mind that scenario."

"You're still mad at him for drinking you under the table aren't you?"

"I have no idea what you mean," his words were muffled as he spoke into the mattress.

A thought struck her, and she sat up. Moving carefully she began to pat the sheets. He turned his head to face her. "What are you doing?"

She grinned at him. "The sheets are clean."

His eyebrows rose. "I'll be damned. They actually did it."

"With all the mated couples popping up whoever did this could make a fortune," she said inspecting the fitted sheet.

"It was Lief. His magic works best with anything plant based. He literally spun these sheets from magic and cotton." Etain propped his head up on his hand. "The fae have a magic similar to what he used that is woven into clothes."

When she went to crawl toward the head of the bed she flinched. Her body was protesting their evening.

Etain sat up and moved to her side. "Did I hurt you?" he asked, his face a mask of worry.

Moving from side to side her body reminded her of their love making. "You did exactly what I wanted. I will be feeling this tomorrow." She pulled up their blankets and slid inside. She crooked her finger at him. "Come here space heater." She patted the spot behind her.

He laughed. "I see why you really want me," he joked as he got in behind her. As usual, he wrapped his arm around her waist and pulled her close to his body.

Vivi couldn't remember a time in her life where she felt as warm and content. It wasn't just that he was her mate. He was also quickly becoming her best friend.

He was someone she could laugh with and turn to. Not all mates found love within their union. For her to find not only love, but friendship as well made her feel doubly blessed.

"Thank you," she whispered.

He kissed the back of her neck. "You're welcome."

She smiled. She had been thanking Fate, but Vivi didn't think she'd mind if she allowed Etain to think she had been thanking him, after all, she was the one who arranged their mating.

CHAPTER TWELVE

VIVI WAS ALMOST GIDDY AT the prospect of working with Gavriel's blood. She hummed as she slathered jelly on her toast.

"You look like a kid at Christmas," Rheia observed.

"Are you kidding me? I will be the first person in history to observe blood this old under a microscope, there's no telling what I'll see. After I get the proper dosage balanced, I will be working with Magnus, using vampire blood to cure a vampire. It will be a day of firsts all around." Vivi waved her butter knife around as she spoke.

Beth rubbed Gavriel's arm. "She will be chasing you around with a syringe asking for more samples later."

Gavriel's expression became thoughtful. "I have never seen my blood under a microscope before." He turned to Vivi. "If it is truly interesting, please let me know. I would love to see what impresses you."

Vivi had just taken a bite of toast, so she simply nodded. She went to smile at her mate and noticed that he was staring at Meryn who kept rubbing her ears. "Fleas?" Vivi asked.

Meryn just held up a middle finger as her other hand kept rubbing her ear. Aiden looked down. "Baby are you okay?"

"Yeah, but ears are buzzy."

"Buzzy?" Aiden looked at Rheia. "Should she be buzzy?"

Rheia eyed Meryn. "With her, I just don't know anymore. I just hope she's not getting an ear infection."

Scowling, Meryn ate her breakfast with one hand as she alternated rubbing either ear.

Ellie, like Vivi was eating her breakfast with gusto. She seemed just as eager to get a start on their day. If all went as planned the shifter children should be cured soon, and they would see a dramatic improvement with the sick vampires.

As breakfast began to wrap up Meryn popped out of her seat. She looked at Etain. "You got a second?"

"Baby?" Aiden asked.

"Just gotta do something real quick," Meryn replied.

"Why Etain?" Aiden asked.

Meryn blinked. "I thought he was my guard? I mean I can walk around by myself if you like…"

Aiden shook his head. "No, take Etain. Good thinking baby."

Etain stood then bent down to kiss Vivi. "I will catch up with you later at the lab." He looked at Kendrick. "Will you escort my mate and ensure her safety?"

Kendrick nodded. "Of course, I'm heading to

the lab as well. Those elemental tests to determine the type of magic in the virus should be wrapping soon."

Etain stepped away from the table. "After you Meryn."

"Dis a way," Meryn said marching from the room.

"Have fun!" Vivi called after them.

Vivi downed the rest of her coffee and stood. When she looked around she saw that both Ellie and Kendrick were also standing and ready to go.

"Dis a way," Vivi said mimicking Meryn.

Ellie giggled and Kendrick bowed.

It was going to be a great day!

Etain followed behind Meryn fully expecting her to head toward her communication hub. When she turned down the hall that led to the detention cells the hair on the back of his neck began to stand on end.

"Meryn?"

"Just gotta do something."

"Ryuu is going to be upset you didn't tell him you were coming here. You knew very well everyone assumed you were going to the communications hub."

"Yeah, well, you know what happens when you assume."

"No, what?"

Meryn stopped in the hallway and looked at him. "Seriously?"

"What?"

"When you assume, you make an 'ass' out of 'u' and 'me'."

Etain smiled. "That is very clever Meryn. You come up with the most interesting things."

Meryn blinked, then grinned slyly. "Yeah, I do don't I?"

They walked to the end of the hall, and Etain used his palm to unlock the door to the cells. All of Eta, the Elders and the unit leaders of the other units had access to any of the prisoners.

Meryn walked in as if she owned the place. She looked left, then right, then locked in on DeLaFontaine sitting in his cell. She walked over and stood in front of him.

"Well, if it is not the complex little human. To what do I owe the pleasure?" he asked standing.

Meryn frowned and rubbed at her right ear. "I'm not sure."

"Are you here to accuse me as well?"

Meryn crossed her arms over her chest. "Don't play innocent with me. You were literally caught red-handed. You play poor, misunderstood accused with the warriors, but I know better."

DeLaFontaine stared at her for a moment. "You are indeed an odd human."

"So why did you do it?"

He gave a lazy shrug. "Hypothetically speaking, if I truly had a hand in this, I would probably say... Oh, what is the phrase?" He tapped his lips. "Ah yes. To make an omelette one must crack a few eggs."

"And hypothetically speaking, you don't mind cracking certain eggs?"

Again, DeLaFontaine simply shrugged his response. He watched her carefully. "You know. You are more like me than you realize."

"No I'm not."

"Yes, you are. You seem to be able to quickly identify what you perceive to be problems, then you take action in the most direct way possible. One could say you are a bit ruthless," he smirked.

"Only with certain eggs," she retorted.

"Touché," he inclined his head. A smiled pulled at his lips. "How is Magnus' treatment going?"

Etain felt his stomach clench as Meryn stepped back. She spun on her heel and practically ran from the room. Etain had to hurry to catch up.

"Was it something I said?" DeLaFontaine called after them cackling.

When the door to the cells closed behind them Meryn was pulling desperately at the walkie-talkie at her belt. She brought it up. "Stop all treatments! I repeat, stop all treatments! Do not administer the third trial!" Meryn yelled as they turned the corner and ran past the transport tunnel.

When they reached the lab Meryn pounded on the door. They waited a minute before Meryn ran for the infirmary. She went to pound again when the door swung open. Kendrick stood there frowning. "Meryn, what on earth is the matter?"

Meryn wedged her way inside. "Don't give Magnus the treatment!"

Vivi paled. "I already have. It didn't take me long to balance the dosage since I was only working with two samples," she explained. "Why? What's going on?"

Meryn chewed on her lower lip. "I don't know."

"You don't know?" Vivi asked. She turned to Kendrick. "Is this more your thing?"

Kendrick placed a hand on her shoulder, and his eyes widened. "That is fascinating." He looked down. "Meryn are you seeing anything?"

"Just flashes." She swallowed and looked up at him. "And it's all bad."

The door behind them glowed with a flash of blue light before it swung open and Ryuu walked in heading straight to Meryn. "*Denka*, breathe. Your heart rate is too high."

Etain was impressed, from the moment that Ryuu entered the room his presence seemed to expand out in front of him. Vivi walked past Magnus' bed where Caspian and Broderick sat on one side and Marjoram the other. She walked up to Etain and into his arms. He didn't know what was happening, but until he did, he wanted his mate safe at his side.

Meryn chewed on the side of her thumb. "It's probably nothing."

Kendrick shook his head. "If you could see your magic you wouldn't say that. It looks like the Fourth of July."

"Crap," Meryn groaned.

Kendrick's eyes were huge. "Meryn what are you seeing?"

"Fangs and Magnus freaking out."

Everyone turned to where Magnus was lying on the bed. "He seems to be okay Meryn," Vivi said eyeing Magnus' monitors.

"Meryn? Etain? Can we get an update?" Rheia asked over the walkie talkie.

Meryn looked around tears in her eyes. "I'm not

lying."

Ryuu placed a hand on her back. "No one is saying you are *denka*. Everyone here believes you."

Meryn was about to reply when she gasped. "Hold him!" she screamed.

Etain watched in horror as Magnus sat straight up in bed and reached for his brother. Had Kendrick hesitated even for one moment they may have lost Caspian.

"*Immobiles!*" Kendrick shouted freezing Magnus in place.

Everyone stared in horror as their normally kind prince snarled and hissed at them, baring his fangs.

Beth collapsed against Gavriel. "Oh gods! He's feral!"

"Look at his eyes," Vivi whispered.

Etain felt like he was going to be ill. Magnus' eyes were pitch black.

Vivi looked up at him frantic. "What have I done?"

Vivi worked with Kendrick and Gavriel to get Magnus to lay flat. It took them ten minutes of freezing and unfreezing him to get him back under his covers. Every time he could move he tried to attack them.

Meryn sat beside Beth her arm wrapped around her. "S'ok Beth," Meryn reached up and patted Beth's forehead with the palm of her hand. "S'ok."

Beth gave her a teary smile. "Thank you for trying," she said reaching up to hold Meryn's hand.

Kendrick collapsed into a chair. "What just happened?" he asked looking completely wiped.

Vivi stared down at Magnus. "I know I gave him an even distribution of blood."

Kendrick pulled out his walkie talkie. "Code One. Code One. I repeat we have a Code One, all unit warriors report to your assigned locations. This is not a drill."

"What's a Code One?" Meryn asked.

"Emergency on Level One. Aiden and Adriel worked out the code system last week," Gavriel answered sitting down next to Beth lending her his strength.

Vivi turned to Kendrick. "Could the samples have been tampered with?"

He shook his head. "I had spells on top of spells to keep the lab and the samples safe. Nothing disturbed them."

Marjoram smoothed Magnus' blankets. "We need to move him to his quarters. We cannot run the risk of anyone seeing him like this."

Gavriel stood and pulled Beth to her feet. "Kendrick could you shield Magnus from view if I were to carry him?"

"Easily," Kendrick said getting to his feet.

Caspian wiped his eyes and shook his head. "No. I will do it. He is my brother." Broderick rubbed his back. "And we will help you," he added looking around the room for support.

"Of course we will," Marjoram replied.

"We need to go. Everyone will be heading to the Rioux quarters for an update," Gavriel advised them.

Vivi jumped when Etain wrapped an arm around her. She had been absorbed in going over every step she took, but she couldn't think of anything that would have caused this.

"Come along my love. We can discuss it further with everyone at Magnus'." Etain walked with her toward the door. Behind them, Caspian and Kendrick lifted Magnus from the bed. With Broderick manning the doors, they hurried as fast as they could to the resident quarters.

Once inside Caspian, Broderick and Marjoram kept going to get Magnus settled in his own bedroom. Etain sat them down in a love seat as Aiden rushed over and scooped up Meryn looking relieved. "I thought the Code One was for you," he whispered burying his face in her hair. When he raised his head, he looked at Gavriel. "What happened?"

Gavriel looked around the room. Everyone, including Avery and Warrick, was huddled in the antechamber. Sebastian looked completely shaken. Hal walked over, led the squire to a chair and made him sit down.

Gavriel took a deep breath. "About twenty minutes ago Magnus had a violent reaction to his first treatment for the virus."

Adriel looked from Gavriel to Vivi and back. "Violent how?"

Gavriel met his eyes. "He looks feral." Gasps were heard all around the room.

"But he's not, right?" Beth insisted looking to Vivi.

Vivi buried her face in her hands for a moment before looking up. "I can't say for sure."

Etain placed a supportive hand on her back. "Remember, she is trying to treat an impossible virus with an experimental method, there are no certainties."

"Damn this virus!" Beth exploded vehemently.

Gavriel's eyes turned red in the face of his mate's anguish. Vivi knew a lot of his anger stemmed from the fact that there was nothing he could do to help her. With a soft voice that contradicted his visible anger, he comforted his mate. "Beth my love, remember to try and stay calm for the baby's sake. It is only his first treatment, maybe this has to happen before he gets better," he said reasonably.

"Do you really think so?" she asked looking up at him with desperation shining in her eyes.

"It is as Etain said. We are facing an unprecedented situation. I believe that anything is possible." Gavriel held Beth close.

Etain turned to Meryn. "Do you think DeLaFontaine had anything to do with this? Is that why you went to see him after breakfast?"

Everyone turned to Meryn. Aiden frowned. "She did what?" Meryn shook her head. "No, well he may, but that wasn't why I was there. All through breakfast my ears kept buzzing, and I kept seeing a picture of DeLaFontaine in his cell. When I went to see him, the buzzing stopped but then flashes of Magnus started coming. DeLaFontaine was too damn smug. He even asked how Magnus' treatment was coming. There's no way he could have known we were doing that today."

Aiden looked around. "The only ones who knew about today's treatment are sitting in this room."

Avery leaned forward his eyes darting around.

"What about listening devices?" he whispered.

Kendrick shook his head. "Every time I cast a soundproofing spell it would short out any listening devices. Even if they had one in here before we arrived, it would be toast by now with the number of spells cast per day."

Aiden waved around the room. "So right now we're covered?"

Kendrick nodded. "It was the first thing I did when we got back here."

Gavriel looked to Aiden, then they looked around the room. "What are our first steps?"

"We need to determine what happened with Magnus. What or who caused it and if it will affect the children and other vampires," Vivi suggested first.

"That's pretty much it, in a nutshell," Ellie agreed.

Meryn turned to Kendrick. "What did you see when you looked at my empathy?"

Kendrick rubbed his eyes. "I think I witnessed a premonition happening from a magical perspective." He blinked. "It was incredible. There were flashes of pinpoint light going off everywhere."

"That shit hurt," Meryn grumbled.

"Premonitions aren't supposed to hurt Meryn," Kendrick said looking at her closely.

"Maybe they wanted to make sure I was paying attention," Meryn suggested massaging her temples.

Kendrick hesitated then gave a slow nod. "That might actually be a viable explanation."

As Gavriel turned back to Vivi, the door crashed open. Nigel and Neil practically tumbled through the doorway. Kendrick frowned and looked as if he were about to admonish them when Nigel fell to his knees and vomited in the corner. Kendrick jumped to his feet quickly moving to their side, his face like a thundercloud.

"Nigel!" Meryn exclaimed. She spun looking around the room until she spotted Rheia. "Help him!"

Rheia and Ellie were already moving. Ellie knelt beside Nigel while Rheia spoke in soothing tones to Neil. She turned to look at Kendrick. "They're in shock."

The state of the twins snapped Sebastian out of his own despair, and he rushed to Rheia's side. "What do they need?"

"Blankets and some Blessed Chamomile," Rheia answered. Sebastian gave a quick nod then practically ran from the room.

Kendrick bent down and gently pulled Nigel to his feet. One arm wrapped around Neil, the other Nigel as he steered them to a sofa. He sat down with one twin on either side. "You're safe boys. No one and nothing can harm you here." Avery moved to sit on Neil's other side, and Meryn got up to sit on the other side of Nigel.

Ellie scrunched up her nose. "I don't suppose your magic can take care of that mess will it?" she asked pointing to where Nigel had gotten ill.

Law stepped forward. "I'll take care of it." Moments later, the air was fresher, and the sweet sick smell was dissipating.

Nigel opened and closed his mouth. "Minty fresh. Thank you," he said weakly.

Kendrick looked from one twin to the other. "What happened?"

Neil's eyes were still huge. "B-b-b-b," he stuttered.

Avery rubbed his back. "Take a deep breath," he suggested.

Nigel turned to Kendrick. "We were taking care of the refuse tube like you asked when..." he swallowed hard looking green again. "We were dredging it with our magic when we found something." He covered his mouth with his hand and swallowed again. "It was a body. Or what's left of one, it's been bloating and rotting in sewage and refuse for a while."

"Gods!" Declan exclaimed looking a bit sick himself.

"Another victim?" Adriel thought out loud.

Neil just shook his head back and forth still unable to speak. Nigel looked at Kendrick. "It's Augustus Pettier." His words fell flat in the room.

"That is impossible," Gavriel started.

Nigel gave him a tired look. "Neil and I have been studying his picture to watch out for him in the camera footage for Meryn. Chunks are missing from the corpse, but it's definitely him."

"B-b-b-b," Neil stuttered. Kendrick pulled his head onto his shoulder and whispered a spell softly. Neil's face relaxed. "Warm," he said blissfully.

Sebastian and Ryuu rushed in. Sebastian was holding a thick blanket while Ryuu carried a large tray with tea. Kendrick stood and scooted the twins together before wrapping the blanket around them. He sat in the chair next to the sofa. Meryn patted their blanket awkwardly.

"How could this happen?" Beth asked.

Meryn frowned. "His murder or the refuse tube?"

"Both," Beth replied.

Meryn pursed her lips. "Rheia or Ellie will have to confirm it, but if I had to guess I would say that Augustus Pettier has been dead this whole time. From what I understand of the process, the reason why the refuse tube backed up was because it was detecting vampire cells breaking down slowly. It recognized them as living matter and wouldn't empty."

Rheia turned to Ellie. "I am not doing an autopsy on a corpse that has been rotting in shit. No way, no how."

Ellie shuddered. "Ditto."

An extremely loud alarm sounded. "What now?" Kari demanded looking flustered.

Kendrick turned to Adriel and Aiden. "That's the alarm I set for the lab." Both men left the antechamber running, Declan and Colton right behind him.

Broderick came from Magnus' bedroom looking spooked. "What was that?"

Beth looked up at her father. "Someone broke into the lab."

He frowned furiously. "Again?"

Meryn snorted then covered her mouth to hide her giggle. Vivi had to admit, though it was a dire situation, Broderick's reaction was comical. Broderick smiled at Meryn and sat down next to his daughter. She leaned in, and in a low voice explained what was going on with Nigel and Neil.

Ryuu handed first Nigel, then Neil a cup of tea. He stood and looked around the room. Beth followed by Kari got the next cups. Vivi thought Beth looked like she was two seconds from completely unraveling.

"This was supposed to be a happy day," Beth whispered as she stared down into her tea.

Meryn tapped her fingers on the sofa's arm. "Nigel, does anyone else know you found the body?" Nigel shook his head.

Kendrick looked at Meryn his eyes wide then he began to chuckle. "Little genius."

Vivi glanced from one to the other. "What?"

Kendrick bowed in his chair. "Allow me?" he asked Meryn.

"Sure."

Kendrick straightened. "If we can secure the body without anyone else the wiser, then the killer will have no idea that we know they exist. They will think we're still looking for Augustus Pettier. It may give us the upper hand."

Law exhaled. "I'll go secure the body from where the twins left it." He turned to Gavriel. "Where do you want it?"

Gavriel grimaced. "Do we even have a morgue?"

Beth shook her head. "We cremate our dead in Noctem Falls."

Gavriel eyed Rheia and Ellie. Rheia scowled. "I will take a look to see if I can determine the cause of death, but that's it."

Gavriel looked relieved. "I will take it." He turned to Law. "Could you assist her? After she has determined all she can learn from the body, take it to the cremation chamber to be cremated. We will store his ashes respectfully until they can be handed over to his sister."

Rheia stood slowly. "I was really hoping that by this time we would have been celebrating everyone's recovery."

Law looped his arm through hers. "We'll get there."

Rheia looked over her shoulder. "I would say to send Colton when he gets back, but he has a weak stomach. Make him stay here. I won't have the energy to baby him later."

Gavriel gave her a sad smile. "We will ensure he stays here."

Vivi sat back and closed her eyes. How had everything gone so wrong? When they heard Aiden calling for Goddard and Viktor over the walkie-talkie, everyone looked around worriedly. It took the men thirty minutes to return. All four men looked exhausted. When they sat down Adriel turned to Ellie and Vivi. "What?" Vivi asked.

"All the blood collected to treat the children and the sick vampires is gone." Adriel sat leaning forward his elbows on his knees. He rested his chin on his laced fingers.

"The stone!" Vivi gasped.

Aiden shook his head. "If you're talking about the black and gray thing, it's still in the mini-fridge on the opposite wall. But Goddard confirmed all of the blood from the walk-in refrigeration unit is gone. He said he helped bring it down from Level Six after the blood drive and saw where it was stacked. It's all gone."

Gavriel turned milk white. "My blood?"

"It's right here!" Vivi announced pulling the injector cartridge from her lab pocket. "I stuck it there when we got that panicked call from Meryn. It never made it back to the refrigeration unit."

Gavriel let out a shaky breath. "Thank the gods,"

he whispered reverently.

Ellie simply buried her face in her hands and wept. Grant pulled her close his lips pulled back in a snarl. "Give me just five minutes with DeLaFontaine," he begged.

Colton looked around his eyes narrowing. "Where is my mate?"

"She went to go play with a rotting body that has been marinating in shit for the past couple weeks. Did you need her for something?" Meryn asked.

Colton's eyes widened. "She's what?"

"She went to see if she could determine a cause of death for Augustus Pettier. Did you need to go to the infirmary to be with her?" Meryn eyed Colton.

He shook his head looking a bit green. "No, I think she can handle it. She does have a guard right?" he asked quickly.

Meryn nodded. "Law went with her."

"Good," Colton said sitting back.

Vivi watched as Gavriel turned to Meryn and mouthed, 'thank you'. Meryn winked at the interim prince. Evidently, Meryn knew how to handle Colton.

Kendrick's jaw was clenched as he stood. "I am going to head to the lab to ensure that whoever broke in didn't disturb my testing plates."

The twins unravelled themselves from their blanket. "We'll come too."

Kendrick looked touched. "You two can stay here and rest."

Neil shook his head. "We want to stay near you," he declared unabashedly.

Kendrick's cheeks tinted pink before he cleared

his throat. "Then come along." The boys sprang up from the sofa and followed him out the door.

Vivi couldn't bear to face Beth. "This is all my fault."

"I don't know about that," Meryn responded. "Maybe whoever took the blood, took it because they believed you were on to the right track. Maybe you are totally right, and they are freaking out."

Beth nodded. "She's right. Don't blame yourself. I know that my uncle would say the same thing."

Vivi knew they meant well, but not only had she created Magnus' treatment, she physically injected him with it causing his current state. No matter what, she knew this was on her.

She turned the cartridge with Gavriel's leftover blood in her hands. "I need to head to the lab as well to start testing. I wish I knew how a shifter would react to the older blood. They did so well with Viktor's blood, and he was only fourteen hundred years old. The blood we collected was twice as old."

"We still have the injectors upstairs that you prepared. So whenever you would like to move ahead with the third trial either on the shifters or vampires, we can," Ellie reminded her.

"Can't you just inject a kid and see what happens," Meryn suggested.

Vivi stared. "Meryn, I can't test on the children."

Meryn looked confused. "Why not? Wouldn't it be the quickest way to find out what will happen? Same thing with other vampires, just jab em and sit back and watch."

"Meryn, that's unethical and probably illegal,"

Vivi explained.

"Oh. Never mind then," Meryn said toppling to one side on the twins' blanket. She sat up then looked down at the blanket smiling. "Kendrick spelled it so it would be warm. Score!" She stood and began to twist until only her face was visible at the top of the blanket roll.

"My favorite delicacy. The Meryn Roll," Aiden teased picking her up. "Come on, I'll lay down with you for your rest period." He nodded to them then headed to their quarters.

Adriel stood. "I'm canceling the Code One and sending the men back to their usual posts." He held his hand out and helped Eva to her feet. Eva looped her arm with his. "I'll check in with Stefan. When y'all enacted the Code One the pack surrounded the hospital. I want to make sure they know that it was cancelled."

Ellie wiped her eyes on her sleeve. "I should go check on the children." Grant cupped her cheek. "How about after you do that we'll pick up Benji from Adora and watch a movie before dinner? Just the three of us?"

Ellie just wrapped her arms around Grant's neck hugging him tight. "That sounds like heaven."

Grant stood and easily swept his mate into his arms. "Then let's go. The sooner you check on the kiddos, the sooner we can see Benji."

As Grant was carrying her from the room, she looked over his shoulder at Vivi. "If you need anything just call."

Vivi shook her head and waved. There was little to be done at this point except testing, and that she could do on her own.

Beth set her tea cup down. "I want to sit with Uncle." She drew in a ragged breath. "Though I don't know what good it will do."

Broderick patted her knee. "It may do more good than you realize." He gave her a sad smile. "When we were getting Magnus into his own bed Caspian made the off comment that his behavior had upset you. Magnus actually calmed down a bit. I think, deep down, he's still in there. We just have to help him find his way back."

"Thank the gods!" Beth whispered.

Vivi sighed wearily. "I'm heading to the lab."

Etain stood and took her hand. "We may take a slight detour, so if you need either of us reach out using the walkie-talkie."

Micah stood. "Until we find the one who broke into the lab, I'll act as Vivi's guard."

Gavriel nodded before turning to Beth. "Let us go see Magnus."

Vivi and Etain left the Rioux estate with Micah in tow. When she went to head towards the lab, he tugged on her hand. "I would like to go to Level Six before you sequester yourself in your lab."

"Why?"

He shot Micah a look. The warrior walked to the far side of the hall to give them a bit of privacy. Etain looked back down at her. "Because you need a break away from here. You have spent every moment since your arrival either in the lab or in meetings. Allow me to take you on a date. We can pretend this entire, horrible situation isn't happening for a while before returning to reality." Etain held both of her hands in his. "It is my responsibility to ensure your happiness, and right now you are not happy."

"So we just forget that Magnus is ill and go on a date?"

"Was Magnus ill this morning?" he asked.

"Yes."

"Will he be ill tonight?"

"Yes."

"Will he more than likely be ill tomorrow?" Etain continued raising an eyebrow.

"You know he will be," Vivi responded sourly.

"Then I don't think taking an hour out of your day to get away will harm him. It may actually do you a bit of good to clear your mind and start fresh."

"I hate it when you make sense," she grumbled.

He gave her hands a quick tug pulling her forward and off balance. As she fell against him, he quickly captured her lips. His kiss at first was gentle, but both of their hungers soon took over. When she inadvertently moaned he stepped back. The love she saw in his eyes humbled her. Not once since meeting him had he complained that she was putting others first. In fact, he had only gotten upset over the fact that she wasn't taking proper care of herself.

"You're too selfless," she said reaching up to touch his lips.

"Is it truly being selfless if serving others is what brings me happiness?" he asked.

"Try to put yourself first a bit more. You should have gotten a mate who would help you curb that, and look out for you, but you got stuck with me. I can barely keep track of myself," Vivi let her hand drop feeling worse for having put words to her feelings.

Etain thumped her between the eyes. "Stop that!" She glared at him. "Did you and Hal create the 'Thump Vivi' club or something?"

He just stared down at her smiling. "You need to put yourself first a bit more. You should have gotten a mate who would have the time to see to your health, not spend his day serving an entire city. But, you got stuck with me. I can barely keep my own home clean and feed myself, despite being over a thousand years old."

Vivi's mouth dropped open. When he said it, it sounded ridiculous. "How did you do that?"

His lips twitched. "I don't know what you mean." He looked up the transport tunnel. "Are you ready to experience fine dining on Level Six?"

"I love you."

His eyes widened in surprise at her sudden statement before he smiled wide. "And I love you too Vivian Vi'Aerlin."

She took his hand. "Not Princess Vivian?"

He shook his head. "To me, the fact that you are taking my last name trumps your royal status."

"We still need to register that," she reminded him.

He grinned down at her and pulled her into the tunnel. "I already have Rex drawing up the paperwork."

Etain called out to Micah, and he joined them as they floated up to Level Six. Vivian couldn't help smiling. She would be changing her name for the third and final time in her life. She couldn't wait to be Vivian Vi'Aerlin.

CHAPTER THIRTEEN

E TAIN HAD A BOYISH GRIN on his face as he led her to the vendor who operated at the edge of the eating area. He sat her down and went to the stand. Micah stood behind her waiting. When Etain returned and handed her a paper wrapped item she smiled in delight. "Crepes! I love crepes!"

Micah leaned in and took a bite of her treat. Licking his lips he groaned. "Damn that's good." He looked around. "Be right back." He jogged off to another food stand.

"Are strawberry and chocolate okay?" Etain asked.

"Perfect. I could eat these everyday and be happy," she closed her eyes happily and took another bite.

Etain nudged her and pointed. She looked over to see that the crepe vendor was watching them anxiously. "She knows who I am," Vivi asked in the barest of whispers. Etain kept smiling but gave a slight nod.

Vivi took another bite. "Gods! These things are amazing! Can we come here more often?" she said in a louder voice.

The crepe vendor covered her face with her hands in delight and began to clean her tiny stand in a fit of happiness.

Etain smiled wide. "Of course my love," he answered. Under the guise of kissing her cheek, he whispered in her ear. "Softie." He sat back and continued eating his own snack.

Micah came back over and sat down on her other side. "You have to try these!" Micah held up a long, skinny orange stick.

Cautiously she took a bite and chewed quickly. "What is that?"

"Good?" he asked eyeing her knowingly.

"Better than good."

"They're sweet potato french fries dipped in a brown sugar and cinnamon glaze. They are my ultimate weakness," he confessed.

"I can see why."

She and Micah exchanged bites so they could each enjoy the other's dessert. Etain finished his and simply sat at her side with his arm draped across the back of her chair.

They were just walking past the hospital, about to head back down to Level One when a tall, dark-haired wolf shifter stepped in front of them. "Is this her? The murderer?" he demanded.

Vivi gasped. "The what?" she whispered.

Etain and Micah moved to stand in front of her. Micah eyed the man a confused look on his face. "Cainan, this is the amazing doctor I was telling you about. The one who developed the treatment for the children. You said you thought she must be an amazing person and wanted to meet her. I don't understand the change in attitude."

"That was before I knew who she was, who she really was. I heard her name on that announcement they made about Prince Gavriel taking over, how she was a DuSang. A murderer born of a murderer!" he raved.

"My mate is no murderer," Etain said cordially.

Vivi felt her blood turn to ice. She knew without looking that Etain's expression would be murderous. She knew she was right when the shifter took a step back.

He recovered quickly. "Don't you think it's strange that Prince Magnus was fine until she arrived? How do we know she didn't do this to him?" Gasps were heard all around them. Vivi looked to their left and right and realized that both shifters and vampires had closed in around them to watch what would happen.

Vivi brought her hand to her throat. Little did he know his words stuck at her very core. She had hurt Magnus, just not in the way he was implying.

"See! She looks guilty!" he crowed.

"Would you please refrain from saying hateful things about my mate? I will happily turn her pain, into your pain," Etain offered almost off-handedly.

Cainan paled, but persisted. "Do you know who her father was? What he did?"

Etain nodded. "Of course. I was here for it."

Cainan was about to respond when Stefan pushed his way through the crowd. "What in the hell is going on? Etain? Cainan?" He looked from one to the other.

Etain's eyes never left the angry shifter in front of him. "Your pack member feels it necessary to say terrible things to my mate hurting her very soul.

For that alone I could rip out his spine." Etain's even voice made the violent words that much scarier.

Stefan's eyes widened at Etain's demeanor. "Cainan, you want to tell me what this is all about?"

"She's a DuSang, Alpha. Her father killed my brother!" he exclaimed angrily.

Vivi pushed slightly between Etain and Micah to face the shifter. "My father killed many people, including my own mother. But I am not him." She straightened her back as the realization truly hit her. She was not her father, and she would not be bound by his guilt. She had her own mistakes to bear. She refused to be weighed down by his any longer. In a louder voice, she repeated her words. "I am not my father. I heal. I don't kill. I was raised by a shifter, Halbjorn Bergson and I would never do anything to disappoint him."

Cainan refused to accept her words. "Your father killed my brother and most of my pack all because he didn't want to admit that his supposed mate left him for a shifter, her true mate." Low murmurs spread out around them.

Vivi stared at him. "How do you know that?"

"Because it was my brother who she left that tyrant for. He stole their pure happiness and their lives because he didn't want to be 'shamed'!" he growled low.

Stefan frowned. "So correct me if I am wrong. But you're snarling and being rude to the woman who would have been your baby niece?"

Cainan stopped mid-growl as his eyes widened. "Baby niece?"

Around them, wolves and vampires alike began

to chuckle. Stefan's words had knocked the wind right out of the angry shifter. He put his hands on his hips. "Yes, baby niece you idiot. She would have been raised with our pack had her mother and true mate lived."

Cainan stared at her, a goofy look on his face. He turned beet red and began to rub the back of his neck when he looked back in her direction. "Sorry about that."

Micah exhaled loudly clutching at his chest. "You can't do stuff like this to me! I am a delicate individual." More chuckles were heard as the tension practically evaporated.

Cainan really looked at her. "Macario, my brother beat DuSang in the end." He gave her a teary smile. "Halbjorn was the name of my brother's best friend. If he raised you to be a healer and not a killer, then you have become my brother's legacy."

Etain and Micah stayed in front of her but stepped to one side so that she could face her uncle. He gave her a shy smile. His warm smile turned to one as horror as he leapt forward.

Vivi was confused until a sharp, biting pain blossomed in her midsection. She looked down and froze. There was a finger wrapped handle sticking out of her shirt. Shouts and screams erupted as Cainan crashed to the ground with someone at her side causing the handle and fingers to disappear as a jagged edge dagger emerged from her body. She looked up to see her mate staring at her in terror. "Etain, there was something on my shirt." Why was she finding it so hard to talk? She felt woozy, then she was staring up at the ceiling. Etain's lips were moving, and he looked so frantic. She reached up and traced his lips. She loved his lips. "Love you," she said before closing her eyes. Those crepes must have made her tired. She was just going to rest her eyes for a bit.

"Etain, there was something on my shirt." His mate looked down at her stomach baffled seemingly unaware of the growing bloodstain. Her words unfroze his muscles, and he caught her as she fell. He cradled her in his arms. "Micah!" he screamed. "I need help!"

Micah knelt across from them. "Set her down Etain, I need to see the damage," he instructed.

Etain had to fight every instinct to set her down. Micah quickly ripped the fabric of her shirt aside and sucked in his breath. He held his glowing hands over her wound.

She reached up and touched his lips, just as she had before. "Love you," she said before she closed her eyes.

"No! Micah, do something!"

"I am, but it's not working! We need Ellie or Rheia or Dr. St. John. She's not healing Etain. I can only sustain for a few more minutes, then she's going to bleed out."

Stefan knelt beside them. "I called down to Level One. Rheia is waiting for you in the lab. She said to stay out of the infirmary," he advised.

Etain scooped her up in his arms. "With me

Micah?"

"Go!" Micah yelled.

Together they ran for the tunnel and shot down to Level One. Etain didn't look back. He knew Micah would be there. The hallway flew by before he knew it he spotted Colton standing at the door holding it open for them. He ran inside.

"Here!" Rheia yelled pointing to a gurney.

He set her down and was immediately pushed out of the way. When he pulled his hand back to punch Tarragon both Adriel and Grant grabbed him on either side and dragged him to the wall.

"She needs me!" he yelled.

"She needs the doctors more!" Adriel shouted in his face.

Etain felt his world spinning out of control. "Why is this happening?" he asked. Grant and Adriel each wrapped an arm around him to hold him steady. But neither of them had an answer to his question.

Tarragon stepped back and looked around the room. "Kendrick can you come here?"

Kendrick hurried over, and Tarragon pointed. "Can your magic detect any foreign substance in the wound?"

Kendrick placed a hand on Vivi's shoulder. He pulled it back growling. "It's an anticoagulant and blood thinner."

"Dammit!" Tarragon shouted then turned back to his patient.

"What?" Etain asked. "Why is that bad?"

Kendrick walked over and placed both hands on his shoulders. "The mixture of an anticoagulant and blood thinner in a wound this deep in a vampire is fatal. Unlike shifters, fae and witches, vampires react horribly to both substances. This wound was meant to kill her," he explained slowly, in an even voice.

Etain shook his head. "That is unacceptable."

"We agree," a voice said from the door. Gavriel and Caspian hurried over to the gurney. "We would like to use a similar method to the one Vivi has been trying with the virus treatment. If Caspian and I both donate our blood, we may be able to prevent a bond from forming." He turned to Etain. "There is a probability that she may form a bond to one or both of us, but as we will only be sharing a few drops each to counteract the anticoagulant and blood thinner it should not happen. That being said, she does not share our bloodline, so we also run the risk of our blood acting like a poison and killing her. But as the four royal families are closely related we believe it has a very good chance in working. Are those risks you are willing to take?"

"Yes! Gods, yes! Anything, just don't let her leave me," he begged.

Gavriel gave a nod and turned to Caspian. "As there is a substance in her wound preventing it from healing, I believe that the best method would be to drip our blood directly into her."

Caspian nodded. "I believe you are right."

They each took a breath and using a claw from the opposite hand, they opened deep cuts on their wrists. Etain watched as each drop of their blood seemed to take an eternity to fall. After a few minutes, Etain struggled against his best friend and unit leader. "Well!"

Gavriel and Caspian licked their wrists closed.

Gavriel turned to Rheia. "Blood pressure?"

Rheia watched the monitor. "Rising! Thank god! It's rising!"

"Rising is good?" Etain demanded.

Micah's hands stopped glowing. He looked up tears in his eyes. "Rising is very good. Her wound is closing." Micah swayed a bit, and Declan propped him up. "Good work Casanova," he said, bumping his shoulder.

Etain felt his legs go, but he didn't fall. His brothers wouldn't let him.

"We have you," Adriel said quietly.

Etain rested his forehead against Grant's shoulder and let the tears fall. He refused to let the room see them, but he didn't mind if his brothers saw. When he needed them the most, each member of his unit had been there to support him. He would never, forget that.

"Can I get a fucking update!" an irate voice demanded out of no where. Etain lifted his head and found himself smiling. The tiny human had a way of spilling light into their darkest of moments.

Gavriel picked up his walkie talkie. "I will update Meryn. Etain why do you not take Vivi to your quarters where she will be more comfortable? There is a large, frantic squire desperate to see the both of you, and he is losing his mind as we speak."

Etain straightened. "I can move her?"

Rheia leaned against her mate looking exhausted. "She may be slightly tender, but she's perfectly healed." She pointed down. "Not even a scar."

Etain rushed forward to confirm for himself. The edges of her ripped shirt were bloodstained and the only proof of the ordeal he just lived through.

Adriel stepped up behind him placing a hand on his back. "Her attacker?" he asked in a low voice.

"Stefan and his pack member Cainan have him on Level Six," Micah replied. "You'll never believe who it is." Etain looked up. "Who?"

Micah's eyes hardened. "That damn tunnel escort."

Etain went to turn to his unit leader and Adriel tightened his grip on his shoulder. "Do not worry brother. No matter what the council may say, his death is already a certainty."

Etain gave a nod in acknowledgement and gently picked up his mate cradling her close. He faced the room. "Thank you, all of you."

Rheia waved off his thanks. "It's what family does."

Her words shook him to the core. For the first time in centuries, he truly felt surrounded by family.

"Put her here! No! Wait, there! No, wait!" Hal was practically walking in circles in their family room.

"Hal."

"Maybe here, so she's closer to the kitchen," Hal continued.

"Hal," Etain repeated trying to get the squire's attention.

"But she should be in a bed." Hal looked around the room.

"Hal!" Etain practically shouted.

Hal turned to him his eyes wild. Etain swallowed hard. The man's fear mirrored his own state not too long ago. "She's okay. Gavriel and Caspian saved her. She's just fine, not even a scar. Come look."

Hal stumbled over on unsteady feet and looked down. Tears dripped down his nose to pool on Vivi's belly. Hal reached out and traced the blood on her shirt. "The one who did this?"

"Will be taken care of, you have my word. My brothers are seeing to it," Etain swore.

Hal looked him in the eye. "She is my entire world." His frank statement just about destroyed Etain, because he knew exactly how he felt. "As she is mine," he replied.

"Take her to your room. I'll make her favorite hot chocolate for when she comes around," Hal said gruffly wiping his cheeks.

"We will be out as soon as she wakes so you can see her," Etain promised.

Hal nodded. "Get her out of those clothes and washed up. She shouldn't have to see that."

Etain couldn't help but agree. "I will."

He carried his mate to their master suite and carefully balanced her against his body to open the door. Once the door closed behind him; he headed straight to the bathroom and stripped her gently. He wrapped her in a bath sheet and walked out to lay her on their cushy floor in front of the fireplace before switching the logs on. She would be nice and warm while he cleaned up the mess.

His hands shook as he cleaned the blood smears from the bathroom floors and fixtures that her clothes had left behind. He wrapped up the offending, bloodstained shirt and pants in a towel and pushed it between the toilet and the wall. He'd take it out to Hal to be incinerated later. He stripped himself of his clothes and went back to lift his mate in his arms where she belonged.

He set her on the long bench and took his time washing her hair and body. When he got out he quickly dried them with a towel before tucking them under the covers. He pulled her close and allowed himself to face what happened. He was glad her hair was already wet. She would never know that the thought of living without her had driven him to tears.

Vivi woke up and blinked. She felt Etain's arm around her waist, and they were both naked. She went to sit up and winced.

Etain stirred beside her. When he saw her eyes were open he popped straight up like a Jack in the Box startling her. "You're awake," he said breathlessly.

Vivi slapped his arm. "You scared the crap out of me. What the hell is wrong?" She rubbed her stomach. "Did we have sex again? I'm kinda sore and not in a good way."

Etain's almost maniacal laughter had her edging away from him about to bolt for Hal. "Etain, what is it?"

He simply fell over her and pinned her to the bed. "You almost died," he choked out the words.

"What?" Vivi asked. Then images of a handle near her midsection flooded her. "Oh, yeah. There was something sticking out of me."

"Something? It was a dagger!" Etain pulled back his eyes flashing.

Vivi looked down at her belly. There wasn't even a pink line showing where her wound have been. "Well it looks like I'm okay now." She sat up and stretched her arms over her head. "I should get back to the lab."

Etain released an unintelligible string of curses. He reached over to his side of the bed and tapped a small alarm clock looking thing. "Hal, I need you in here."

She looked over at her mate. "Really? You're calling Hal in?"

The door swung open and Hal filled the doorway. "Is she okay?" he demanded rushing over.

Vivi gave an indignant peep and pulled the blankets up to cover her chest. Hal rushed over and sat on the bed. He tried tugging the blankets down and she fought with him. "Hal!"

"Is she bleeding?" Hal asked looking frantic.

"Hal! I'm fine, for the love of the gods believe me. I am fine." Vivi continued to tug at the blanket.

Hal turned to Etain. "Truly?"

Etain nodded. "Yes, but she feels like she should return to the lab." Etain crossed his arms over his chest.

Hal's head swung around. "Oh, she does, does she?"

"I feel fine. No lingering side effects to being stabbed besides being a bit sore. I think you're both overreacting."

"A bit sore." Hal gave a short laugh. "A bit sore she says!"

Etain nodded pointing at her. "See what I mean!"

Hal turned back to her. "You almost died. If it were not for Gavriel and Caspian, you would be dead. Forgive us for thinking you should stay in bed a few hours!" he roared.

Vivi pinched the bridge of her nose. Her mate and her squire had somehow formed an alliance and were ganging up on her. "Guys, I wish I could share with you how I feel. I don't really remember the attack so it's not impacting me the same as the two of you." She took in their haggard appearance. "My poor mate and Hal. The two men who I love the most in this whole world, I'm sorry you were put through this."

Hal simply engulfed her in a hug. "Nothing else can happen to you Baby Girl. My heart won't take it."

She pulled back and smiled at him before turning to her mate. "I don't plan on going anywhere for quite some time." She rubbed her belly. "Gods, it's a good thing I wasn't pregnant." She looked up to watch all color drain from the two men. "No." She shook her head. "No," she repeated firmly. "It's highly unlikely that I would get pregnant this quickly." Etain began to tremble. "Isn't it?" Hal stood and ran from the room yelling for Sebastian.

Vivi went to get out of bed and Etain just about lost his mind. "Stay!" he ordered.

"I'm not greeting Sebastian naked!" she yelled back.

"Fine! I will get your clothes, but stay right there." Etain jumped from the bed and went to the small bag she had yet to unpack. He pulled out random things and brought them over.

She quickly got dressed and watched as Etain fumbled with his shirt buttons. "Come here, I'll do them," she offered.

Etain staggered over. "You're fine," he said, almost as if reassuring himself.

"Yes, I'm fine."

"She's here!" they heard Hal shout a second before the room flooded with people. Vivi gave Etain an 'I told you so' look before pointing to her clothes.

Micah, Kendrick and Rheia hurried over. "What's this about being pregnant?" Rheia asked.

Vivi shook her head. "We don't know for sure."

Sebastian stepped forward holding a stone. "One way to be sure."

Vivi hesitated. What if she was?

"Vivi, love, please hold out your hand. We need to know if you're pregnant." Etain said in an even voice.

Vivi held out her hand and Sebastian dropped the stone into the center of her palm. There was a short burst of light, but then it began to flicker. She looked around the room. "What does this mean?"

Kendrick moved quickly placing a hand on her shoulder. "Not on my watch," he swore.

Vivi looked around. "What?"

Rheia sat on her other side and took her hand. "Vivi, honey, you're losing the baby," she explained in a very calm voice.

"No, I'm not." She turned from Hal to Etain. "I'm not!" she protested.

Rheia squeezed her hand. "You need to stay calm.

If you get upset it will hinder Kendrick's magic."

Vivi's throat constricted, and tear after tear began to fall. "I can't lose my baby, not when I just found out they were there." She looked up at Etain. "Save our baby!"

Her words vaulted him to action. He knelt between her knees where she sat at the edge of the bed. He placed his palms over her womb and his hands began to glow a soft golden light.

Minutes dragged by, but the tiny light in her palm continued to weaken.

"He's here," Micah said entering the room out of breath. While Kendrick and Etain had been working to save her baby, Micah ran for help.

Vivi looked up to see five fae unit warriors striding in. They formed a semicircle around Etain. The tallest turned to her. "My name is Sulis Vi'Er-london. Will you allow us to share our light with Etain?" He pointed to the men behind him. "We all felt it when he began to share the light of Éire Danu, it would be an honor and a privilege to assist in saving the newest child of the fae."

"Please," she croaked her voice breaking. "Please help him."

The men placed a hand on Etain's broad back, and their hands began to glow. Vivi had never seen anything more beautiful in her life. Though each warrior's hand glowed with a golden light, no two were the same.

Etain's light was bright and sure. Sulis' was warm and slightly orange in color. The other men's lights ranged from yellow gold to amber in hue. The longer they shared their light, the stronger the pregnancy stone glowed.

When it finally began to pulse with a steady light, the men around her stepped away. Kendrick wiped the beaded sweat from his brow. "She's a fighter. You will have your hands full with that one," he said smiling.

Etain rocked back on his heels grinning. "A baby girl?" he asked.

Kendrick nodded. "She already has a definite personality. She's quite sassy. I think I am going to adore her."

Sulis reached down and helped Etain to his feet before offering him his forearm. "Congratulations brother!"

Vivi leaned against Rheia. "I'm going to be a mother." It was still sinking in. She was almost afraid to say it out loud. She stared down at the glowing pregnancy stone. "It doesn't seem real."

Rheia gave her hug then stood. "Trust me, it will get more and more real as time passes, especially when you get to the cravings and hourly pee breaks." She winked trying to make Vivi smile.

Sebastian dabbed at his eyes with a napkin. "Why don't you hold on to the stone for a while," he suggested.

Vivi's hand clenched around the stone. "Thank you."

"Okay people, let's give them some space!" Hal boomed.

Vivi was grateful. She just wanted to spend time alone with her mate. Hal herded everyone out then turned to them. "Make sure you're ready for dinner. You need to eat," he sniffled. "Especially since you're eating for two now." He shook his head. "My baby girl is having a baby girl." His eyes widened, and he turned closing the door behind him. Through the door they heard Hal yell. "Sebastian I need those baby websites!"

Once they were alone Etain dropped down on the bed beside her. They both stared straight ahead not saying a word. Vivi opened her hand and stared down at the light. "A daughter," she said softly.

"I'll need an army to keep her safe," Etain muttered.

Vivi rested her head on his shoulder. "You can be her guardian angel commanding the other angels to keep her safe."

"Angels?" he asked.

"The fae warriors. They looked like a host of angels when they walked in. Somehow I knew everything would be okay." She wrapped her arms around his waist and he tucked her under his arm. "Thank you for saving our baby."

"I would have given her my life to ensure she would make it."

"That's what the light was, wasn't it. Your life."

Etain hesitated then nodded. "That's why Micah ran for the men. They helped shoulder the burden. Instead of me giving everything, a bit was taken from each warrior."

Vivi felt her stomach plunge, and she looked up at her mate. "Are you... are they going to die now?"

Etain chuckled and shook his head. "No, my love. A quick trip back to Éire Danu will replenish our light. As soon as the portals are working we'll be just fine."

"Thank the gods!" she whispered low.

Etain pulled her backwards onto the bed. "And Micah Sageson. Without him, I would have lost you and the chance to see our daughter born."

"We need to do something nice for him," she suggested.

Etain gave a slow nod. "I have something in mind, but I need to speak with Adriel first."

She snuggled in close. "Today is the first day of the rest of our lives."

Etain tipped her head back and kissed her gently. "And I intend to enjoy every second, for tomorrow isn't promised and every moment a treasure to be safeguarded."

Vivi knew there were dark times ahead, but she wasn't afraid. She had her mate and her new friends to walk along beside her. No matter what the future had in store for them, she knew they had the strength to see it through.

EPILOGUE

"I CAN'T HELP IT. YOU INSIST on turning the shower to the 'lava' setting," Aiden complained as he and Meryn entered the antechamber in Magnus' quarters later that evening before dinner.

"It is not that hot," Meryn protested.

Aiden held up his hands that were still a bit pink. "And I'm a shifter."

Meryn crossed her arms. "Yeah, a big shifter baby," she huffed.

Kendrick cleared his throat. "Actually Aiden, as you are taller and closer to the shower head, the temperature is of course warmer since it hasn't been cooled by the air. By the time it reaches Meryn it could be significantly colder."

Aiden blinked. "Seriously?"

Meryn stamped her foot. "That's not fair! No wonder I can never get my showers hot enough."

Aiden grinned down at her. "The advantages of being tall."

Meryn looked over at Kendrick. "Could that be why Aiden doesn't think his farts or feet smell? His big nose is too far away?"

Meryn's question silenced the room. Aiden turned red and he just closed his eyes shaking his head. First Declan, then Colton busted out laughing. Rheia gouged Colton in the ribs and turned to Meryn. "It may be a shifter thing. At times, I'm pretty sure a feral crawled up Colton's ass and died."

Meryn scowled. "This is bullshit. My air smells like feet, funk and farts and his air smells like shampoo!"

"Meryn! Stop! I beg you!" Colton wheezed holding his midsection.

Aiden smiled down at his mate. "I do love your shampoo."

Meryn tapped her chin thoughtfully, and Aiden's smile evaporated. "What are you scheming?"

Meryn's eyes widened as she put on an innocent face. "Me? Scheme?"

"What are you thinking?" Aiden asked.

"Nothing."

Aiden scrubbed his hands over his face. "Gods," he muttered.

Etain leaned down. "I love you," he whispered.

Vivi fought a smile. She was pretty sure her mate was thankful he hadn't gotten stuck with Meryn. Vivi honestly believed that Fate knew what she was doing, because no one fit Meryn like Aiden, just as she couldn't imagine being with anyone else besides her mate.

She winked up at him. "You just love me because I'm smexy."

Etain tilted his head to one side. "What is smexy?"

"It means smart and sexy," she explained.

"Then I'm smute!" Meryn declared.

"Smute?" Vivi questioned.

"Yeah, smart and cute."

Vivi eyed the small human. "Are you sure about the smart bit?"

Meryn glared at her. "Are you sure about the sexy bit?"

Vivi stuck out her tongue and Meryn reciprocated.

Etain wrapped an arm around her. "So dignified," he chuckled.

Meryn pointed to her belly. "Congratulations on Vi-three two-point-oh."

"Huh?" Vivi asked.

"Well your name is Vivian, but you go by Vivi. Then you changed your last name to Vi'Aerlin, so that's like three 'Vi's. So your kid is Vi-three two-point-oh." She gave her a sly smile. "Or maybe Bella, if she turns out to be a sparkly fae vampire."

Vivi's mouth dropped. "That's low."

Meryn giggled. "Fine. No sparkly vampires."

Vivi rubbed her temples. "Great, now that image is stuck in my head."

"At least she isn't calling your baby a jackalope," Beth said.

Vivi couldn't help but laughing. "A bunny with fangs," she looked from Beth to Gavriel. "That's too much."

Beth sighed. "I know."

Vivi turned to Gavriel. "Any word as to what may have happened at the entry door?"

Gavriel shook his head. "No one saw anything. Marek said one moment he heard the commotion coming from Level Six when you were attacked then nothing. He woke up on the floor, his head splitting and the Grand Hall door was open. We are doing a level by level head count, but that will take some time."

"Yeah, because there are a shit ton of people on the census," Meryn added.

Gavriel gave her a droll look. "It is a pillar city Meryn."

Meryn rolled her eyes. "I keep envisioning people hibernating in little caves like bees in a beehive. Stacked up in little tubes."

Beth laughed. "When the virus is cured, I will take you on a full tour of the city. There are whole towns on each level you haven't seen yet."

"Nah. I think I'll just stay in my bat cave. People irritate me," Meryn said shaking her head. Beth rolled her eyes.

Etain leaned down. "I'll be right back."

She looked around and noticed that Adriel, Micah, Grant and Declan were waiting by the door. "Be safe," she whispered.

"Always."

Vivi watched her mate walk out with his fellow unit warriors and smiled. Whatever they were up, to she'd find out about later. For now, she had a midget to torture.

Micah stood shoulder to shoulder with his unit brothers staring down at the tunnel escort who was kneeling at their feet.

"Why?" Declan asked.

The tunnel escort's eyes darted from warrior to warrior. "Why did you bring me down here?" he asked looking around. They had taken him out of his detention cell and were now standing below Level One in the Pits.

Declan punched him across the jaw. "We are asking the questions. Why did you attack Vivi? What do you know about the Grand Hall door being open?"

"Nothing!" the escort shouted.

Etain knelt down. "You see? I do not believe you. One way or another, I will get the answers I need. Torture is inevitable. As to how long it lasts and how much pain is inflicted between now and then, that is up to you," Etain informed him pleasantly.

Micah watched as the tunnel escort began to shake in the face of Etain's polite threats. He couldn't blame him. If his friend's anger was directed at him, he knew he'd be a babbling mess.

Adriel turned to him. "Micah, if you would please."

Micah looked down at the escort. "You should have answered the question." He extended his hand and allowed an electric current to flow through him to the escort. The man writhed on the floor.

"Enough," Adriel said.

Micah pulled back his magic.

"Now. Once again. Why did you attack Vivi? And what do you know about the door being opened?"

"Okay! Okay!" the escort sobbed. "DeLaFontaine promised he would make me his heir if I killed Vivian DuSang."

"Did he say why?" Grant asked.

The escort shook his head. "Only that she had to

die. That she was too close."

"And the door?" Etain prompted.

"All I know is that I was to come down here, create a platform and go up to the Greeting Hall. After that I was to find Vivian and stab her," he looked around. "That is all I know. I swear!"

Adriel turned to Etain. "Your call. DeLaFontaine will be killed for his part in this. We do not need this parasite's testimony."

"You cannot kill me! I have to go before the council!" the escort screamed.

Etain stared down at the escort and smiled. "The council is not here. The virus locked down the city remember?" He pulled the long sword from the scabbard at his waist. "You almost stole my mate from me. I had to watch my unborn daughter's light flicker as she fought to cling to life. What made you think you would not die?"

"For the crimes you have committed against the city, her royals, my brother, his mate and his unborn child. I sentence you to death." Adriel declared before leaning down. "Or did you forget I was a royal now and could do such a thing?"

The escort's mouth opened before Etain sent his head bouncing across the hall. Micah stared down at the growing pool of blood. "We're just lucky I learned some of the cleaning spells from Kendrick when we set the royal quarters to rights."

Etain lifted his sword toward him, and Micah whispered a low phrase removing the blood from blade. Etain slid the sword back into the scabbard and turned to Adriel. "What trouble could we face for this?"

Adriel shrugged. "Probably none. Both Aiden

and Gavriel have mates after all."

"We all do," Grant murmured then looked to Micah. "Sorry."

Micah forced a smile. "It's quite alright. The way things are going, I'd prefer to meet my mate much, much later. Definitely after this virus is cured and the city is back to normal."

Adriel gave him a funny look. "Have you not been having nightmares?"

Micah kept cool. "Some odd dreams here and there, nothing too bad." He could not share his dreams with his brothers, no matter how desperately he wanted to.

Grant clapped a hand on his shoulder. "Don't be like us. Share your fears, we can help."

Micah shook his head. "I'm good, big guy." He looked up. "You better get back to your mates. The last thing we need is for them to ask Meryn to search for us with her drones."

Grant gave a quick smile. "That human is most amusing."

Etain looked down, and Micah waved him off. "I'll take care of it. We're firing off the cremation chamber for Augustus. I'll sneak him in after that. No one will be the wiser."

Etain looked relieved. "Thank you."

"Go give that gorgeous fire-headed mate of yours a kiss for me," Micah joked wagging his eyebrows.

Etain shook his head and patted him on the back as he walked out. Grant, Adriel and Declan all gave him a nod before floating up to Level One.

Micah looked down. "Just me and you old man. Let's get your head and float you to the cremation chamber."

Micah used his magic to lift his head and bring it to sit on top of the body. He levitated both and used a spell to clean up the mess. Using another spell to ensure their invisibility, he made his way to the large crematorium.

Flashes of his nightmares plagued him even during the day now. He fought to hide the effects of his sleepless nights. Evenings like this would drain him further.

Unlike his brothers' nightmares, his saw the face of his mate clearly. He saw exactly how she died. There was no hidden assailant, no enemy to fight. She simply looks up at him and whispers that she is sorry before collapsing, allowing herself to die. She chooses death over him. How could he possibly share that with his brothers?

For the millionth time in the few short weeks he had been plagued by his nightmares, he begged the universe to keep his mate away from Noctem Falls.

Stay away and choose life!

Thank You For Reading!

I hoped you enjoyed MY ANGEL!
For a full listing of all my books please check
out my Official Website www.alaneaalder.com

I love to hear from readers so please feel free
to follow me on Facebook , Twitter, Goodreads,
AmazonCentral or Pinterest.

Hug me please!!

SEND ALANEA A
HUG!

LEAVE A REVIEW

**If you liked this book please let others
know. Most people will trust a friend's opin-
ion more than any ad. Also make sure to
leave a review. I love to read what y'all have
to say and find out what your favorite parts
were. I always read your reviews.**

IMPORTANT!!

As you know Facebook strictly controls what
shows up on your newsfeed. To ensure that you
are receiving all my latest news and teasers you can
to sign up for my newsletters so you will receive
regular updates concerning release information,
promotions, random giveaways and future Live
events.

THE ALANEA CHRONICLES

Volume 1, Issue 1   March 2014

I typically send only 1–2 updates per month and won't flood your inbox, promise! ;)

OTHER BOOKS BY ALANEA ALDER

KINDRED OF ARKADIA SERIES

This series is about a shifter only town coming together as pack, pride, and sloth to defend the ones they love. Each book tells the story of a new couple or triad coming together and the hardships they face not only in their own Fated mating, but also in keeping their town safe against an unknown threat that looms just out of sight.

Book 1- Fate Knows Best
Book 2- Fated to Be Family
Book 3- Fated For Forever
Book 4- Fated Forgiveness
Book 5- Fated Healing
Book 6- Fated Surrender
Book 7- Gifts of Fate
Book 8- Fated Redemption

BEWITCHED AND BEWILDERED SERIES

She's been Bewitched and he's Bewildered…

When the topic of grandchildren comes up during a weekly sewing circle, the matriarchs of the founding families seek out the witch Elder to scry to see if their sons' have mates. They are shocked to discover that many of their sons' mates are out in the world and many are human!

Fearing that their future daughters-in-law will end up dead before being claimed and providing them with grandchildren to spoil, they convince their own mates that something must be done. After gathering all of the warriors together in a fake award ceremony, the witch Elder casts a spell to pull the warrior's mates to them, whether they want it or not.

Each book will revolve around a unit warrior member finding his destined mate, and the challenges and dangers they face in trying to uncover the reason why ferals are working together for the first time in their history to kill off members of the paranormal community.

Book 1- My Commander
Book 2- My Protector
Book 3- My Healer
Book 4- My Savior
Book 5- My Brother's Keeper
Book 6- My Guardian
Book 7- My Champion
Book 8- My Defender
Book 9- My Angel
Book 10- My One and Only
Book 11- My Solace

THE VANGUARD
We Hold the Line.

Book 1- Inception

Printed in Poland
by Amazon Fulfillment
Poland Sp. z o.o., Wrocław